The Hook and the Eye

The Hook and the Eye

First published by Ian Fleming Publications in 2025
Registered offices: 73-74 Berwick Street, London W1F 8TE

www.ianfleming.com

003

Copyright © Ian Fleming Publications Ltd 2025

Raymond Benson has asserted his right to be identified as the author of this Work in accordance with the Copyright, Designs and Patents Act 1988

Felix Leiter, James Bond and 007 are trademarks of Danjaq LLC, used under licence by Ian Fleming Publications Ltd

The Ian Fleming logo and the Ian Fleming signature are both trademarks owned by the Ian Fleming Estate, used under licence by Ian Fleming Publications Ltd

Print ISBN: 978-1-915797-59-9
eBook ISBN: 978-1-915797-60-5

A catalogue record for this book is available from the British Library

This book is sold subject to the condition that it shall not, by way of trade or otherwise, be lent, re-sold, hired out, or otherwise circulated without the publisher's prior consent in any form of binding or cover other than that in which it is published and without a similar condition including this condition being imposed on the subsequent purchaser.

Typeset in 11/15pt Sabon LT Std by Six Red Marbles UK, Thetford, Norfolk

Printed and bound in Great Britain by Clays Ltd, Elcograf S.p.A.

EU Authorised Representative: Easy Access System Europe,
Mustamäe tee 50, 10621 Tallinn, Estonia, gpsr.requests@easproject.com

Ian Fleming's
FELIX LEITER

in

The Hook and the Eye

by

RAYMOND BENSON

IAN FLEMING PUBLICATIONS

Contents

Author's Note	vii
Chapter 1	1
Chapter 2	6
Chapter 3	13
Chapter 4	26
Chapter 5	37
Chapter 6	47
Chapter 7	59
Chapter 8	67
Chapter 9	75
Chapter 10	88
Chapter 11	101
Chapter 12	112
Chapter 13	121
Chapter 14	131
Chapter 15	141
Chapter 16	151
Chapter 17	157
Chapter 18	165
Chapter 19	177

Chapter 20	184
Chapter 21	194
Chapter 22	206
Chapter 23	217
Chapter 24	226
Chapter 25	233
Chapter 26	241
Chapter 27	247
Chapter 28	253
Chapter 29	262
Chapter 30	270
Chapter 31	278
Chapter 32	284
Chapter 33	291
Chapter 34	304
Chapter 35	307
Acknowledgments	313
About the Author	314

Author's Note

Felix Leiter appears in Ian Fleming's first, second, fourth, seventh, eighth, and twelfth novels. Ignoring the actual dates of the original publications of these works, Bond historians have long conjectured when in the real world the events in these stories may have occurred. In the late John Griswold's excellent study, *Ian Fleming's James Bond—Annotations and Chronologies for Ian Fleming's Bond Stories*, the author speculates that Fleming's second novel, *Live and Let Die*, actually takes place in January and February of 1952. *Moonraker* happens in May 1953. The action of *Diamonds are Forever* is between July and August 1953. Many online fan sites have adopted this perceived timeline (or very similar ones) as gospel. Given this conceit, Felix Leiter's mishap with the shark in *Live and Let Die* transpired at the end of January 1952. He doesn't appear in a Bond novel again until July 1953 in *Diamonds are Forever*. Thus, the following tale takes place in between those two works, during the last half of 1952 to be exact.

Real highways, hotels/motels, and restaurants around the USA that existed in 1952, as well as the states of

AUTHOR'S NOTE

landmarks such as Carlsbad Caverns National Park, were utilized in the text wherever possible. The New York headquarters of Pinkerton's Detective Agency (the name "Pinkerton" without the apostrophe-s was used interchangeably) was indeed located on Nassau Street in lower Manhattan in that era. Robert Pinkerton II did spend time in both the Chicago and New York offices.

According to the latest U.S. government Consumer Price Index data to adjust and calculate for inflation, in 1952 one dollar would equal a few cents less than twelve dollars in 2025. Thus, $100 in 1952 would be the equivalent of $1,198.76 in 2025, and so on.

1
November 3, 1952

New York, New York

I'm holding in my hand the fate of the world and I don't know what the hell I should do with it.

I ain't kidding. The destiny of the goddamn planet earth is sitting right here in the palm of my left hand. My only hand, I might add. The right one is replaced by aluminum and stainless steel. It hasn't even been a year since I lost it. Ten months. It feels like a lot longer than that, but at the same time it's as if it happened yesterday.

Without a destination in mind, I walk away from the unmarked federal detention center in lower Manhattan where I just paid a visit to a new resident. I don't know how long the inmate is going to be there. They'll be moving the traitor to another secret location in a day or two, likely to disappear into one of the many red tape labyrinths of the justice system and never be heard from again.

Striding aimlessly eastward, I cross the park, wander into the domain of City Hall, and float amidst the multitudes pouring in and out of the building. It's where the mayor, the City Council, the Board of Estimate, and the presidents of the five boroughs work. All the bureaucracy of New York City is so close I could touch it, but at this moment I just want to get away from it all. The Civic Center building? Who cares? I do consider stopping by the Pinkerton's office on Nassau Street, which is practically *right there* at the edge of City Hall Park. Instead, I decide to head toward the entrance to the Brooklyn Bridge. Everywhere you look the streets are crowded with New Yorkers going about their midday business as usual. Taxi cabs, cars, and buses noisily remind me that the city will just keep plugging away, no matter what.

There's no question that I'm struggling with how I feel about the woman who did a number on me. Don't get me wrong—I've been through this kind of thing before. I've been around the block a few times. Women come, women go. It's true, though, that she managed to get under my skin. I'm mad as hell at her for doing so, and also for what she did afterward.

I grasp the thing in my hand tightly so I won't accidentally drop it when I turn my wrist to note the time on my Omega Bumper wristwatch. Just after eleven. For a brief moment I have a memory flash of purchasing the watch in Washington, D.C. in '48, a present to myself right after I'd agreed to work for the newly formed CIA.

A brisk wind wafts off the East River. I return the object to my left trouser pocket so I can use my good hand and the hook in tandem to button up my trench coat, the same one I'd bought in Paris not long after joining the feds. All of that *really* seems a lifetime ago, and yet it encompasses a little less than four years. Quite a bit happens to you if you blink for a second.

The pack of Chesterfields is in my coat pocket. I tap out a cigarette, stick it in my mouth, and fire it up with the Ronson lighter I've had since I was overseas. The thing still works great. It has the Marine Corps seal engraved on one side. I had my surname—*Leiter*—engraved on the other as a joke.

After inhaling the much needed nicotine, I limp-walk along the sidewalk across Lafayette and—oh, did I mention my leg? Not only do I not have a right arm and hand, but I'm missing a third of my left leg below the knee. I'm a regular circus sideshow act, folks. That clopping sound on the pavement is from a joint corset leg made of wood and stretch leather. It's got an articulated foot with a hinged ankle. No one really notices it on first glance because my trouser leg covers the prosthesis and my shoes match. But, as I said, I do limp. Can't help it. People observe my shuffle and the right hook, and they immediately throw an involuntary expression of pity at me. It happens all the time. In response, I simply grin at them as if it doesn't bother me at all. They think I'm an injured war veteran. I suppose I am, just not from the kind of war they're imagining.

Shoot, it was part of the job, I keep telling myself. The luck of the draw. The way the cookie crumbles. That's life, buddy. *Que sera, sera.* All those clichés apply, so pick one.

As I turn south on Pearl Street, I consider going to Fulton Market and perhaps grabbing a sandwich for lunch. Maybe. I'm not really hungry. Not after that talk I had. It left me with a hole in my stomach. Or maybe it was my heart, I don't know. A stiff drink would be more appropriate. It wouldn't be the first time I've had a couple of bourbons before noon.

Ah, to hell with it. *Whatcha gonna do?* as my old man back in Texas used to say whenever he got frustrated. The store was quiet today—*whatcha gonna do?* The milk's gone sour—*whatcha gonna do?* Keep your chin up, son—*whatcha gonna do?*

Well, he's long gone. *Whatcha gonna do?*

I move farther along Fulton toward the East River. Even though it's chillier near the water, I want to see it. At first I think maybe I could be alone here, but, no, if you're outdoors in Manhattan you're never alone. Around me there are women bundled up in coats doing their shopping at the market. Many of them push strollers. There are no older kids about, it's a Monday and a school day.

And tomorrow is Election Day. I've always wondered why that isn't a national holiday. So many people who could and should vote have to work and can't get to the polls. I always make it a point to vote. I have a thing about my country, you see. I'll do my duty first thing in the morning and help send Ike to the White House. There's no question about him winning. Stevenson has his supporters, but Ike won the world war. That counts for something.

I finally get to the edge of the seaport and the Fish Mongers Association joint, drop the cigarette butt and step on it, and then stand there gazing at the water. Boats and ferries move both ways, up and down the river, under the bridge carrying passengers, goods, whatever.

It's kind of peaceful. I like it.

But I'm troubled by what I have in my pocket. How it got there over the past month has been a roller coaster of a journey full of mysteries, bizarre twists, and betrayals.

I pull the item out and hold it in my hand again.

It really could change the world. All I have to do is . . . sell it. And, hey, it would change *me*, too. I mean, don't get me wrong, I'm not hurting for money. But this tiny thing could make me richer than sin. A foreign power would pay me millions of dollars for this bauble.

Of course, if I did that, I'd be a traitor to my country.

I know the object is dangerous. In fact, it's perilous as hell. It's a key to unimaginable death and destruction. Several people have died already because of it. Shoot, I almost died myself a couple of times.

I also fell for a woman on the way to attaining it. Who could have predicted *that*?

Never mind about the heartache, Felix, I tell myself. *Whatcha gonna do?*

I stare at it there in my palm.

Millions of dollars.

So what should I do with the damned thing?

2
January 31–July 28, 1952

St. Petersburg, Florida

My thoughts go back a little over three months to the beginning of this strange adventure in my so-called illustrious career. A bit of reflection is warranted.

First, though, let me tell you about my fun-filled vacation in Florida!

I spent way too much time in a hospital in St. Petersburg, recuperating from The Mishap. That's how I refer to it—The Mishap. Sounds like the title of one of those cheap Hollywood crime movies that feature cynical, hardboiled detectives, crooks, and seductive, but dangerous dames. I love those pictures. Anyway, The Mishap . . .

My job was supposed to be as an "observer" for the CIA on a case that involved a SMERSH operative based in Harlem. SMERSH is a Soviet outfit that runs counterintelligence agencies. One of the group's tasks is to assassinate Russia's enemies—spies, political figures, you name it. Sometimes they even kill off their own people if somebody screws up. Suffice it to say, they're not very nice.

This Harlem gangster also had businesses in Florida

and Jamaica. The British Secret Service was handling the bulk of the operation, and it turned out the agent they'd sent was a friend of mine. He was one of the best men on their team, a Double O, in fact. Those guys are the tops. I'd first met him in France while I was still working as part of the Joint Intelligence Staff of NATO in Paris. Several months after what I refer to as the Casino Job, I was transferred back to the States and put through the works in Washington in the fall of '51. It all happened quickly before the New Year—the brass moved me to New York and I started working out of the tiny CIA branch there. A cozy one-bedroom garden-level apartment on Bank Street in Greenwich Village became my residence amongst the jazz clubs and all the up-and-coming Bohemian artists and weirdos—not that I minded that, I thought it was great. I settled in for an interesting stint in Manhattan. It beat D.C., that's for sure.

The Harlem case was already on the CIA's radar and by mid-January I was assigned to it. The FBI had jurisdiction; like I said, I was simply supposed to be an observer, but I never could sit on my hands. Once my limey pal got to New York, I made sure I shadowed him. We hit the bars and restaurants, drank as if the world would end tomorrow, and still managed to do the work. When my buddy, and a girl that was involved in the matter, arrived in St. Petersburg for the next phase of the mission, I met them there.

I admit I made a mistake. I went off alone during the night to sniff around the Harlem guy's worm and bait warehouse in St. Pete. It was full of exotic sea creatures, some of them pretty dangerous. I should have waited for my British friend, but I didn't. To make a long story short, the big man's henchman caught me and fed me to a shark. The bastard fish took off my right arm and lower left leg. Moments of horror that lasted an eternity. The pain ... well, yeah. I still have nightmares about it. I find Haig & Haig is good medicine for that, but it only goes so far.

I really don't know why, but the man didn't let the shark devour all of me. He got me out of the water—I don't remember any of that part—and his buddies delivered my bloody body to my cabana at a Treasure Island beach resort with a note that read, *He disagreed with something that ate him.* Ha ha. Very funny, fellas.

That was the end of the observing.

The Mishap occurred at the very end of January, so I spent the next few months in St. Pete "on leave." First there was the hospital where doctors saved my life. My face got lacerated and other parts of my body were scarred up, too, so they had to do a lot of skin grafting. That was no fun at all. I do recall the moment when I learned that I no longer had an arm and foot. At first I was monumentally distressed, let me tell you. But then I thought about some of the crap I saw in the Pacific during the war. Hell, I was at the Battle of Iwo Jima in '45. I saw men get blown to bits. Some of them lived to tell about it, and, believe me, you wouldn't want to be in their shape and attempt to have a normal existence.

So, with all things relative, I guess I was lucky. I wasn't completely eaten alive and the villains didn't finish me off. I was allowed to continue my life and serve my country another day.

But I had a long, hard road ahead of me.

It took three months for my stumps to heal well enough to be fitted with prostheses. The Veterans Administration was in charge of that, and I have to say they took good care of me. My prosthetics doc, a guy named Karolewski, fixed me up with stuff from a company called Hanger. The "below knee leg," or BK Leg, as I mentioned before, was made of wood and stretch leather. I had to don a thick wool sock over the stump, and I had to build up tolerance on the skin to be able to wear the thing and walk. I had to build up calluses. It was very uncomfortable in the beginning, but over time I got used to it.

On a day when I was in a good mood, I jokingly mentioned to Dr. Karolewski that I could use the BK Leg as a wooden club and beat a bad guy over the head with it. The doc looked at me and said with complete seriousness, "You actually could. Especially with the shoe on it." By golly, he was right. I stored that information in the back of my mind, and then I thought of something else. "Can you fashion a little secret compartment where I can hide a knife?" I asked him. The man shrugged and nodded. So, ladies and gents, I do indeed carry a six-inch trench dagger that I've owned since I was a kid. My father had it during World War I and he gave it to me. It combines a simple knuckle-duster guard with a short, sharp blade. Very thin, lightweight, and potentially deadly. The compartment is on the lateral side of the leg so all I have to do is bend down, easily open it with my left hand, and pull the dagger out by a short string loop attached to the knuckle-duster hilt. I didn't know if I'd ever have to use it, but it's better to be safe than six feet under.

The Above Elbow Upper Extremity Prosthesis was more complicated and required a hell of a learning curve to operate. The figure eight harness took a while for me to master putting on by myself. That was a whole week of training. The VA arm is made of aluminum, stainless steel, leather, wood, and lamb's wool for padding. It's a dual control, cable-operated miracle of design that works with geometry and one's own shoulder muscles. I had to intimately get to know the function of the two cables, the harness, the body control motions, and the sequence of operation like the back of my ... well, you know.

The arm's two-cable system works by shoulder flexion. Mind you, essential shoulder flexes have to be accomplished in concert to manipulate the cables and perform basic tasks. I can raise the forearm, but then I have to lock the elbow in position. Only then can I open and close the terminal device—that's the hook, or pincer—again with a different shoulder flex. To lower the forearm, I first have to unlock the elbow. Then there's the act of extending the full arm. All of these things take subtle contractions of both shoulder blades and flexing the shoulders.

The elbow can lock in eleven positions. I just have to remember the cycle—pull my shoulder and release it to lock the elbow, and then repeat the motions to unlock it. How high I lift my upper arm or my forearm is dependent on the amount of strength I use to flex. Normal tasks require only a pound or two of effort.

Man, it took some time getting used to. At first I had to take it one command at a time. It was a month of practice, therapy, and just plain *work* to get to where I could use my prosthesis smoothly and do it without thinking. Now I can raise, lock, grasp, unlock, and lower in a second or two, as well as use the hook damn near like a hand. I found that one of the most difficult things was to tie a shoe! That required too much concentration. When I heard that many amputees would give up on that and wear loafers, I said, "Sign me up for a pair."

Speaking of the terminal devices, there are a number of hooks I can use for different tasks. You just unscrew the one that's currently on the forearm and replace it with another. For example, I've got the regular pincer-like hook. I also have one that's just a ring and it can be used to pull and push the steering column shift on a car (learning to drive with a prosthesis was a *whole* different challenge). By the way, I *prefer* a manual transmission over an automatic. I could make it easy on myself and simply drive an automatic, but my love of autos won't let me. I've made it a point to master the column shift, goddamn it!

Then came the difficult exercises of learning to aim a pistol and shoot a target with my left hand. I'd lost my gun arm. Let me tell you, I was terrible at it. Still am. I started going to a range to practice every damn day as part of my physical therapy, and I never could hit the mark. I worked with a VA trainer, too, and the guy was very patient with me. I think I got more frustrated with my aim than with any other aspect of my rehabilitation.

Finally, it was time. The car I'd been driving in Florida before The Mishap was an old Cord that had been impounded by the CIA. I didn't mind. It was on its last legs anyway, I got a little dough for it, and I had another car back in New York. So, on July 28, I headed home on the Silver Meteor, the train that goes all the way up through Tampa, Savannah, Richmond, D.C., Philadelphia, and ultimately to Penn Station.

It was great to be back in the land of the living.

3
August 1–August 13, 1952

NEW YORK, NEW YORK

The CIA had been gracious enough to keep me on the payroll and also make sure my apartment in the Village remained untouched. I felt indebted to Associate Deputy Michael Brinkley, my handler in New York. I'd only just met him when I was put on the Harlem SMERSH job, and we were getting along swimmingly until I became fish food.

The New York office was a tiny ground-floor storefront on Second Avenue, between 51st and 52nd Streets, disguised as an accounting firm that wasn't accepting new clients. It acted as a splinter off the main HQ in Washington. In January, the branch consisted of Brinkley, another officer named Johnson, a secretary called Marion, and me. We never worked in the office. Only Marion was present on a daily basis to make and receive phone calls and manage incoming reports from Washington. If Brinkley wanted to talk to us, we might meet there in an adjoining room that had a table and chairs and a couple of filing cabinets. That's it. Otherwise Johnson and I were supposed to be working out of the country on assignments.

Associate Deputy Brinkley and I had a meeting scheduled for August 1. After so many months away, I already had a bad feeling about it before I walked in.

Michael Brinkley's face registered pleasure to see me with a wide smile and bright eyes ... until the sight of the hook poking out from under my suit jacket sleeve caused him to blink rapidly a couple of times. The grin faltered ever so slightly. I get that a lot from people, both from those I don't know and from folks I knew prior to The Mishap.

"Felix! My God, come in!" he said as he stood. He automatically held out his right hand to shake mine and then realized his error. He quickly switched hands, and I clasped his with my left.

"Hello, Michael," I said. "Good to see you."

"Likewise, likewise. Please, please sit!"

Michael Brinkley was in his forties, fit, and not a bad looking fellow with a military cut of hair and brown eyes. He was a superb example of a CIA officer who appeared to have everything going for him. He wore no wedding ring and I didn't know if he was once married or what, but I imagine he had no problems with the ladies. In the short time I was reporting to him last January, I knew him to be competent and driven.

Once we were sitting at the table across from each other, Brinkley's expression displayed concern. "How are you feeling, Felix?"

I gestured with my good hand to go away. "I'm fine, Michael. Really."

"Tough few months, eh?"

I shrugged. "You could say that. But I'm here. I can manage quite well. There may be a little less Felix than before, but I'm still the same guy with the same enthusiasm for the Agency." I held up my hook. "*This* is not going to stop me, Michael. I'm more than ready to get back to work."

Brinkley nodded and his eyes redirected to the manila folder on the table in front of him. He opened it to a bunch of typed pages with the CIA letterhead.

"We appreciate that, Felix." He studied the words in front of him as if he were analyzing sales reports. Then he looked at me and asked, "How would you describe yourself now?"

That was an odd question. "Uh, two inches over six feet tall, straw-colored blond hair, grey eyes, keeping thin at a hundred and seventy-eight pou—"

He held up a hand. "That's not what I meant, Felix."

"What did you mean?"

"How do you *feel*? How do you evaluate your ability to do the job you were able to do seven months ago?"

"I think I just told you, Michael. I'm still the same officer with the same brain and same attitude. I'm not bitter, if that's what you're asking. Bad things happen. It's the business we're in. I'm still alive. Michael, I'm ready to get back to work. Is that what you want to hear?"

He looked down at the paper again. "You have a terrific history, Felix. You enlisted in the Marines in '42, served in the Pacific arena, and you remained in the corps for three years after the war ended with a rank of

Staff Sergeant. Why did you do that? You didn't want to go home?"

I looked away and gave him another shrug. When I did that, my prosthetic arm involuntarily raised off the table. I'd have to watch how I moved my shoulders! "I didn't have much of a home to go back to. My parents were already gone. The retail men's clothing shop my father owned was sold. A sister and her family lives out west. No, Michael, the Marines became my home. I like serving my country. I thought I'd make a career of it until I got called into that meeting with the recruiter from Allen Dulles' office."

"Why do you think you were singled out to join the CIA?" Brinkley asked.

"I suppose I was good at analytics. I had a knack for strategy and evaluating what the enemy might have in mind. Leadership skills that maybe impressed people with ranks and pay grades higher than mine. I don't really know, sir, I'm guessing. They never said. But I was happy to get the offer. I thought it would be interesting work, so I left the Marines and went into a different kind of government service. Michael, why are we talking about all this? You know my history."

"Yes, yes, I do. I'm just trying to get a sense of your ... disposition ... now."

"Like I said, I'm ready to get to work."

Then Brinkley looked a bit sad. All of a sudden, I knew exactly what he was about to say, and then he went and said it.

"Felix, I'm sorry to have to tell you this, but the word

has come from Washington that you can't be an officer like before."

I felt as if I'd been slugged in the chest. "Sir?"

"As you know, Felix, the CIA needs men in the field to be at the top of their game. With your, uhm, disability, you can't operate at the kind of capacity as someone..."

"Someone *whole*?"

"Felix..."

"Michael, I'm going to the gun range every damn day. I'm practicing shooting with my left hand. I'm getting there. I get better all the time. And I'm quite mobile."

"I'm sorry, Felix. There's nothing I can do. They've made up their minds and that's all there is to it. But hold on!" He held up a finger. "That said, we're prepared to offer you a job in the analytics division in Washington. With your keen mind, you'd be able to study intelligence reports and analyze them, make valuable suggestions, help policymakers with their decisions, and—"

"A desk job, in other words."

Brinkley paused a moment, smiled in acquiescence, and nodded. "It would be a really *nice* desk job, Felix."

"I like it here in New York now. I'm not sure I want to go back to D.C. And I sure as hell don't want to be sitting behind a desk, day in and day out, looking out a window."

Brinkley leaned back in the chair and studied me. After a pause, he sighed.

I blurted, "What? Is that final? I have no say in the matter?"

"I'm afraid so. You know, I had a feeling this was how

you'd react. If you don't take the transfer, I am authorized to give you a very reasonable severance package. I made sure it takes into account your, uhm, pain and suffering."

"Well, thanks, I guess."

"Don't kill the messenger, Felix."

Actually, I was seething inside. "Oh, I'm not upset with you, Michael. Just with the bureaucrats and the upper brass."

"Felix, I'm going to mark you down as a possibility for the Reserves. Those are former operatives who are called into duty in case of a crisis or—"

"I know what they are. I'd appreciate that."

"I can't promise anything on that. They may say no."

"I understand."

He uncovered a white envelope that had been underneath the papers in the folder. He slid it across the table to me. "That has the details of your generous severance. Taxes are already taken out." He shook his head. "It's unbelievable how the IRS doesn't discriminate. You'd think CIA employees could get some kind of break, but no." I detected some history of bitterness there, but I said nothing. "Anyway," he continued, "it should be enough to hold you for a few months until you land on your . . . uhm, until you get your bearings."

"I'll be okay, Michael," I said, not bothering to open the envelope. "I have a little nest egg inheritance from my family. And I've been saving money. I'm not a big spender."

"I understand you like to buy cars."

"Well, some men are golfers, others are mountain climbers. I like to buy a car and drive it for a year and then trade it in for a new one."

"That's an expensive hobby."

"So are women."

That made Brinkley laugh. "What are you driving now?"

"A 1951 Packard 250 Mayfair." I held up my hook. "I got it cheap in D.C. before I moved here. Glad I didn't drive that one to Florida last January. I've already learned to operate a shift in the steering column. Just need a little more practice. I'm in the market for something with a little more *oompf*, though."

I started to stand and he held up a hand.

"Wait a second, Felix ... Have you ever thought about private detective work?"

That stopped me in my tracks. "No, I haven't. But now that you say it, I like the sound of it. Why?"

"Hang on a second. Don't move." He stood and went out of the room. I heard him talking to Marion for a moment, and then he came back with a piece of paper he had scribbled on and gave it to me. Printed in bold letters was the name PINKERTON, followed by an address on Nassau Street and a phone number.

"Pinkerton's Detective Agency?" I asked. "Really?"

"They're national. They've been around a long time."

"Aren't they based in Chicago?"

"Yes. But they have an office here and it's huge. Big building down by City Hall. There are rumors that Robert Pinkerton II—he's the boss now—is going to move the national headquarters to Manhattan by the end of the decade. I know Robert personally and can give you a recommendation. Think about it."

A thousand voices went through my head, but the loudest one was proclaiming that I was now a free man. I didn't have to answer to the government anymore.

I answered, "I will," and put the paper in my jacket pocket. I stood and held out my left hand. "Thank you, Michael."

He gave me a firm handshake. "Stay in touch, Felix. I hope we'll stay friends. Let's have lunch sometime."

"Okay, but you're buying!"

*

Pinkerton's National Detective Agency was established way back in the mid-1800s by Robert Pinkerton. I knew of many of the organization's exploits. In "olden times" they did a lot to protect stagecoaches from robberies, they hunted Butch Cassidy and his Hole-in-the-Wall Gang, tracked Jesse James, and, as the world moved into the 20th Century, were contracted by the U.S. government to break union strikes and labor organizers. That latter stuff, I know, didn't do much for the Pinkerton reputation. They had to rebrand a bit, but there's no question that the company had done very well for themselves. There are offices in many major cities and the one down on Nassau Street in Manhattan is nothing to sneeze at. I can get there from my Village apartment by walking southeast on Greenwich Avenue to Seventh Avenue and descending into hot subway Hades at Christopher Street, to take the IRT downtown all the way to the stop just west of City Hall. A walk east across the park and I'm there. Takes twenty minutes if the trains are operating properly. A bus works, too, but that's much slower.

I took over a week to ponder my buddy Michael Brinkley's advice. Was being a private eye something I wanted to do? Hell, I didn't know. To help me consider the pros and cons, I spent a few evenings in Pete's Tavern—easily one of my favorite dives, located in the Gramercy Park neighborhood just northeast of Greenwich Village—and sampled many a martini, alternating with highballs of bourbon and branch. Of course, it wasn't real branch water, it was likely just from the tap. Real branch water comes from high up a natural stream in Kentucky, where the water filters through underground limestone. I've had maple water substituted for branch water in joints that carry it—that's pasteurized sap from maple trees—and it isn't bad at all.

It soon became clear that if I wanted to work in law enforcement of any kind, at least talking to Pinkerton's was a good idea. What the hell else was I going to do? Be a doorman at a hotel? Sell insurance? Go into retail like my old man? No, thanks.

I called the number Brinkley gave me. Before I knew it, I had an interview set up on August 13. Apparently, Brinkley's recommendation had done the trick.

Robert Pinkerton II conducted the meeting himself. He's the first Robert Pinkerton's grandson, a tall and somewhat big, heavy guy in his fifties. Quite a commanding presence and serious in temperament. He sat behind a large oak desk in an office that resembled an English gentleman's library. Leather chairs, oak and almond wood paneling, table lamps with broad lampshades, and numerous books on shelves. Behind him on the wall hung an abundance of photographs depicting the agency's achievements, portraits of his grandfather with politicians of yore, and a framed banner that read, *The Eye That Never Sleeps*. The place had a pungent, but not unpleasant, odor of sweet tobacco.

We talked about my background and he seemed impressed. He liked the fact that I was a Marine for seven years and was in the CIA until The Mishap. He offered me a cigarette out of a silver case with a big "P" engraved on it. They were all Lucky Strikes—not my favorite—but I took one, and he stood and lit it for me. He then picked up a Holmesian Meerschaum pipe—yes, of course he did—and fired it up. Obviously, this was the source of the room's smell!

"Mr. Leiter," he said, "I don't know if you are aware of what we do at Pinkerton's these days, but it's not like what you might see in the movies. Our detectives are not Sam Spade or Philip Marlowe. We don't do a lot of criminal investigation anymore—some, certainly—but it's not our main focus. You see, the FBI has become larger and stronger over the past twenty years or so, and they handle that kind of thing—what we used to do before the public even knew J. Edgar Hoover's name."

"Doesn't matter to me," I said. "I can do some door-bashing, tail wayward husbands . . . whatever you need."

"We don't take adultery and divorce cases anymore. We find that stuff too seedy. We mostly do private protection services and security work. Our new guys start off doing night jobs at warehouses and hotels. You know, 'night watchman' scenarios. Sometimes you get assigned to bodyguard VIPs." He nodded at my prosthesis. "Can you be an effective bodyguard with that?"

"I don't see why not." I raised the hook. "Mr. Pinkerton, I may be missing my right arm, but this thing is strong. But again, I should emphasize my experience in the CIA. I'm good at spotting criminals and figuring out what they're up to. I have a mind for detail."

"I don't doubt it. Let me ask you this—do you know anything about horse racing?"

"I've seen some. I may be a Texan, but I don't know anything about horses. I grew up in the city, in Dallas."

"Doesn't matter. We will eventually need someone to be on our Race Gang squad that investigates crooked horse racing. You'd shadow two other detectives to learn the ropes and you'd go up to Saratoga Springs often. Does that interest you?"

"Sure, if that's what you need."

Pinkerton wrote something on a pad of paper, saying, "Well, let's see how you do with the entry level stuff." He then nodded at my good arm. "How are you with a gun now?"

"I go to a range almost every day to practice. I'm teaching myself to be a lefty. It's only been a couple of months."

He nodded and then rubbed his chin as he looked at me. Didn't say anything. That made me a bit self-conscious, but I let him stare. Finally, he said, "Mr. Leiter,

I think you have some interesting qualities that could be an asset to Pinkerton's. You don't really fit the type of man we usually employ, given your disabilities. However, your situation just might be the kind of cover you need in being a private investigator. I don't believe criminals would suspect that a man with a hook and wooden leg could possibly be a detective. That, combined with your law enforcement experience, I feel makes you an ideal candidate for us. What do you say?"

I gave him one of my "boyish grins" that so many people tell me I present. I've never thought of my face as "boyish," seeing that I'm not fourteen anymore, but if my boyish grin gets me places, then I'm going to use it.

"Would I have to come here every day? Work in an office?" I asked.

"Depends on what jobs you're doing. We do have investigators that work out of their homes. Freelance, so to speak. On the payroll, but they're paid only when they're on assignments. The Race Gang would be a regular salaried position. You would start out with some freelance spots, though. There are temporary offices in the building you'd be able to use if you need to interview clients and such."

"I think that would suit me fine, Mr. Pinkerton. Let's see how it goes. Then we can talk about the Race Gang after I get the hang of this kind of work."

"The starting spots will be security and night guard jobs. Could be boring and tedious."

I gave him that grin again. "I'm a light sleeper."

The man stood and, wisely, held out his left hand to me. "Well, we're the 'Eye that Never Sleeps.' Welcome to Pinkerton's, Mr. Leiter."

"The *hook* and the eye," I added, gripping his palm and sealing the deal.

4
August 14–September 2, 1952

NEW YORK, NEW YORK
I spent the rest of August continuing therapy at a veterans facility in Greenwich Village and practicing shooting with my left hand at a gun range located at the New York City Police Headquarters on Centre Street near the area they call "Little Italy." You might ask how I'm entitled to use the police range and how I can maintain a license to carry. First, let me explain that when I was still with the CIA, officers technically weren't allowed to carry concealed weapons within the United States. However, certain palms could grease other palms under the table and I managed to obtain a permit that was good in D.C. and in New York state. When I became a civilian after The Mishap, my federal credentials greased the way in very strict New York City for me to keep my license, albeit with many restrictions. But the name Pinkerton opens doors. The detective agency had a special relationship with the police department and exceptions could be made on a case-by-case basis. Given my CIA history, my disability, and my current employment as a private investigator, somehow enough influence and

favors were exchanged to allow my license to remain. I owed that to the standing of my boss, Mr. Pinkerton. His sway extended to the fellas who ran the gun range at the Centre Street building.

Yeah, the other officers practicing at the range stared at me. They wondered what I was doing there. I was sure they quietly made jokes about me because I heard some snickering. Yuck it up, fellas. Learning to ignore gawkers was part of the recovery process.

Unfortunately, at that time my aim was still terrible. I wasn't hitting bullseyes, I was shooting bull's *tails*. *Whatcha gonna do?* Keep practicing!

My days of using a shoulder holster are over. Wearing one plus the prosthesis harness at the same time is unmanageable. I went for a gun-belt holster similar to the one that I already owned, except I purchased the Left Hand model as opposed to the Right. It's a Clark Holster, the Combat model, attached to my right waist side so I can cross-draw with my left hand. It works. Cross draw holsters seem to be popular with plainclothes law enforcement. It allows me good access to the gun in all positions—standing, sitting in a chair with arms, or in a car. This wouldn't be practical for a gun on my left hip and drawing with the left hand.

I've got the right piece, too. When I first joined the CIA they outfitted me with a High Standard HDM, which was something Bill Donovan loved and gave his OSS boys. I always found the barrel too damn long, so starting in 1950 I carried an old Iver Johnson Safety Automatic Hammerless Third Model. It's a lovely five-shot, double action revolver with a 3.25 inch barrel and a blued finish. Uses .38 S&W caliber. I liked it before The Mishap, but it's even better for me afterwards.

Any gun I use now has to be easy to operate with one hand. It being my left and non-dominant hand made it a challenge, but I'm getting better at it all the time. The way you get the cylinder to load and unload is by what's called a "top break" mechanism. I can flip up a toggle release that lies on the gun's centerline at the top-rear of the weapon. It's the easiest gun to unload. There's a central hinge, low at the front of the frame. Aggressively flipping forward the top-front half of the revolver actuates a cam that automatically lifts and ejects any cartridges. The rear of the cylinder is widely exposed for easy reloading. I can snap it open and flip it shut with a vigorous flex of the wrist, or even by knocking the top of the barrel against my thigh, my side, or any fixed object. It's a bit cumbersome to do so, but I can hold the opened gun between my knees to reload or set it down on the ground or a table. It's not really "hammerless"— the hammer is shrouded under an added cover. That's an excellent feature for a concealed carry gun because the hammer can't snag on clothing when drawing it from under my jacket, and the gun can be fired from inside a pocket or a coat without the action getting jammed on the fabric.

The Iver is *perfect* for me now that I'm a lefty.

The rest of my days and nights were devoted to Pinkerton's. My first assignments were acting as a security guard for various businesses. I worked in the so-called

Jewelry Center around Maiden Lane and the Diamond Market on Chatham Square facing the entrance to the Manhattan Bridge. I protected some fur trade shops along Seventh Avenue between 36th and 40th Streets. Nothing ever happened. I simply stood around and pretended to look tough. To tell the truth, if I dressed in my brown Worsted-Tex "British Lounge" model suit made by Botany 500 with the German Shepherd dog's head on the label, and topped off the outfit with my fedora, that prosthesis sticking out of the jacket sleeve appeared rather sinister. I was told I looked like some kind of exotic gangster from a *Dick Tracy* comic strip! My sharp, standard pinstripe suit in dark flannel that I wore as a CIA officer still worked, too. My old man—who ran a men's clothing shop—taught me that it was important to dress as if you were the president of a major corporation. The classier you looked, the more formidable you'd be.

Those were all day jobs. Sometimes I was a night guard at a warehouse or office building. I didn't have to wear a suit then, just a casual short-sleeved dress shirt and trousers. And, of course, the Iver at my side.

It was all pretty dull and tedious. No wonder many private dicks I knew were heavy drinkers. Given my condition and what I'd been through, you would think that I might experience the "dumps" as a matter of course. For a short period after The Mishap, the St. Petersburg hospital staff gave me goddamn barbiturates to supposedly make me "feel good," but all that stuff did was make me want to jump out of a fourth story window. No, when

I'm down, a few courses of my beloved bourbon and water or neat Scotch whisky usually do the trick in picking up my spirits, but I know I can't overdo it like some of those guys I'm talking about. Sure, a binge every now and then is a lot of fun, even if it makes me feel like a morgue tenant the next day. I just have to make it a point to *be careful*.

Besides, I was told by the doctors and nurses that they were impressed by my naturally buoyant disposition. The pretty nurses would turn red and hold their hands over their mouths when I told them ribald jokes, but they did laugh! One doctor said that if I can keep my sense of humor, then I would make it just fine. After all, as I said before, I didn't die that night in the bait factory. I've always tried to make the best of what I have to work with and I continue to do so.

On August 28 I got assigned to be the night guard at the Ansonia Hotel on the Upper West Side, a grand old seventeen-story building that was beginning to decline in stature. It had permanent residents as well as transients. My job was to sit downstairs in the lobby, answer phone calls from residents and act as a concierge (which rarely occurred), and mostly make sure people coming in were legitimate. After midnight, the place was dead. Frankly, the lack of interesting occurrences annoyed me. After two nights of that drudgery, I armed myself with some paperback potboilers that I'd never got around to reading before such as *The Postman Always Rings Twice* and *The Lady in the Lake*. Those passed the time.

Then, on September 2, something happened that was a catalyst for the events of the next two months.

I'd begun my shift at ten o'clock. The phone on my desk rang at just after eleven. A woman in a fourth floor room reported disturbing sounds that had been going on for a half hour in the room next door to hers. Number 405. First they might have been moans and groans of pain, she said. Then there was talking between two men in another language. This escalated into what sounded like a fight. Crashing noises and more cries of pain. I figured they were a couple guys who'd had too much to drink and that I could break it up without placing a call to the cops. I quickly moved to the elevator with the hotel master key in my pocket. When the ridiculously slow elevator finally arrived on the fourth floor, I limped as swiftly as possible down the carpeted corridor.

A muffled gunshot resounded from the room in question.

My left hand went to the Iver at my side as I approached Room 405. I drew the pistol and knew I'd have to use the hook to grasp the master key. I knew better than to stand directly in front of the door. Someone inside had a firearm and I didn't want to get plugged myself. Standing to the side, I shouted, "Open up! Hotel security!"

The door swung inwardly and a tall man burst out of the room like a bull bolting full speed out of a pen. He slammed right into me and knocked me down. I didn't get a good look at his face. In those few seconds I discerned that he wore a black T-shirt and black pants, was likely well over six feet, and was bald. I wasn't hurt and I still had the gun in my hand. Twisting my body so that I was lying on my stomach, I watched him run toward the elevator.

"Stop, or I'll shoot!" I yelled at his back, but he kept going. I aimed the pistol, took a bead on the guy, and squeezed the trigger. The shot echoed deafeningly in the corridor.

I missed, damn it.

The man skipped the elevator and instead went through the stairwell door next to it. I knew that by the time I managed to get up and chase him down the hall, he'd be downstairs. By the time I got to the ground floor, he'd be on the street and might as well be a ghost.

Residents, including the woman next door, were peeking out various doors in the hallway to see what was going on. As I stood, I told the neighbor lady to call the police. I then bellowed to everyone else, "Go back inside! I'm hotel security. Police are on the way. Nothing to see here."

I then turned to the open doorway of Room 405 and stepped inside, my weapon still in hand.

It was a two-room apartment with a living space and kitchenette and the bedroom through a door on the left. A man lay on his back in the middle of the floor. At first glance he looked to be in his thirties or forties, dark hair, Caucasian. He was dressed in pajamas. A bright red splotch was spreading on his chest. His face was a bit bloody, as if he'd been punched a few times. A lamp lay on its side on the floor and there were other signs of a scuffle. More telling was a bloody rag that was half-on, half-off his face, tied around the back of his neck. The man had been gagged.

A pair of pliers lay by his bare feet. Three of the victim's toes were mangled.

The poor guy had been tortured, but with the gag the perpetrator had made sure the screams hadn't awakened everyone on the floor.

I holstered my weapon and took a deep breath.

The lady next door stuck her head in the doorway and gasped. She was maybe in her sixties and was dressed in a nightgown.

"Ma'am, go back to your room, please," I said.

"Is he dead?" she asked.

"I think so. Did you call the police?"

"They're on the way. Oh, Lord . . ."

"Did you know him?"

"He just moved in a week or so ago. We said hello a couple of times in the hallway, but I don't know his name."

"All right. I'm sure the cops will want to talk to you. Go on now."

When she was gone, I went to the bedroom. The bed was unmade. The victim could have been asleep when the killer arrived. No one had entered the building after I started my shift. The shooter must have already been in the hotel somewhere or he'd come in an unauthorized entrance like the loading dock.

Then I noticed something unusual.

Sitting atop a small table was a suitcase opened to

reveal radio equipment. My CIA training kicked in and I immediately recognized it as a Type 3 Mark II clandestine suitcase transceiver from World War II days, commonly known as a B2. In other words, it was a spy's radio set, actually one that had been developed in the U.K., but models had proliferated around Europe after the war. It consisted of a receiver, a transmitter, and a power supply unit, plus a box of spares and accessories. The transmitter was located in the center top of the suitcase with the receiver below it. The spares box had a Morse key mounted on the lid.

He'd been using the table as a desk, for a chair sat in front of it. Pads of paper, pens, and pencils were spread on the table next to the transceiver. I leaned closer to the top notepad and saw scribbling in a language I thought might be Polish. I couldn't read it, but two names in English popped out.

MARKO.

IVY.

A voice called out from the other room. "Police! Anyone here?"

They'd arrived. I raised my voice, identifying myself as hotel security, and said I was in the bedroom. A uniformed officer with a gun in hand peered inside. I raised my hand and hook and said, "Pinkerton's Detective Agency, sir. I'm the hotel night man."

He asked for identification. Once he saw my credentials, he told me to relax. I went back to the front room where two other cops were examining the body and searching for evidence. The first guy asked me what happened and I told him the whole story. He then ordered me to go downstairs to my post and wait. They would talk to me further later. Obviously, a Pinkerton's detective was not law enforcement, and the police were going to take it from there.

Back in the lobby, I sat at my desk thinking about the room upstairs. Was the resident some kind of spy? With all the news in the last couple of years about Julius and Ethel Rosenberg, David Greenglass, Harry Gold, and other Americans who passed nuclear secrets to the Soviets, I couldn't help but think the dead guy upstairs was one of them, too.

About an hour later, two newcomers entered the hotel. The men were dressed in suits, the standard federal agent uniform that I recognized. One of them approached me and flashed a badge.

"Federal Bureau of Investigation," the guy said. "We're looking for—"

"Fourth floor, Room 405."

"You're the night watchman who interrupted the crime?"

"Yes."

"We'll want to talk to you. You'll be here a while?"

"Until seven a.m."

The man nodded and then did a double take at me. He looked familiar, about my age, had a military haircut, and was built like a former Marine.

His face registered surprise. "Leiter?"

"Yeah?"

"Felix Leiter! My God, I don't believe it!"

Then I knew who he was. He had been in my regiment, the 21st, during the war. We were on Iwo Jima together. "Steve Sandlin, as I live and breathe. How are you?" I stood and held out my left hand.

Sandlin had already stuck out his right and then realized his mistake. As we shook, he eyed the hook and asked, "Jesus, Felix, what happened to you?"

"Long story. Better get on up there. There's something you need to see."

It was around three in the morning when the ambulance arrived to take the body away. The cops wrapped up the scene and the G-Men returned to the lobby. One of Sandlin's men carried the B2 suitcase.

I spent another half hour telling them my side of the story, and then I asked my buddy, "The guy was a spy, you think?"

"Could be. The question is whose side was he on?" Then Sandlin gave me his card. "Felix, let's get together, what do you say? Get a drink or something? I want to hear your long story. We can certainly meet here in the city, but I'd love it if you came out to Rockville Centre. It's beautiful. There's a car dealership in my town you've got to see."

That got my attention. "I'd like that, Steve."

We saluted each other for old time's sake.

After he left, I was excited. Unexpectedly, I had fallen into a *bona fide* mystery.

5
September 6–8, 1952

ROCKVILLE CENTRE, NEW YORK
My 1951 Packard 250 was olive green and had a silver flying goose hood ornament that teenagers might have called "ginchy." The car was kept in a garage down on Houston Street. Not a terrible monthly fee to park it, and it beat having to find spaces on the streets every damn day. I took the Packard out only when I felt like going on a practice drive, usually upstate. Working the "three-on-the-tree" column-shift three-speed manual transmission wasn't easy with a prosthesis. During the rehabilitation and therapy period in Florida, I struggled like a dog to be able to do it. I had to raise the forearm, lock the elbow, grasp the shift, and use shoulder flexion to move the lever. If I had to do *anything else* with my right appendage in the car while I was driving, I had to unlock the elbow first and lower the forearm.

In D.C. I also had a sweet red 1948 Pontiac Silver Streak convertible that I sold when I moved to New York. I wanted another convertible and was thinking about getting one. What can I say? I love cars. One can never have too many cars.

I took up Steve Sandlin's offer to come out to Long Island for a visit. He was off work on Saturday, so I got the Packard out of the garage and made the drive. I crossed the Manhattan Bridge into Brooklyn, sped along Flatbush Avenue through Queens, and got to Rockville Centre in an hour and a half.

We met at the Lincoln Inn for a surprisingly upscale lunch that Sandlin insisted on buying. Ribeye steak, mashed potatoes, a vegetable medley, peach cobbler, and more martinis than I care to admit imbibing prior to getting back behind the wheel of an automobile! But that was several hours later, so I was okay.

We spent the first half hour catching up. I learned all about his life after the war, and he listened to *my* story with his jaw open so far it practically touched the table. He was appropriately sympathetic but I waved him off and told him I was fine. Then, since I was the inquisitive type, I immediately asked about the incident at the Ansonia Hotel.

"Well, this is all on the QT, Felix," Sandlin said. "I suppose I can tell you a few things since you were the first man on the scene and former CIA to boot. I guess you know how to keep secrets."

"Of course, and who knows, maybe we can help each other, Steve."

He shrugged and brought his voice down. "The dead man was named Titov. Gregory Titov. We still don't know a lot about him except that he was a Polish immigrant. He and his parents entered the country through Ellis Island in the thirties when he was fourteen. We're still looking into his background and studying the radio equipment he had in his possession. But I think your instincts were correct, Felix. The guy was likely a spy for the Soviets. In fact, he may be a part of a cabal that's attempting to steal state secrets and deliver them—or sell them—to the Russians. We know there are others in New York, too."

"Others like him, or other cabals?"

"Both. We just haven't identified them yet. Titov had a license to operate a ham radio, but he didn't have one in the apartment. There are many ham radio operators in the city, and many are non-English speaking. The FBI tries to monitor that kind of traffic, but there's so much of it. The case is now in our hands. We like to sniff out spies, it's part of our directive. Don't know if you've noticed, Felix, but we have a leaky faucet. The Rosenbergs, that guy Greenglass . . ."

"Jeepers, how leaky is it?"

"Felix, there are multiple groups out there. We've got Russian spies, Chinese spies, Korean spies, British spies, French spies . . . everybody wants a piece of world power. That reminds me . . . Have you ever heard of the Promethean Movement?"

I sat back in my chair and lit a Chesterfield. I offered him one and he took it. "Yeah," I answered as I flicked my lighter and ignited our cigarettes. "I came across them when I was in the CIA. Why? Aren't they defunct?"

"No, there are small factions of Prometheists continuing to operate in Poland and Ukraine," Sandlin said.

I knew that Prometheism was a political and cultural

movement that developed in Europe in the 1920s and 30s. It was fiercely anti-communist, a real sect that indeed existed in Poland, Ukraine, Georgia, and other Eastern European and Eastern Bloc countries after the formation of the Soviet Union. As I understood it, the Prometheists took their name from the Greek god Prometheus. They fashioned an ideology and strategy devised to combat Soviet imperialism. Underground groups attempted to sabotage, politically hinder, and thwart aggression. Sometimes they were successful. More often not.

"Are you sure about that?" I asked. "They still exist? They were active in the early half of the century, but after the war the movement lost much of its strength, especially when Europe was partitioned off. You know, when the Soviets gained a lot of territory and populations were placed under the control of the U.S.S.R."

"Right. Nevertheless, we know that small factions of Prometheists continue to operate, and their allegiances tend to favor whatever country they reside in."

"Was this man Titov a Prometheist?"

"That's what we're trying to find out. We do believe that Prometheists are recruiting spies in America to steal state secrets for themselves."

I thought about that. "That makes sense. There were a lot of intellectuals associated with the Prometheists. Very smart people. Scientists and such. I mean, sensitive government secrets can be dangerous enough in the hands of *stupid* people, so I appreciate the concern. Is that what you're thinking?"

Sandlin shrugged again. "More or less."

On the way out of the restaurant, he gave me directions to Bill Frick Motors on Sunrise Highway, about a five minute drive away. "Don't get lost in there, Felix. You want me to come with you and make sure you don't lose your shirt?"

"I think I can handle myself. Steve, it was great to see you."

"Likewise. Let's keep in touch."

This time he stuck out the correct hand.

When I pulled up in front of Bill Frick Motors, I saw a big banner in the storefront window that read: ORDER YOUR STUDILLAC TODAY! I didn't know what a Studillac was, but I figured I should find out.

Yes siree, it was pretty much a car lover's dreamhouse. Frick himself was there, and he pegged me for a mark as soon as I started looking at something called a Fordillac.

"It's a Ford with a Cadillac V8 engine," he said, grinning like a Cheshire cat. "A hundred-and-sixty horsepower, three-hundred-and-thirty-one cubic-inch four-barrel, available in manual or automatic transmission. Engine and chassis upgrades are also available."

I couldn't help but laugh. "Sounds pretty wild, my friend."

Frick introduced me to his partner Phil Walters, who as "Ted Tappett" raced Midgets and jalopies around Long Island, and then switched back to his given name when he started driving sports cars. Bill Frick himself was also a road racer and loved to build race cars. I got his whole life story right there on the sales floor.

"So what is this Studillac that's on the sign?" I asked.

"Ah!" He wiggled his eyebrows. "I'm starting to work on those now, but they won't be ready for about six months. I'm going to take Studebaker Starlight and Starliner coupes and switch out the engines with two-hundred-and-ten horsepower Cadillac engines. You'll get the poise and attractiveness of the Studebaker with the power-packed performance of the Cadillac engine. I reckon it'll be capable of a hundred-and-twenty-five miles per hour."

"What about the transmission?" I asked, totally intrigued.

"Your choice. Manual steering column or manual floor shift. I might put in a dual range Hydramatic."

"You mentioned coupes, but can you do a convertible?"

Frick wrinkled his brow. "Hadn't planned on that."

He showed me pictures of what he had in mind and I was practically salivating. "What do I have to do to sign up?"

"Three hundred dollars down and you're on the list."

I rubbed my chin with my left hand as I eyed those photos. "Man, oh, man ..." I said. "I think I'm in love, but I really want a convertible. You sure you can't do one?"

Frick closed his eyes and tilted his head up at the ceiling as if he were attempting to receive some kind of divine guidance. Then he looked at me and said, "Mr. Leiter, I convert these things, and the word 'convert' is part of the word 'convertible.' How about if I agree to do this but only under the condition that this is a one-off and our little secret?"

NEW YORK, NEW YORK

On Monday I phoned Michael Brinkley and told him I wanted to talk to him. He said he was busy but could spare me a few minutes that morning. I took the Third Avenue bus uptown, walked over to Second, and before long I was back in my old haunt. Marion greeted me warmly. She also looked lovely with her sparkling green eyes and auburn hair done in a bouffant. For a brief moment I wondered if she might like to go for a coffee or something with me now that I wasn't working in the office anymore. Would a woman want to go on a date with a guy with only one hand? Should I ask her?

That was an issue. Whether or not I could maintain my way with the opposite sex. My self-confidence in that regard still had a ways to go.

But Brinkley opened the door and stuck his head out of the other room before I could act on my impulsive insanity. We greeted each other, went in, and settled behind the closed door.

"Good to see you, Felix! How are you getting on at Pinkerton's?"

"Swell. I mean, so far some of the jobs have been a little dull and tedious, but I may be moving to their horse racing squad soon."

"That sounds like it'd be right up your alley. You're a native Texan, right?"

I chuckled. "I was born in Texas and I grew up in Texas, but I was a city boy. I know which end of the horse is which, but that's about it. I appreciate you putting in a good word for me, though."

"Well, I'm happy you landed someplace good, Felix."

"Thanks. Listen, Michael, I wanted to tell you about something." I asked him if the FBI had shared anything with the CIA about the alleged Russian spy who was shot and killed at the Ansonia Hotel. Brinkley immediately furrowed his brow.

"The FBI doesn't share a damn thing with us. And for that matter, we don't share a damn thing with them. At least we try not to. And they try not to. It's just the way of the world. Russian spy? To answer your question, I don't know anything about it. Speak to me."

"Look, I'm probably not supposed to be telling you this," I said, "but seeing that I have more loyalty to the CIA than the FBI, I will." I proceeded to give him the whole story—everything I knew about Gregory Titov, the communication equipment he had in the hotel, and the fact that he was murdered by an unknown assailant. I mentioned my Marine pal, Steve Sandlin, and how he and the feds showed up that night and took over the case from the NYPD.

"I've heard of Sandlin, but I don't know him," Brinkley said. "He's supposed to be a good man."

"He is. Solid as they come. No complaints about him at all. If I have to rub elbows with a G-man, I want it to be Steve."

"Still . . ." Brinkley said, as he wrote some of what I said on a pad of paper. "I'm none too happy that the FBI *didn't* share this information with us. We're looking into spy rings that are quite active in the United States, too, and there are some right here in New York. We look at their overseas handlers, of course. Hell, I'm working on a case that might very well involve this guy Titov. Did the FBI fellas mention anything about accomplices?"

"No. Although, like you, they're looking into other possible spy activity in the city."

Brinkley rubbed his chin and looked at me with a squint. He was considering ... mulling something over ...

"What?" I asked.

"You know, I could maybe hire you for a job."

I blinked. "How's that?"

"Hear me out. Totally legitimate. Through Pinkerton's. The CIA could come to Pinkerton's and say, 'We need a private detective for some work here in the U.S.' You know, the CIA is not supposed to work stateside. But there's nothing that says we can't hire some freelancers to do it for us."

This got my heart racing. The idea that I could work for the Agency again was cause to sit up and listen. "Keep talking."

"You're a private detective now, Felix. How good are you at surveillance?"

"Are you kidding? I'm ex-CIA!"

Brinkley nodded. "I need a guy followed. I want to know about his activities. What he does. Who he sees. Where he goes. He might be one of the dead man's accomplices or maybe a member of a rival network."

I gestured with my hand and hook. "I'm all yours. Tell me more."

"I'll give Robert Pinkerton a call. We'll arrange

something. It'll be a genuine Pinkerton's assignment, but the CIA, or rather an alias of mine or one of our front businesses, will be the employer. And ... I'll have to check with Washington on this, but maybe ... just maybe ... this could help you get on the CIA Reserves if you do a good job. Sound okay to you?"

"It does."

"The target is a man named Karl Adamski."

"Sounds Polish. Just like Titov."

"Uh huh. He lives in Greenwich Village."

"So do I."

"Give it a day or two for me to get hold of Pinkerton. We could very well be working together again real soon."

6
September 9–18, 1952

NEW YORK, NEW YORK
Pinkerton took me off the Ansonia Hotel duty and, true to Brinkley's word, I was placed on a surveillance job to follow and observe Karl Adamski. The client paying for the assignment was an "attorney" named Parker, but I knew he was really Brinkley. It was such a cloak and dagger set-up that for the first time since I joined Pinkerton's, I really felt like a private detective.

Adamski lived in a five-story brownstone on Mercer Street close to Bleecker. You know, Greenwich Village is a maze. It's not laid out in a nice, intuitive grid like the rest of Manhattan above 14th Street. The reason, as I understand it, was that back in the olden days, the Village was an individual settlement. They had designed their own streets, so there's a real confusion and odd arrangements of thoroughfares. The City eventually absorbed the Village, of course. The neighborhood's eastern border is Sixth Avenue, more or less, and from there to the East River is the Lower East Side. That area is a completely different ball of wax. I've heard some people refer to it as the "East Village," and by the same token, they call Greenwich Village the "West Village," but that's not official in any way. Maybe someday it will be.

I picked up Adamski on September 11 as he departed his building on Mercer and walked down the street to a newsstand. He was in his thirties, my age or thereabouts, medium-height, not a bad-looking guy, dressed in non-descript clothing. He wore a grey pork pie hat over short brown hair. An ordinary Joe, if you ask me. Was he a spy out to do damage to the United States? Considering how David Greenglass also looked like a regular Joe, then I supposed anything was possible.

Over the next three days, I made note of where Adamski went when he left his apartment. From what I could tell he wasn't employed, that is to say, he didn't go to a job. He went to buy groceries, he picked up newspapers, he'd go to restaurants and diners, and he went to an old bar on the Lower East Side called McSorley's Ale House. It was on 7th Street just off Third Avenue and it was nearly a hundred years old. It was known to be a hard-drinking Irish bar for men only. No women allowed—not even the woman who owned the place.

There was good ale there, though, and it was the only thing they served. I'd sit and watch the guy as he sat alone at the bar or at a table. He never spoke to another person except the bartender, who seemed to know him as a regular. Adamski would drink exactly two pints of ale, and then he'd leave after an hour (I timed him, too). I was beginning to think I might need to use my nifty collection of lockpicks and get inside his apartment sometime when he was at the bar. After all, I wasn't learning a damn thing about him so far.

On Saturday the 13th, however, Adamski didn't go to McSorley's. He was dressed in a suit, so he was obviously doing something different that night. I followed him to an apartment building on MacDougal Street just below Bleecker. I loitered across the street and smoked a Chesterfield until he emerged from the building accompanied by a girl.

Even though I was across the street, perhaps some fifty feet away, I could see that she was peachy. She looked to be in her late twenties or early thirties and had dark brown hair. Dressed in a full swing skirt with a bright red flower pattern and a tight bodice that matched, and formed a tiny "wasp" waist.

Our potential Russian spy was on a hot date!

They started walking up MacDougal toward Washington Square. I rushed across the street and opened the outer door to the dame's building. I examined the mailboxes in the inner foyer to see if I could determine what her name might be. The little tags by each of the twenty-four boxes for the building listed only a surname and first initial. Not much help. There were all kinds of American names like Peters, Franklin, Ward, and such, maybe an Italian or German one like Leone and Reinhardt ... but then I noticed the one surname I thought might be Polish. "Wysocki, D." Would Adamski be dating another Pole? Could that be our girl?

I didn't want to lose the couple, so I darted out the doorway and onward up MacDougal. I spotted them a block ahead, so I clopped along at a good pace until I was some thirty feet behind them. They reached Washington Square and then headed west on Washington Place. After a half-block or so, they entered an Italian restaurant called Marta. I knew then that I'd have to kill an hour or so, but not wander too far away. I bought a newspaper, and then I meandered over to Washington Square and sat on a bench. Quite a few people congregated on the square at that hour. Men played chess on stone tables in the lower west corner. Other couples strolled arm in arm around the space. Some teenagers smoothly glided over the pavement on roller skates. The square had one of the more peaceful and pleasant atmospheres of any of the Manhattan landmarks. I lit a cigarette, opened the paper, and acquiesced to the mood. The sun had already set, but there was enough illumination from the street lights for me to pretend to read.

With perfect timing, I eventually got up and walked to the corner of MacDougal and Washington Place just as Adamski and his date left the restaurant. From there I followed them west to Seventh Avenue South near where I lived on Bank. I was amazed to see them enter the Village Vanguard, one of my favorite music clubs.

You might say I'm a jazz aficionado. Even before I moved to New York, whenever I visited I often made trips to the Vanguard, Birdland in mid-town, and way up to the clubs in Harlem, too. I never went in for the ingrained prejudice that so many of the folks I grew up with in Texas had. And, heck, I just love the music. I even wrote articles about Dixieland Jazz for the *Amsterdam*

News. I'd like to get back to doing that again, although I'm not sure how I can use a typewriter now.

The Vanguard presented a lot of folk music, poetry readings, and Broadway-style music, but jazz was becoming more popular among white audiences every year. The Vanguard allowed mixed races in the audience, and there was never any trouble.

That night, though, the Vanguard didn't have a jazz show. The headliners were Betty Comden and Adolph Green, the couple who wrote musical movies, most recently *Singin' in the Rain*. The placard in front of the club stated that they were in town for a short time from Hollywood and were reviving their act, "The Revuers," with some new backup singers. The club was sold out, unfortunately, so I had to kill more time and wait for Adamski and his date to leave.

It was after eleven when the crowd poured out of the club. I caught up with the couple and, unsurprisingly, Adamski walked the girl home to MacDougal and then he went to his own place on Mercer.

The 15th was a Monday. It was around four in the afternoon that I picked up Adamski walking east from his place. When he turned uptown on Third Avenue, I had a hunch he was heading for his ale house, and sure enough, he went into McSorley's. As nonchalantly as possible, I went in, too, and ordered one of their signature ales for myself. Adamski sat alone again, this time at a table. It was beginning to look like business as usual when a man entered the joint and took a seat across from Adamski. He was middle-aged, wore a suit and glasses, and he reminded me of my biology teacher in high school. The guy ordered an ale and then the two men spoke softly in Polish for a while as they drank. When the newcomer finished his ale, he shook hands again with Adamski, got up, and left. Adamski ordered his second ale, as usual.

That, however, was my cue to find out who that other man might be. I quickly left money on the bar and hurried outside. The man, who I dubbed "Biology Teacher," was standing at the corner of Third and 7th attempting to flag a cab. One showed up after a minute. He got inside and the car pulled away from the curb.

Fortune must have been smiling on me, for another cab pulled up to the corner just as I approached and raised my prosthesis to signal the driver. Two women got out of the back and paid the man through the window, and I got inside.

"Please, see if you can catch up with the cab that just left," I said to the driver. The man shrugged and took off. He stepped on the gas and zig-zagged through traffic for a minute until he was directly behind the other taxi. It wasn't long, though, before Biology Teacher's cab pulled over to the curb at 37th Street and stopped. I asked my driver to do the same. Biology Teacher got out, handed over his money, and began to walk west on 37th. Once I was on the pavement, I followed him at a safe distance. The man crossed Lexington Avenue and kept going, so I did the same. He seemed to be trekking across town, for he crossed Park Avenue, too.

Biology Teacher finally stopped walking when he was

near Madison Avenue. He went up the steps of a large, ornate building and disappeared inside.

It was the headquarters of the Consulate General of Poland.

I supposed that made sense. The issue for me was that Poland was currently under communist rule. The U.S.S.R. had its iron thumb on the country. I had nothing against Poles. There had been three in my regiment in the Marines and I liked them a lot. I knew Polish folks back in Dallas, Texas. Wonderful human beings. The cuisine was fabulous, too. One of my favorite restaurants in Washington, D.C. when I was there was a fairly new Polish joint called Old Europe. It was a tragedy that Poland had been in the wrong place, geographically, at the wrong time during the war. The country didn't deserve to be ruled by the Soviets.

On the 17th, a Wednesday evening, I followed Adamski as he picked up the girl again. They were dressed for another evening out and walked over to Sixth Avenue. They stood and waited at a bus stop. I figured this was what most folks did in Manhattan. Taxis could be pricey, depending on the destination, even for a date. As nonchalantly as I could, I loitered near the stop. When the bus finally came, they got on.

Just before the door closed, I rushed to the opening and boarded, too.

The couple had gone farther back into the bus. I took a seat at the front and focused my eyes out the windows. Don't know if they noticed me or not, but I didn't give them a reason to.

The bus headed uptown on Sixth. Maybe Adamski and the girl were going to a Broadway show. Ten minutes later, after the bus pulled over at various stops, we were midtown. We passed Bryant Park on the right and kept going. The couple finally stood when the bus stopped at 52nd Street. I played it cool until they were off and on the pavement, and then I quickly muttered to the driver, "Oops, my stop!" and rushed down the steps and out the door.

Staying twenty feet behind them, I trailed them west to Broadway and, to my surprise, to the jazz club Birdland. Adamski and the girl went down below street level and inside. The marquee announced that Count Basie and His Orchestra was playing. Hot dog! Count me in!

Inside, the place was hopping. An opening act I didn't know was already on the stage, but I found a stool near the bar in the back where I could observe the entire room. Adamski and his date sat at a table where I could watch them. Eventually Basie came on with a sixteen-piece band and the crowd went nuts. It was a great show.

I noted that Adamski and his girlfriend never touched each other. They didn't hold hands. He never put his arm around her. In fact, I realized that was also the case when I'd followed them the other day as they walked on the Village sidewalks. They weren't very romantic. When saying goodbye at her door, he never kissed her, not even on the cheek. Come to think of it, Adamski seemed almost wary of her, as if he wasn't sure he should be with her.

The next evening, the 18th, I followed Adamski from

his place on Mercer to his usual haunt, McSorley's Ale House. Since I had timed his visits there, I knew I had at least an hour before he would head back to his apartment. I hailed a cab and had him drive me to Mercer to save precious minutes.

I had already checked out the mailboxes and knew that Adamski lived in apartment 18 on the fifth and top floor. The lockpicks I use fit into my belt buckle, an accessory I had made when I was in the CIA. While the picks were never going to open a safe or any other highly sophisticated locks, they'd usually get you past a door. I didn't need them yet, though, because another resident of the building happened to be exiting as I approached and pushed past him as if I lived there. There was no elevator, the building was a walk-up, so I trudged up the stairs five flights and quickly found apartment 18. That's when the lockpicks came in handy. Prior to The Mishap, I'd gotten to be pretty good at using them, but with my hook they were more of a challenge. Picking a lock took delicate maneuvering.

Damn, it was tough.

It was all in the *feel* of the pick working the tumbler. Switching from the right to left hand for that subtle touch was tricky.

I needed to practice more. It took a hell of a lot longer than usual, but I finally succeeded and got inside, luckily without being seen. Of course, I knew damn well that what I was doing was illegal. No warrant to search his property. Nothing I found, if anything, could be used as evidence against Adamski. Hell, I could likely be arrested for breaking and entering. But, given that I was unofficially working for the CIA, investigating spies who wanted to cause damage to the United States, I doubt there was a jury in all of New York who would find me guilty. Especially since Senator Joe McCarthy was spouting all that alarmism and all of America was afraid of the Reds. I justified my actions as "for the good of the country."

The place was a typical New York bachelor pad. Small, tight, one bedroom and a living room with a kitchenette. It was neat and uncluttered. Smelled of cigarette smoke and there were plenty of butts in an ashtray on a coffee table. I hadn't seen him smoke on the street, but he and the girl had done so inside Birdland. After a cursory examination of the front room, I knew to move to the bedroom, because that's usually where the good stuff was.

Talk about hitting the jackpot! Sitting right there on the guy's dresser was another Type 3 Mark II suitcase transceiver. A B2 just like Titov's. It was closed, so I opened it to make sure it was what I thought it was. Brinkley's suspicions were correct: Adamski was a spy.

Even more interesting was that next to the B2 was a new Hallicrafters HT-20 shortwave radio. The guy was a ham operator. I knew that this type of receiver was also a transmitter, and, sure enough, there was a table microphone next to the machine. Attached to the back with a clip was a long coil of wire. It was, of course, the antenna. I noted that the bedroom window was close by. I figured Adamski uncoiled the wire and hung it out the window, allowing it to dangle down the exterior of the building when he wanted to use the radio.

I snooped around the work area and found more writings in Polish. I couldn't read a thing. A book style calendar sitting near the transmitter caught my attention. There was Polish scribbling on some of the dates that I couldn't discern, so I flipped the page to October to see more of the same.

But on the 3rd he had written a question in English: HURRICANE?

October 3 was only a couple of weeks away. On the same page, the date October 31 was circled but nothing was written there.

I then turned another page to November and ... *whoa*! Written in English on November 1 was the question: IVY? I remembered that word from Titov's notes in his apartment. Who the hell was "Ivy"? From the question mark, it implied that Adamski didn't know if he would see Ivy on November 1 or not. Was Ivy the girl he was seeing or someone else? And why did Titov also note Ivy's name? Thinking back to Titov, he had also written the name "Marko." Maybe "Hurricane" was also someone's name? A nickname, perhaps?

Finally, on November 2, a Sunday, Adamski had written: MCS 7 p.m. That was a new one, and I had no idea who or what that meant, either. Nevertheless, I stored all these dates and things in the filing cabinet in my head. *Hurricane. Ivy. MCS.*

Then I noticed an envelope with an American Airlines logo on it propped next to the lamp on the dresser.

Opening it, I found a round trip ticket on October 27 from New York LaGuardia to Dallas on American, and then a flight from Dallas to Santa Fe, New Mexico, on Pioneer.

I glanced at my Omega Bumper and knew it was time to leave before Adamski came home. But my ticker was beating fast with excitement when I left his building because of what I'd found.

New York City was a nest of spies, and I was going to help uncover them!

7
September 19, 1952

NEW YORK, NEW YORK
Brinkley met me for lunch at Pete's Tavern in Gramercy Park. I'd phoned him earlier that morning to tell him about what I'd found at Adamski's apartment. I was already in the second booth nursing a bourbon and branch and smoking a Chesterfield when he arrived.

"Isn't this the place where O. Henry used to write?" he asked as he plopped into the seat across from me.

"It is," I said. "Back then it was called Healy's Café. We're sitting in his booth, as a matter of fact. He wrote 'Gift of the Magi' right here. Or so they say."

Brinkley told the waiter to bring him two gin and tonics. He didn't want a meal. I ordered a hamburger and fries. He said I'd have to pay because he was short on cash.

"I'll buy you lunch, Michael," I told him.

He shook his head and said, "No thanks, just give me the scoop."

I told him what I'd learned. He had no problem with me using lockpicks to enter Adamski's apartment. Brinkley said he would have done the same thing.

"I think there's no question that Adamski is a spy, just like Titov," I said.

The waiter brought the food and drinks. Brinkley clinked my glass with his, said, "Cheers," and took a hard, long swallow. I'd never seen him do that before.

"Damn, Michael, you nearly downed half your drink," I said.

He just grinned. "Hair of the dog."

"Okay. I've been there." I tapped his glass again and we both laughed. "There's something else."

"What's that?"

"He met with someone at the Polish Embassy." Then I told him all about Biology Teacher, McSorley's, and the Consulate General of Poland.

Brinkley merely nodded and started on his second drink. "I'm not surprised that he's in contact with someone at a commie-run embassy. I'll use your description to try to find out who he is. It may or may not mean anything. Adamski's a Polish-American. We're not too concerned about the embassy. We have people looking at their people. The FBI has people looking at their people. If there were any red flags we'd know about it. More interesting to me is the girl he was with. Do you know who she is?"

"I'm not sure, yet. She might have the last name Wysocki, but I haven't verified that." Brinkley's head slightly cocked. "Does that name mean anything to you?"

He frowned. "No. Sounds Polish, though. Could be important, but maybe not. If she is, she might be part of the spy ring. See if you can find out who she is. And I want you to keep watch on Adamski."

I shrugged. "I will. Do you have any idea who Ivy is? Or Marko? Or Hurricane? Or MCS?"

"Haven't a clue," Brinkley said, "but I'll shoot it up the ladder. Maybe someone in Washington knows who they are. Interesting about the ham radio. I'll bet he transmits at night to avoid interfering with radios."

"Or televisions, if anyone in his building owns any," I added.

Brinkley downed the rest of his drink quickly and stood. "Good work, Felix. Keep it up. You're doing great. And listen ... don't involve the police or the FBI. This is between us. This is CIA business. Got it?"

"Sure, Michael, whatever you say."

Then he was out the door. Short and sweet. I figured guys like Brinkley who were above my pay grade would know what to do with what I told him. It was funny how all he'd wanted was a liquid lunch. His vehemence for exclusivity was a bit much, too. He wasn't a newspaper reporter. Did he need a scoop that badly?

That evening, I did my duty and was out on the street again to follow Adamski. He left his apartment dressed in a jacket and tie and walked in the direction of MacDougal. I wasn't surprised that he had another date with the same girl. When she came out of her building, my thumper did a little somersault. The dame wasn't exactly what I'd call gorgeous, but she had a sexy quality in the way she moved that was extremely attractive. She had *attitude*. This time she wore a white blouse and a red skirt with white polka dots on it. The heels were not too high, but tall enough to make those ankles and lower calves tantalizingly defined.

The couple gave each other an innocent hug. Once again it didn't appear to me that they were anything but friends. Either that or Adamski was too timid to display affection in public. Most men wouldn't have been able to help themselves.

I was happy to see that their destination was the Village Vanguard. It was my lucky night, for pianist Art Tatum was the headliner and I was able to buy a ticket. Once I was inside the heavenly venue, I wondered why I didn't come more often. It was the kind of place that made you feel good just being there. Since my last visit, owners Max and Lorraine Gordon had classed up the joint with white tablecloths and waiters wearing tuxedos. I propped myself up on a barstool to get a wide-angle view of the room, ordered a vodka martini the way my limey pal in England does, and lit a cigarette. Adamski and his date had snagged seats at a table near the stage and weren't about to go anywhere. Thank goodness there was no reason for me to do anything but enjoy the show. Tatum, who was a little drunk, played a fiery set with bassist Slam Stewart and guitarist Everett Barksdale, and the audience loved it.

After the concert, I followed the couple at a fair distance as they strolled at a leisurely pace down Seventh Avenue, presumably back to MacDougal and the girl's apartment. At one point she gestured to him to take a left on Bleecker Street, which shot diagonally to Sixth and was thus a shortcut.

The time was close to midnight. There were still plenty of people out and about on the major avenues, but that wasn't so on that narrow one-way street. I couldn't say for sure, but I think I was alone with them just ahead of me. Minimal illumination. No traffic.

As the couple approached Sixth Avenue, a vehicle shot past me and pulled up alongside them. Even though it was in shadows, I recognized the shape of the vehicle as a Buick Roadmaster. Hard to say what year, but it was a recent one. A dark figure got out the passenger side and moved aggressively toward Adamski and his date. He was tall, dressed in black, and wore a white hat. The guy held out his arm in front of the pair. Because of the blanket of shade over everything, it took me a couple of seconds longer than usual to realize the man was holding a gun. He gestured toward the car, speaking Russian or Polish—I couldn't tell from my distance. Adamski backed away, shouting back at him.

"*Get in the car!*" the man with the gun demanded in English.

My left hand pushed aside my jacket to reveal the Iver in its holster at my waist. Despite the newness of not being able to use my accustomed right hand, I managed to draw the gun in a fluid, speedy maneuver with my left. The practice was paying off.

It happened very quickly. Adamski reached beneath *his* jacket and drew his own pistol from a hidden holster.

Any pedestrians nearby would have likely described the noise as that of a loud firecracker on the Fourth of July. But I knew better.

The girl screamed.

Adamski's body wavered and started to sink.

I ran toward them. Not easy with a prosthetic leg.

Adamski fell on his back.

The shooter growled something at the girl and then moved back to the car.

"Hey!" I called.

The killer's eyes met mine. They were glints of reflected light from a streetlamp on the corner. I then understood that the white hat I thought I'd perceived was not a hat at all.

He was bald.

My God, he was the same guy who'd murdered Gregory Titov!

I aimed and shouted, "Stop!"

He ducked to get into the Buick just as I squeezed the trigger.

The round passed over his head and hit the exterior brick wall of a townhouse behind him. I'd missed again.

By then, the assassin was in the car and it was speeding toward the corner. In the light of the streetlamp, I saw that the Buick was either black or brown. The driver ran a red light and turned left on Sixth. They were gone.

I holstered my gun, turned, and went to Adamski and the girl. She was on her knees on the sidewalk, bending over the body, visibly upset. An unfired Colt Police Special lay on the pavement beside him.

"Are you hurt?" I asked.

She didn't move. Her mouth was open, frozen in shock.

"Ma'am. Please. Let me help you." I reached out and gently placed my left hand on her arm. I kept my hook down, so as not to alarm her. "Can you stand?"

She did so, but she stepped away from me with both hands to her face.

"You're not hurt?" I asked again.

"No," she managed to say. Then she pointed at Adamski. "That man shot him."

"I know." I squatted to my knees and gave the victim a quick scrutiny. A red blotch spread across the middle of Adamski's shirt, just like what had happened with Titov. The killer was a damned good shot. I had no doubt that Adamski was dead.

The girl began to back toward the corner of Sixth Avenue. She turned to run.

"Wait! Ma'am!"

She hesitated, not sure what to do. The woman was scared to death.

I went to her. "What's your name?"

"I . . . I . . ."

"Ma'am, please. My name is Felix Leiter. What is your name?"

"My name? . . . Dora . . . Dora Wysocki."

I'd been right about the mailbox.

"Listen, Dora." I pointed to the phone booth there on the corner. "I need to call the police. You need to stay here."

"I can't. No . . . no! I can't talk to the police!"

"Why not?"

"I must go! Please." Unsurprisingly, she spoke with

a European accent. "Thank you for your help, but . . . I must go!"

"Dora, wait. I'm a Pinkerton's detective, but I'm not law enforcement. I can help you."

She placed a hand on my chest. "Please. Don't tell them my name. Forget about me!"

Dora Wysocki turned and ran down Sixth. There was no way I could catch her, especially when she dangerously darted across the avenue in front of the bright headlights of traffic. A cab driver had to slam on his brakes to avoid hitting her.

I stuck around for the police to arrive. With a mind to protect my assignment, I simply described the killer and the Buick the best I could. The cops didn't seem to be aware of a second gunshot, and I wasn't about to tell them I had discharged my concealed weapon anyway. They took down a full statement, said I didn't need to come to the station, and told me I could go by the time the ambulance took the corpse away.

I hadn't mentioned Dora Wysocki.

8
September 20–30, 1952

NEW YORK, NEW YORK
Over the weekend I tried phoning Brinkley, but he wasn't in the office. I didn't have his home number. There was no mention of Adamski's murder in the newspapers on Saturday or Sunday. On Saturday afternoon, I walked down MacDougal past Dora Wysocki's apartment building to see if I might spot her on the street. I wasn't sure if Brinkley would still want me to find out more about her after what had happened, but *I* sure wanted to. I had my suspicions. Was she part of Adamski's spy group, whatever that was?

On Sunday I did catch her leaving the building. She walked over to Sixth Avenue to a neighborhood grocer. She bought some produce and carried it home in a bag. I figured even spies had to eat. She didn't appear to be itching to leave town, so I gave up and waited until Monday to talk to Brinkley.

It was a short phone conversation. Once again, he wanted me to keep tabs on her and see if she met up with anyone. He had heard about Adamski's murder, and in fact there was finally a short piece in the *Times* about it that morning. According to the writeup, police had no clues as to a motive or the identity of the perpetrator—described, as I'd told the cops, as a tall, bald man, but that wouldn't be much help to anyone. I could walk down any street in Manhattan at any time during the day and see a few tall, bald men. The paper described the victim as a Polish-American who had lived in Manhattan for several years. No profession given. Not much there. No mention of his own gun.

On Wednesday morning, Dora went on a long walk around the Village and Lower East Side. I tailed her from a distance. The weather had turned a little cooler, so I had on my trench coat and fedora. She wore a light jacket and a scarf around her neck. After an hour it was apparent that she was simply wandering. First she went up to Washington Square Park and sat on a stone bench. She threw bread crumbs to pigeons from a small paper bag she had brought along. This was followed by a spell of people-watching. I thought maybe she was waiting for someone, but no one showed. She did appear to be melancholic. Was she grieving for her friend?

Dora eventually got up and walked up to E. 8th Street. She stopped in a women's clothing store and browsed for twenty minutes. From there she strolled east past Broadway and over to Astor Place. She turned north at Third Avenue. I continued to follow her, but I was convinced she wasn't going anywhere for a rendezvous.

She turned back west when she reached 14th Street. I reckoned she was circling back to the Village to head home, but she stopped at the Horn and Hardart cafeteria at 14th and Irving Place. Lunchtime. The idea sounded pretty good to me, too. I wondered if she would recognize me from the other night if I went inside as well. Would it be a bad idea to be seen? I hemmed and hawed about it until I came to the conclusion that if I was going to find out anything about her, I might need to make contact again. I threw caution to the wind and entered the cafeteria.

Horn and Hardart is an inexpensive and rather fun way to get a meal. You insert coins into the slots by the little windows displaying what you want and then pull out the dishes. I got a chicken salad sandwich—with "all white meat!"—for forty-five cents, a side of fresh spinach for fifteen cents, and a cup of "Horn and Hardart's Gilt-Edge Coffee" for a dime.

I sat near the windows facing the room. Dora was across the floor sitting catty-cornered from me. She had some kind of sandwich and coffee, too. At one point, she looked straight at me. I turned my head as if to gaze out the window, hoping she wasn't studying my face. I laid odds that she probably recognized me, but she didn't register a reaction. Perhaps she had seen my hook and was eyeing me out of curiosity. A lot of people did that. When I jerked my eyes back to her, she was facing forward again.

Come to think of it, I was pretty sure she'd seen my prosthesis that night.

She finished eating before I did. She put away her tray, donned her jacket and scarf, and walked toward the door.

Her eyes were on me the whole way, her face expressionless.

I knew then that she had made me. Did it matter? Hell, I didn't know. My assignment had no clearly defined parameters.

One thing that played heavily on my mind, though, was that she was so damned fetching.

Several days went by and there was more of the same. Endless walks around lower Manhattan, occasional stops at eateries, and a bit of shopping. Dora was the picture of an ordinary single woman in the city. One day she took a bus uptown to the Metropolitan Museum of Art. She stayed exactly two and a half hours, and then rode another bus back to the Village. On the last evening of the month she went alone to the Village Vanguard to see Pearl Bailey perform. I decided not to be *too* obvious in case she spotted me there, so I didn't buy a ticket. In fact, I thought it might be the perfect opportunity for me to have a look at Dora's apartment.

I flagged a taxi to take me to MacDougal and Bleecker in a hurry. It was easier this time with the lockpicks. My left hand was developing the touch. They got me in the building's front door and into her one-bedroom abode on the third floor.

The place was tastefully decorated with a feminine flair that was quite the contrast to Titov's and Adamski's apartments, and, hell, to mine, too. Women naturally keep their places clean and tidy. Hers smelled nice, too. A nice perfume subtly permeated the living room and bedroom. Made me think that if I got close to her, *she* would have that same fragrance about her ... in her hair, on her skin ...

The living room didn't contain much of interest. There were some books in both English and Polish. What looked like a handmade Cepelia tapestry depicting Polish buildings adorned a wall. A framed photo on the bookshelf displayed a much younger, teenage Dora in front of a building with the word *biblioteka* on it. I knew enough Polish to know that was a library. Oddly, the photo was torn in half. There was a sliver of another person's arm along the tear. Had Dora intentionally removed her companion?

I was actually relieved that I didn't find a B2 transceiver or ham radio in the bedroom. In fact, there was nothing sinister or suspicious in sight. No communication equipment of any kind. Just more feminine decorations, clothing, and furniture. Dora's apartment was homey and comfortable.

Another framed photo on the dresser featured the teenage Dora with a young man about her age. It was a faded black and white picture that must have been from the late 1930s. They were in front of what I knew to be the famous Syrenka Mermaid Statue that was on a bridge over the Vistula River in Warsaw, Poland. Dora was dressed in a traditional Polish dress with ribbons. *He* was wearing the uniform of a Soviet soldier.

It was obvious from the glow in the teens' eyes and their arms tightly clutching each other's waists that they were in love.

Had been, rather. It was a long time ago.

I began to feel remorseful that I had encroached on Dora's privacy. I hadn't found a thing that indicated she was up to no good. Nevertheless, I still had a job to do, so I continued to snoop around.

A tin box on the dresser invited me to open it. Inside were a couple of hand written letters in slit-open envelopes. The return address on them revealed that they were from Ava Spence in Odessa, Texas. *Odessa, Texas?* I knew that Odessa was a small oil town in the western part of the state. It was in the middle of desert-like flatland and close to the New Mexico border. I'd been through it as a kid. My father once joked that it should be called "Odessalation."

I opened the most recent one and saw that some of it was written in Polish and the rest in English. Same handwriting. Dated last May.

It read—

Dear Dora—
I am writing in both English and Polish because I want to keep fluent in what we learned as children.

  It has been too long since we communicated.

  Because we are sisters—yes, I believe we still are!—I will tell you this news. A man named Bork has asked me to marry him. He is a bartender. I have not given him an answer yet. I do like him. He would, of course, never replace Don. I still miss Don Spence and his kind eyes and easy laughter. It is hard being a widow on this ranch, though, and it would be nice to have male companionship once again.

I wish you would perhaps come visit me in Texas so we can talk face to face and hopefully bury this cancer that has grown between us. The past is the past! Many years have gone by since what happened in Warsaw. I have told you a million times that I never meant for Bogdan to be harmed. Please try to understand. Can't you forgive me?

But then I ask the same of myself. Can I forgive you for what you did to me? I am trying, Dora. I really am. But it is hard. You meant to hurt me and you did. My husband was so distressed about it that he had a heart attack.

But I will move forward if you can.

We were once so close.

It was signed, *With sincerity, Ava.* I felt rather dirty reading it, so I put it back.

Dora and Ava ... sisters. Interesting.

The other envelope contained several pieces of torn stationery. The same kind as the letter I'd read. I poured out the fragments on the dresser top and examined them. Sure enough, they made up another hand written letter from Ava. What could have caused Dora to tear up a letter from her sister?

I carefully laid the pieces together like a jigsaw puzzle.

The note, dated December 12, 1949, was short and not very sweet.

Dora, why? WHY? How could you have done this to me? Don is my HUSBAND!

—Ava

At the very bottom of the tin was a folded, worn newspaper clipping. It was a small item in Polish, made up of two columns of two inches each. The paper had colored with age. The header read: *Rosyjski żołnierz zamordowany w pobliżu uniwersytetu.* I couldn't make head or tail of it, but I did see the name BOGDAN APALKOV amidst the text. Dora or someone had written in ink in the margin: *August 12, 1939.*

Why were these three items—and *only* these three items—contained in the tin?

Spotting a pen and notepad on the dresser, I carefully transcribed the clipping's headline and a bit of the first paragraph onto it, tore off the sheet, and put it in my pocket. Then I placed the tin and its contents back where I'd found it.

Personal keepsakes. Frankly, none of my business. The pitfalls of private detective work, digging through the confidential lives of individuals. Again, I felt a bit slimy.

After cursory sweeps of the closet, under the bed, and in the chest of drawers, I verified there was nothing else of significance pertaining to my mission.

As I left the building, I wondered if anything I'd seen meant a damn thing. The rift between these sisters was likely irrelevant to the matter at hand. It didn't shed light on why Dora had been so afraid of talking to the police that night. After all, Adamski was murdered right in front of her eyes.

This mysterious woman's behavior was indeed puzzling. I had to know more.

9
October 4–14, 1952

NEW YORK, NEW YORK

On Friday the 3rd, the *New York Times* sported a headline at the bottom of the front page that read: BRITAIN'S FIRST ATOMIC TEST IS SUCCESSFUL OFF AUSTRALIA. The piece went on to say that they had exploded the bomb in the Monte Bello Islands, fifty miles off the northwest Australian coast.

Pinkerton phoned me mid-morning that day to say that I was temporarily pulled off the "Parker" case to perform guard duty on Saturday at General Dwight D. Eisenhower's home, located near Columbia University on the Upper West Side. Eisenhower was the president of the university but, more importantly, he was the Republican candidate for president. The election was just a month away.

Apparently all of Washington was in a tizzy because of the news about Britain. The United Kingdom had just become the third nation in the world to possess nuclear power. Ike was in town and was holding meetings and briefings at the Morningside Drive home that day. The FBI, the New York Police Department, and Pinkerton's

Detective Agency were tapped to supply security for the candidate. The NYPD force was too busy protecting the metropolis and could spare only ten men. The FBI offered three. Pinkerton's threw in another three, and I was one of them. The Secret Service did not supply protection for presidential candidates.

Ike's home was a large red and white townhouse that faced Morningside Park. Columbia's law school was behind the residence, and the rest of the campus was west of that on the other side of Amsterdam Avenue. The street was lined with limousines that had brought representatives from the White House and the Joint Chiefs of Staff.

The fact that Britain now had the bomb was a concern because the U.S. had not shared any of its nuclear secrets with anyone. Churchill had announced last spring that the U.K. was beginning the development of their own weapon and would likely test the thing in the fall, but folks here were skeptical. At least Britain was an ally. This was going to help us against the Soviets, wasn't it? We were definitely in a conflict with the U.S.S.R., even though for the past few years we've been calling it a "Cold War."

For my shift I was stationed across from Ike's home. Around midday, a man in plainclothes crossed Morningside, past the obvious uniformed police presence, and headed my way. He was carrying two cups of coffee. I grinned and waved my hook at him when I recognized the guy.

"Steve Sandlin, what in blazes are you doing here?" I asked.

"Felix, would you believe I had to come up to supervise my two men guarding the general?" the FBI man replied. He handed me one of the cups. "Here, I thought you could use this. I saw your name on the list."

"Thank you, sir. Much appreciated." I took it with my left hand and saluted him with the hook. I nodded to the mansion. "What gives?"

"As you can imagine, inside and in D.C., everyone is on high alert. The world is changing rapidly, my friend."

"You said it. What do you make of the Brits' test?"

"If you ask me, they obtained a lot of information from spies who stole our work from Los Alamos in New Mexico. The Brits have their own physicists, don't get me wrong, and their man Penney is brilliant. Still, it's disconcerting how much gets leaked. We have a priority to catch all the Russian spies who do that kind of thing, but—" he chuckled "—protecting the next president of the United States is more important today."

I was very tempted to tell Steve what I had been doing for Brinkley, but my loyalty to the CIA, and Brinkley's admonition to keep my job between only us, prevented me from doing so. However, I did ask, "Have you learned any more about that man Titov?"

"Yes. You remember me telling you about the Prometheists?"

"I do."

"Titov was a Prometheist. He had ties to a small group of them in Poland that consists of some politicians, scientists, and military men. That means he wasn't working for the Russians. There are some who might ask the question, 'If Prometheists are against the Soviets, wouldn't that mean they're allies?' The answer to that is 'no.' The Prometheists have their own agenda. They're still spies working against the U.S. They want to steal our secrets, too, for their own use."

"I see." I wondered if he knew about Adamski. Surely he did.

"We're continuing to work at identifying the rest of the Prometheist spies in the U.S. Titov was in cahoots with someone here in the city. There was a guy killed in Greenwich Village a couple of weeks ago . . ."

"Karl Adamski," I said.

Sandlin cocked his head and grinned. "Oh, you know about him?"

I shrugged. "I saw it in the paper."

My friend wagged a finger at me. "Felix, I know you were a witness. Your name was in the police report. You gave them a description of the killer."

What could I say? "That's true, Steve. I was there. What, you wanted to see if I'd come clean? I was at the Village Vanguard that night and so was he. He left after the show, and I did, too, and I happened to be walking behind the guy on the street when it happened." It was the truth, if not the whole truth. Again, Brinkley's orders were ringing in my ears. Then I simply played dumb. "Are you saying he was one of the spies?"

"As a matter of fact, we're beginning to think Adamski might have been in league with Titov. Nothing certain yet. We're having a little tug of war with the CIA on that case. Our team has official jurisdiction, though. We're looking into Adamski's background. Does the name Jan Bartosz mean anything to you?" He spelled it for me.

"No. Who's that?"

"Before Adamski moved to Manhattan, he lived in the Bronx. Jan Bartosz, also a Pole, was his roommate. Bartosz has a red flag in our files. He was a person of interest in a murder of a Russian diplomat in Poland six years ago." Steve shrugged, smiled, and held out his hand. "So, we get back to work and do our jobs. I have to run. Nice to see you, Felix."

"Thanks for the coffee, Steve. Stay in touch." He started to walk away but I thought of something else. "Hey, Steve."

He turned. "Yeah?"

"Was the U.S. expecting this atomic test? Did they know about it?"

"We knew it was imminent. They kept the date a secret, though. The Brits called it 'Operation Hurricane.' See you later."

As he crossed Morningside Drive, my heart rate bumped a bit.

Karl Adamski had written the word "Hurricane" on his calendar ... on October 3. *He* had known about the test.

*

Dora seemed to be staying in a lot, so on Tuesday I took the opportunity to go uptown to the New York Public Library on 42nd Street and Fifth Avenue. The impressive building with its two stone lion guardians always aroused in me the impression that this storehouse of knowledge was as secure as Fort Knox. Inside, I asked a librarian for an English-Polish dictionary. Sitting at one of the massive wood tables in the main reading room on the third floor, I carefully translated the text I had copied from the newspaper clipping I'd found in Dora's apartment. It wasn't surprising to me that the article's heading read: RUSSIAN SOLDIER MURDERED NEAR UNIVERSITY. It didn't take too much mental legwork to assume that the young man with teenaged Dora in that old photo was Bogdan Apalkov. A group of "student radicals and older intellectuals" had attacked him in Warsaw just before the Nazis invaded Poland in '39.

Dora had been in love with him.

Did it mean anything? Was it relevant to my investigation? Were these student radicals and older intellectuals Prometheists? My CIA-trained analytical skills strongly suggested that they were.

It wasn't until Thursday the 9th that I caught her emerging from her apartment. She went to the Caffe Dante, which was on her block on MacDougal. Lovely old bar and eatery that's been there for a few decades. In the summertime they serve espressos and drinks at tables on the sidewalk in front of the place, but the weather had turned to the cooler side so most patrons were indoors.

On Saturday I followed her up to 11th Street, where she had a meal at Gene's Restaurant, another old landmark that served French-Italian fare.

I honestly didn't know what I should do. If Dora didn't do anything interesting by the next weekend, I was going to phone Brinkley and tell him that he was barking up the wrong tree. There was indeed the question of why she refused to stick around at the crime scene when Adamski was shot, but I could chalk it up to the dame simply being afraid to get involved. Some people are like that. They have an aversion to talking to cops.

On Tuesday the 14th, I decided to go to Caffe Dante myself for an espresso and a cigarette. It was around eleven in the morning. The day was a little warmer, so I sat outside with a newspaper. If she came out of her building, I'd see her.

Sure enough, just as I was about to finish, she appeared and walked toward the diner. There was no way she wouldn't see me. I remained still and just pretended to mind my own business.

"Do you live around here, Mr. Leiter?"

Her voice startled me. There she was, close to me. Right in front of my table.

"Hello," I said.

"You remember me, right?"

"I do. And, yes, I do live around here." I gestured with my left arm. "Over on Bank and Greenwich." Innocently, I added, "And you?"

Her head tilted a little and she replied, "You know where I live, Mr. Leiter."

The jig was up, apparently.

"Would you ... would you care to join me?" I gently asked.

"I think I would." She took the chair opposite me at the little round table.

I swirled around and caught the eye of the waiter, then turned back to her. "What'll you have?"

"Espresso."

I ordered for her and asked for a bourbon for myself. It was early, but I think I needed it.

"You remembered my name," I said.

"And you've been following me."

"I have?"

"I've seen you, Mr. Leiter. You were at Horn and Hardart not long ago. I've seen you on my street here. You're not ..." She inadvertently glanced at my right hook and quickly shot her eyes back to mine. "You're not easy to miss."

So much for my surveillance abilities. I was learning the hard way that having prostheses was not conducive to blending in.

"Miss Wysocki, I ... I was struck by what happened when we first met. I suppose I wanted to make sure you were all right."

"You couldn't just talk to me? I thought you might be following me for a reason. You said you were a detective."

Ready for another cigarette, I nodded to her and pulled out my pack of Chesterfields. I offered her one and she took it, and then I lit both of them with my lighter. "Miss Wysocki, I am indeed a detective. I work for Pinkerton's. But I wasn't ..."

The waiter brought the drinks. I held my glass of

bourbon up and said, "Cheers." She smiled slightly and stirred her espresso with a tiny spoon.

Suddenly I was tongue-tied. I didn't know what I should tell her. *Sorry, ma'am, the CIA hired me to find out if you're a spy.* Had I botched the case? Maybe I wasn't ready to be a private investigator so soon after The Mishap. Maybe I . . .

"If you wanted to ask me out on a date, you could have," she said. "I didn't figure you for the shy type."

I laughed. "Shy? Me? Lady, you've got me wrong."

"Well, you weren't going to find out 'how I am' without talking to me."

She had me there.

"Truthfully, I didn't know if I should approach you again or not. How about we start over, then? Hi, my name is Felix Leiter and you can call me Felix."

She smiled and said, "And I'm Dora Wysocki. But for now you can call me Miss Wysocki and I will call you Mr. Leiter."

To my eyes, the woman wasn't beautiful in the glamour and fashion magazine sense, but she exuded a sensuality that was breathtakingly attractive. Her mostly straight brown hair was a single length cut with a curved shape around her face and a deep side part. The length was to her chin and rolled curls puffed out a bit in a bobbed effect. The color complimented her equally brown eyes. Her lips, moist with a light red lipstick, had a sexy, pouty quality that I found irresistible. In fact, she reminded me of a movie actress I'd seen recently, but I didn't know or couldn't recall her name. She was in

Operation Pacific, that war movie with John Wayne that came out last year.

"You're not from New York," Dora said.

"No, not originally."

"I hear a southern accent. It's not pronounced, but it's there."

That made me laugh. "I've tried my damndest to get rid of a drawl. If I have a few drinks it comes out a little stronger. I'm from Texas. But I've lived in Washington, D.C., in France, and I spent some time on a lot of Marine bases in the Pacific."

"Texas." She grinned and shook her head. "I have a sister in Texas."

I played dumb. "Do you?"

"Yes. She's in some God-forsaken small dot on the map in the western part of the state."

"I hear an Eastern European accent from you. German? Polish?"

"I lived in Poland for much of my early life, but I was born here. My parents were Polish-Americans. My father had a job in Poland before the war. We were able to get out when it began *because* we were Americans. I learned to speak both Polish and English as a child."

"Are your parents still with us?"

"They are not."

"Sorry to hear that. Neither are mine."

She didn't pursue that line of conversation. Instead she asked, "Did you say you were a Marine?"

"Yes. Not only during the war, but I remained in

uniform for a few years afterwards. Then I decided I didn't want to be a career soldier."

"So you became a private detective."

I skipped right over the CIA chapter. "Yes."

She took a drag on her cigarette and slowly blew out the smoke. "Mr. Leiter, can a private detective be hired to travel with a client?"

Whoa. What was she getting at?

"What do you mean?"

"Suppose someone wanted to hire a private detective to be a companion—for protection—while traveling."

"Sure. That could be done."

"Is that something you do?"

I shrugged. "I've never been hired to travel like that, but I could do it. I've done a lot of the 'protection' part."

"Mr. Leiter, how much would it cost for me to hire you to accompany me to Texas?"

Holy mackerel! Was she serious?

She went on. "I need to go and visit my sister Ava in Texas. There is something we have to discuss and I must go in person. I want someone from your profession . . . to accompany me."

"Well, Miss Wysocki, I don't know how much it will cost. You'd have to contact my employer, which is Pinkerton's. They would determine what it would cost. I have no say in the matter. You'd also have to pay expenses, you know, travel expenses, lodging, meals, that sort of thing. It won't be cheap. Just airplane flights alone would be pricey."

"We wouldn't be flying."

"No?"

"I'm deathly afraid of flying in a plane. I can't do it. I survived a plane crash in Poland when I was eight years old. When my family left Poland, we were supposed to fly, but I couldn't do it. My father had to arrange a boat trip instead. We would have to travel by train to Texas."

Although I already knew the answer, I asked, "Where exactly is it in Texas?"

"Odessa. It's odd that it's named after a town in Russia. I am prepared to pay your expenses."

I guessed she was going to see her sister to repair the rift between them. That torn-up letter I'd seen could be the impetus for her inquiry. And yet, there were a lot of warning signs flashing in the back of my skull.

"Miss Wysocki, in theory we can do this, but I'd like to know more about what happened that night. Was the man who was shot ... was he your ...?"

"Boyfriend? No. Just an acquaintance. He was Polish-American, too. His name was Karl."

"Do you know anything about why that man with the gun wanted to take your friend away in that car? It appeared to me that the man shot Karl before Karl could shoot *him*."

"It was a complete shock. I thought that thug was going to rob us, but then he insisted that Karl get in the car. I don't know why. I had no idea that Karl had a gun! Then there was the gunshot, and the killer fled in the car. I think that had to do with you. You stopped him from hurting *me* and taking what little money we had."

Did she really believe it was a robbery attempt? She said it with complete conviction.

"Why wouldn't you talk to the police? You were a valuable witness."

"I didn't want to get involved."

"Why not? You still could. You really should go to the police and tell them you were there. It's the right thing to do."

She vigorously shook her head. "I won't do it. I'm sorry. There's nothing I could tell them, anyway. They already know everything that would help them find Karl's killer. Frankly, I don't think they will."

Dora was probably correct about the NYPD not finding Adamski's murderer, but it was possible that the feds would. Did she know about her friend's spying habit?

One thing was certain. The woman was hiding something and maybe I could find out what it was.

And get to know her better, too.

"I'll talk to the boss at Pinkerton's," I said.

10
October 16–20, 1952

NEW YORK, NEW YORK

I told Michael Brinkley on the phone that I needed to give him a report. He suggested lunch at Sardi's, one of my favorite joints in the theater district on West 44th Street. The dining room walls are lined with caricatures of famous actors and actresses, mostly drawn and colored by an artist named Alex Gard, who passed away not too long ago. I beat Brinkley to the restaurant, so, like the tourists, I spent a few minutes examining the caricatures to see if I could spot the actress I thought Dora resembled. I didn't.

I'd been thinking about Dora a lot.

"Hey, Tex, are you looking for your silver screen heartthrob?"

I turned to see Brinkley with a grin on his face. I laughed. "Aren't we all, Michael? Go on, tell me. Who kept you up at night when you were growing up?"

He jerked his head over at a table and I followed him to it. We sat and he said, "I had a thing for Maureen O'Sullivan. You know, Tarzan's Jane."

"Oh, I can understand that completely," I said with a nod.

"What about you?"

"Too many to count, my friend." I gestured to the waiter and ordered a dry vodka martini. "You have that Cresta Blanca vermouth, don't you?"

"Yes, sir."

"Use that, please. And for my friend . . . ?"

"One of your bourbon highballs," Brinkley said. "No, bring two."

We both lit cigarettes and then I told him what had occurred the other day at Caffe Dante. He puckered his lips and blew a low whistle.

"You hit the Vegas jackpot, Felix," he said. "This could be good."

"I don't know, Michael. I mean, Odessa, Texas? She's probably going because it's all about family business with her sister."

He pointed a finger at me. "Felix, listen. Get this in your head. Whatever she tells you is probably a lie."

I blinked at that. "Why do you say that?"

"We don't have enough information yet, but I can read between the lines. I know she's up to no good."

I didn't know what he meant, but I had to agree that *something* was there. Dora indeed had some secrets. There was an air of mystery about her, both in her demeanor and in the way she spoke. The Eastern European accent. Her sophisticated behavior.

I took a full sip of the martini when the drinks came, and then said, "I have to admit I think she's hiding something."

"I want you to figure out what that is, Felix. Personally,

I think she's one of them. It's very possible that she'll lead you to the hub of the spy network."

"In West Texas? Seriously? Come on, do you really think this girl is a spy?"

Brinkley sat back in his chair. "Maybe she's a red herring, but . . ." He leaned forward and whispered, "The name Wysocki was embedded in some coded messages in Polish that Karl Adamski had received and transmitted on that shortwave of his."

"Really? Why didn't you tell me that before?"

"I just found out. I managed to get some of the surveillance reports of ham radio activity in the city. You know, ham radio transmissions can be heard by anyone. Your man was likely talking with innocuous coded messages in Polish."

"So you think I should let her hire me to escort her to Texas?"

"I do."

"Why do you think she feels she needs 'protection'?"

"Don't forget if Adamski was a colleague, he was assassinated on the street. That other guy, Titov . . . he was murdered in his room. If she's part of the gang, don't you think she's a little paranoid about getting bumped off, too?"

"But she hasn't been afraid to go out in public," I said. "She's been going to restaurants and grocers and to music clubs."

"Maybe she doesn't think the killer will do the same thing twice. Have you noticed if she stays mostly on the avenues and big streets with lots of traffic and pedestrians around as opposed to walking on those narrow side streets in the Village at night? Like where Adamski was killed?"

I considered that. "Come to think of it, that could be the case."

"Felix, there's something else I haven't told you. Maybe it's relevant to this case, maybe not. But you might want to know."

"What's that?"

"There's a SMERSH assassin in the country."

My heart skipped a beat. Just the mere mention of that outfit conjured flashbacks of that fish warehouse in Florida. The restaurant, the caricatures, my friend Brinkley ... they all vanished. I suddenly *heard myself screaming*. I was lost in darkness, surrounded by the sounds of splashing water and my own goddamned throaty squeal of terror and pain ...

"Felix?"

Sardi's came rushing back to me in an instant. "What?"

"Are you all right?"

He nodded at my hook. I'd been subconsciously scratching the top of the table with the pincers.

"Yeah."

"I figured mentioning them to you might get a reaction."

"Do you know anything about this assassin?"

"He's in the country and he likely has a team working under him. Probably men he recruited here. It could be that he was the one who killed Titov and Adamski."

"Do you have a description?"

"No. Only a code name. A name you mentioned to me before."

"What's that?"

"Marko."

Once again I felt as if my blood pressure had risen a notch. "That was written on Titov's notes."

"There you go," Brinkley said, his point made. "I didn't know this the last time we met. Our intelligence has a few details about him. He's a sociopath, a killer, and he likes to carry dynamite with him wherever he goes."

"Dynamite? What does he use it for?"

"To blow stuff up, I guess! Sounds insane, if you ask me. Pyromaniac."

"Sheesh. All right," I said. "I'll do the job. But I'm going to offer to drive her in my car, though. Not take the train."

"Whatever works. Tell Miss Wysocki Pinkerton's fee. I have a feeling she'll meet it. Between you and me and Robert Pinkerton, 'Mr. Parker' will add funds to do the job, so it's a job within a job. Pinkerton will be more agreeable to it that way. Again, I don't have to tell you this, but I will anyway. Keep this between you, Pinkerton's, and the CIA. There's some sensitive stuff going on here. Any interference could blow the whole business."

"Whatever you say, pal." I downed the martini and crushed the stub of my Chesterfield in the ashtray. The whole thing sounded a bit mad, but I didn't give a damn.

And if it meant that I could hit back at SMERSH, I was going to do it.

*

On late afternoon Monday, Dora Wysocki met me in one of Pinkerton's temporary offices used by the freelancers. She looked alluring, as always, but she was more conservatively dressed than usual in a black and white rayon dress with a length below the knees, buttoned down the front from the neck to the hem. Combined with the black and grey rounded crown cloche hat, she might have been on her way to church.

"Miss Wysocki," I began after we were both seated, "Pinkerton's is prepared to entertain your proposal of hiring me to accompany you to Texas. Since you have stated you are looking for 'protection,' I must first ask you why you use that word. Protection from what?"

"Mr. Leiter," she answered, "I will be a single woman traveling a great distance. Men who are strangers sometimes behave in an ungentlemanly fashion when they encounter a woman alone. Do you get my drift?"

"I do." I wanted to add, *especially if she looks like you*, but I instinctively knew that was an ungentlemanly thing to say. "Besides that, are you perhaps thinking about what you witnessed that night on Bleecker Street? Are you afraid? Do you feel like you're in any danger?"

She paused and looked down at the purse in her lap. "I might be."

"What makes you say that? I need you to be honest

with me, Miss Wysocki. If I'm going to be your escort and protector, you need to know that you can talk to me in confidence."

She looked up. "I'm afraid that needs to be part of our ... contract. I will hire you to do this, but I must stipulate *no questions asked*."

"Seriously?"

"Seriously. I am a very private person. My business is my business. I don't like to talk about myself or my affairs. I would be the 'boss,' so to speak. You would be following my orders. If you can't agree to that, then I must find someone else."

That made me a little uncomfortable, but it was something I could handle. Yep, she was hiding something. Yep, she had secrets. Well, I did, too. She didn't know that the CIA was hiring me to find out what those secrets were. So, I figured we were both playing that game.

"I can agree to that," I said. "But you would also need to follow my instructions if we really did run into any trouble. After all, that's why you're hiring me. For example, if I say we need to *go* and not stick around someplace, then we need to do it. How soon do you want to embark on our journey?"

"As soon as we can. I have to be in Odessa before October thirty-first."

There was a calendar on the wall. I eyed it and determined that we basically had two work weeks with a weekend in the middle.

"Miss Wysocki, trains to your destination are not a

straight shot. I suggest that I drive you there. In my car. We can stop each night at hotels or motels. Eat at restaurants and diners along the way."

She nodded at my hook. "You can drive?"

"Yes, I can." I held up the prosthesis. "Miss Wysocki, I can do a lot of things with this." I then cross-drew my Iver Johnson from the holster on my side and pointed it at the ceiling with my left hand. "And I can do even more with this."

Dora blinked and nodded.

I had been considering what I would do about my weapon. No permit for the contiguous states. After much back and forth debate with myself, I'd decided, *to hell with it*. I was bringing the gun.

"How long would the trip take?"

"I reckon five days. Providing we don't have any problems. Probably not a good idea to push it, seeing that I *am* driving with a disability. I assure you it's not a problem, though. We'd take our time. And my car is in good shape, it's only a year old."

"When do you suggest we leave?"

I holstered the gun and replied, "Given your deadline, we should probably leave by the end of this week. Maybe Friday at the latest."

"I suppose we should talk terms, then."

I told her what Pinkerton's fee was, which truthfully wasn't terrible. But then I gave her examples of the expenses. The costs of meals, hotels, and gasoline. "Those things can add up," I warned her. "They can often be unexpected and more than you thought you'd be paying. It's just part of the deal when you hire a private detective."

She audibly took a deep breath and exhaled, and then she pursed her lips.

"Is that too much?" I asked.

Dora looked down at her purse again. "I can afford it. I have money. My sister and I, we inherited a ... from our parents ..." She cleared her throat. "They left us with an agreeable inheritance. But it is a large amount of money to spend these days."

"I understand. Do you want to think about it and get back to me?"

"No, no. Let's do it."

"Terrific. Pinkerton's does require a deposit of a portion of the final fee, and I have a contract here for you to sign."

As she looked over the paperwork, I couldn't help feeling excited. It was going to be a *very* interesting assignment. Was it ungentlemanly of me to think about what it might be like being alone with Dora in a car for hours at a time for several days? I considered myself a professional, to be sure, but I was also a man. Couldn't be helped.

Dora signed the contract and then opened her purse. She removed and counted out bills to cover the down payment.

"Let's plan to leave Friday," she said.

"The twenty-fourth it is. We'll need to leave fairly early in the morning. I'll pick you up at your place at eight. Miss Wysocki, think of it as an adventure. You're going on a road trip across America. Hell, you might even have some fun!"

She managed to smile, which made me happy.

*

I offered to escort Dora to the subway. We left the Pinkerton building together as the sun was setting. Walking with such an attractive woman by my side gave me a little lift to my limp!

But as we began to cross Centre Street toward City Hall Park and the subway entrance, I saw the car about twenty yards to my left.

A black Buick Roadmaster.

It was illegally parked at the curb with the motor running. Two figures were in the front. The sun had sunk significantly, so it was difficult to see them clearly.

Was it the same Buick I'd seen on Bleecker Street?

My experience and intuition told me that it was. Certainly ninety percent sure.

Other traffic zoomed past as I paused before crossing.

What were they doing? Were they watching Dora? Watching me? Or waiting for someone entirely different?

Only one way to find out. I made the decision not to alert Dora in case it was a false alarm. As soon as the flow of vehicles ebbed, I indicated that we should set off across the road.

The noise of a messy engine cut through the air and grew louder. It wasn't the Buick, for it remained parked at the curb.

No, wait—a single headlight was coming our way at

a great speed. A motorcycle! Didn't know where it had come from. Must have been farther back on Centre.

We were only halfway across the road. The way that guy was bearing down on us, I knew I couldn't make it all the way.

"Dora! Get back!" I snapped.

She gasped at the approaching cyclist. Pivoting, I quickly turned, grabbed her waist, and hurried the woman back to the curb from which we'd come.

The motorcycle slowed to a stop when it neared us. I thought it was one of the new Harley-Davidson Hydra-Glides, but I wasn't sure.

Then the rider extended his right arm at us.

A pistol!

Instinct saved our lives as I tackled Dora. She screamed with a start. We hit the pavement just as the gun discharged. I forced her body to roll laterally until I ended up on top. Before she could react, I eyed a post office box five feet away from us.

"Move, Dora!"

With a scramble, I managed to pull her up. We crawled to reach the metal mailbox. The damn leg prosthesis slowed me down, but I made it.

The cyclist fired a second time, once again barely missing us before we were somewhat safely crouched and shielded by the box, her back against the metal and my body wrapped around hers. The mailbox wouldn't protect us forever, though. I drew my own handgun and stretched my arm around the left side of the box. But I couldn't see anything from that position. Should

I shoot blindly? There were pedestrians on both sides of Centre Street!

By then, though, the Buick's headlights had flicked on. It darted out onto the road with screeching tires, just as it had done the other night on Bleecker. This new development distracted me from firing my weapon.

The cyclist attempted to get a bead on any part of my body that might be exposed.

Horns honked. Other vehicles were beginning to line up behind the Buick and the motorcycle, unable to go around them.

Then the Buick swerved next to the cyclist on his right side. The car blocked my view of the Harley, but I swear the driver threw something at the cyclist. Simultaneously, the Buick shot forward, turned onto Park Row, and disappeared—just as a *tremendous explosion* rocked the middle of the street. Debris and heat blew at us on both sides of the mailbox. I withdrew my arm and huddled securely with Dora.

In a few seconds it was over. I stood and gaped.

The motorcycle was in flames, lying on its side in the middle of the street. The rider weakly crawled on the road, his clothing ablaze, his screams echoing in the evening air. He almost made it to the opposite curb, but then he collapsed.

My first thoughts were what Brinkley had told me.

SMERSH. Marko. Dynamite. Pyromaniac.

But if the driver in the Buick was Marko, then who was the poor sap on the motorcycle? And why did the cyclist try to shoot us?

More importantly, was I going crazy, or did the Buick driver just save our lives? Had that been intentional? Or were we just bystanders in some feud between the cyclist and the men in the Buick?

"My God, my God." Dora was trembling as she sat there on the pavement, her back on the mailbox.

I squatted again. "Are you all right, Miss Wysocki?"

She nodded.

"We need to get up. The police will be here soon."

Dora stood and gawked at the mess in the street.

Luckily no other cars in the traffic jam had been affected. Drivers were getting out, standing on the street, shouting to each other and anyone around.

"Come on."

I quickly led Dora away from the scene, back toward the southern curve of City Hall Park and then up Broadway on the other side. From there we made it to the subway station and descended the stairs. If any witnesses mentioned that a man and woman might have been involved in the incident, the couple was long gone.

One thing was certain. If the Buick was in fact the same one I'd seen on Bleecker Street the night Adamski was murdered, then Dora Wysocki indeed needed protection.

It also meant there was a disturbing connection between tonight's incident and my assignment to drive her to Texas.

11
October 24, 1952

New Jersey – Pennsylvania – Maryland –
West Virginia – Virginia

I picked up Dora in the Packard at eight o'clock on Friday morning. She was sitting on the stoop of her building, wearing a breezy, striped, grey, red, and yellow wool tweed dress that revealed her calves and ankles, and casual black shoes with a short heel. A suitcase sat on the stone step beside her. An overcoat over her arm and a purse in her lap. As we would be traveling in fall weather, there was no telling what the climate might be. It would certainly be warmer farther south.

"Good morning," she said with what seemed to me to be a forced cheeriness when I got out of the car and opened the trunk. The space was already loaded with my own suitcase and a bag of equipment I deemed essential to take with us—some coils of rope, a few tools, and two flashlights with new batteries. I'd also thrown in four bottles of Haig & Haig Pinch. The spare tire was in good condition. The car was serviced for the journey. It had a full tank of gas and a quart of fresh oil.

I picked up her suitcase and laid it in the trunk. I closed

it and opened the passenger door for her. "Everything okay, Miss Wysocki?"

She exhaled loudly as she got in. "I can't believe we're doing this."

I went around and got in the driver's seat. "Just sit back and enjoy the ride."

And we were off.

I had armed myself with road maps, carefully marking the route I would take. The trickiest part was getting out of Manhattan, into New Jersey, and navigating the spaghetti that was the highway system on the other side of the Hudson. I set about concentrating on getting us through the Holland Tunnel. Once we emerged and had entered New Jersey, I navigated to sprawling Newark. I glanced over at Dora and saw that she was gripping the arm rest on the door and clutching her purse tightly.

"Miss Wysocki? Are you okay?" I asked.

"Yes. I just . . . I admit I have a kind of travel anxiety. That's what a doctor told me when I was younger. I told you I can't fly in planes. Boats make me nervous. You can imagine how difficult it was for me to cross the Atlantic Ocean all those years ago. I don't mind buses and trains. I can ride the subway in the city. When I'm in a car, though, especially on a highway with a lot of traffic, I get very tense."

"I'll take it easy on the gas, although I'm a sucker for fast cars. This Packard can get up to ninety miles per hour, but don't worry, Miss Wysocki, I assure you that you're in good hands. Look, even with my prosthesis, I can handle the shift just fine."

There was something I needed to speak to her about but I was waiting for an appropriate moment. It involved the motorcycle incident down at City Hall Park. Later. I had attempted to talk to Brinkley about it but couldn't reach him. When I called Steve Sandlin's office, I was told he was out of town.

In Newark, I veered south to State Highway 29 and then onto 22, the road that would be more or less a straight shot west across the state to Pennsylvania. The gas tank held twenty gallons and the Packard did anywhere between fifteen and twenty-two miles per gallon. It was possible we could go four hundred miles without filling up.

"Turn on the radio," I told her. The car was equipped with a Motorola "signal seeking" device. "Find some music you like."

She hesitantly did so and I instructed her how to use the selector bar and tuning knob. A piece of classical music eventually came through the speaker. I knew the tune but couldn't identify it. It had an Eastern European feel to it.

"Oh," she said, leaning back into the seat and closing her eyes. "I love this, don't you?"

I faked it. "I sure do. I don't recall the name ..."

"It's by Smetana. *Má Vlast. Vltava.*"

She visibly began to relax some. The music had done the trick.

By that point we had picked up speed. The sweeping melody of the strings was the perfect accompaniment for sailing through the urban landscapes of Hillside,

Union, and Mountainside, and then onward to Phillipsburg. Frankly, I was itching to get away from the densely populated areas and into the country.

While New York City had its fair share of gigantic billboard advertising, especially in the Times Square area, out on the highway one was bombarded by sales pitches. There were monstrous displays for Coca-Cola and Pepsi-Cola, Esso and Gulf Oil, Chevrolet and Oldsmobile, and Libby's and Dole. Nabisco implored us to "switch to Oreo," Kleenex was the only tissue that "popped up," and Texaco service stations hawked a "registered restroom" that was "something a lady appreciates!"

That reminded me to say to Dora, "If you ever need to stop, just let me know. If you get hungry, or thirsty, or whatever, you just holler."

A hint of a smile played on her lips. Her eyes were still closed as she drifted with the music. Then she said, "Thank you. I'm fine for now."

She sure looked lovely there in the seat, all dreamy and vulnerable ...

Concentrate, Felix!

The Smetana piece ended and the music changed to Beethoven. I would have preferred a little Duke Ellington, but I doubted I'd be able to find a station that he'd be on at that time of day. Dora perked up, opened her eyes, and studied her surroundings.

"All these towns in New Jersey run together," she said.

"That will change the farther away from it we get." I shifted to slow down when we approached Harrisburg.

"I am very impressed that you can shift so well with . . ." She let the sentence die.

"My prosthesis? I'm impressed, too. It took a lot of practice."

"Was it the war?" she asked.

"I beg your pardon?"

"The war. Did that happen in the war?"

"Oh. No, no. It happened at the beginning of this year. Right at the end of January."

"*Really?*"

"Yeah."

"I'm sorry. I shouldn't have asked."

"No, it's okay. I don't mind."

"You were in an accident?"

"Uh, sort of. It was a shark, Miss Wysocki. A big ol' shark with very sharp teeth. He bit off my arm and part of my leg. I'm lucky I survived. It happened in Florida. I was on a case." I figured the less details I told her, the better.

"Oh, my goodness. I'm so sorry."

I shook my head. "It comes with the territory. Law enforcement professionals put their lives on the line every day. You never know what might happen."

After a pause she looked at me and said, "Thank you for doing this."

"You're welcome, ma'am."

More silence followed. I then asked her, "Could you reach into my jacket pocket there and get my Chesterfields? I'd appreciate it if you could light one up for me. My appendages are a little busy."

"Sure."

"Take one for yourself, too."

"I will, thank you."

Dora gently reached into the pocket and removed the pack. She deftly tapped out two cigarettes and lit them with the car lighter. I flexed my shoulder to remove my hook from the shift, extended the arm to her, opened the hook and took the cigarette from her hand. Once it was in my mouth, I returned the hook to the shift. That simple maneuver required six steps in manipulating my prosthesis.

"I find it amazing that you can do that," she said.

I shrugged. "Me and millions of other one-armed soldiers. It's not a big deal. Please don't let it bother you."

"Oh, it doesn't. I'm rather fascinated by it." She then put a hand to her mouth. "Oh, I'm sorry. That sounded like, I don't know, something I should not have said."

"It's okay, Miss Wysocki. I know what you meant. You thought that I would think you were gawking. Trust me when I say this—I understand when people are uncomfortable when they see my prosthesis. Once you get used to it, though, you won't notice it."

Maybe she bought that. I admit I do feel self-conscious. Every damn day. But jovial ol' me won't let the world know that if I can help it.

After a beat, to change the subject, she asked, "How far will we go today?"

"I'd like to see how far we *can* go. If we can go four hundred miles, I'll be happy. Five hundred would be better, but that's unlikely at this speed."

"I've never been outside of New York."

"America is a big country. It's full of contradictions. The differences between where we are now and where we're going are vast. What you see around us now is not what the rest of the trip will be like. You'll see some pretty country. Mountains. Plains. Lakes. And, sure, more cities. Prettier ones than what you see here in New Jersey!"

She laughed at that.

"The leaves are turning with the fall weather," I continued. "It's really scenic upstate New York and in New England. But you'll see some of that magic along the way."

She nodded toward a group of trees in a park. "There, for instance."

The radio began to fade in and out as we moved farther west. Dora turned the knob again and found a variety show of music, comedians, and the news. Eventually, though, I thought it was time to broach the subject of the other day.

"Miss Wysocki, see the newspaper on the back seat? It's Wednesday's *Times*. Grab it, would you? Have you read it?"

She did and replied, "No."

"Page fourteen. See the article with the headline 'Traffic Incident Baffles Police?' It's about what happened down at City Hall Park on Monday."

"Oh!" She began to read.

"It says they identified the man on the motorcycle as Jan Bartosz. Did you know him?"

She shook her head. "No. It says he died."

"He did. The driver of that black Buick threw an explosive at him. I think it might have been a small stick of dynamite. The police have no idea what it was all about. They never found the Buick. That name, Jan Bartosz, really means nothing to you?"

"I said no."

"Well, guess what. Jan Bartosz was Karl Adamski's roommate when Karl lived in the Bronx a few years ago."

She audibly inhaled. "I don't know anything about that." Looking at me, she said with intensity, "I knew Karl only after he was living in Greenwich Village."

Since I had to keep my eyes on the road, I couldn't study hers. Usually I can tell if someone might be lying. Still . . .

"All right," I said. "It just seems like Mr. Bartosz was trying to hurt you. Or me."

"And that's why you've been hired to protect me. And not ask questions."

Okay, then. That's the way she was going to play it.

We didn't speak again until we reached the state line between New Jersey and Pennsylvania.

I needed to stretch my legs. "Are you getting hungry?" I asked.

"I could eat," she answered.

We crossed over and entered the town of Easton. "Welcome to Pennsylvania," I said.

I saw a sign for the Lafayette Diner and pulled into its parking lot. Dora went inside to freshen up while I took a moment to walk around the Packard to make sure everything was in tip top shape. My father had impressed upon me to always do the "walkaround" every time you stopped on a long road trip. You never knew when a rock or other debris would bounce off the road and mess up something.

It was then that I noticed a black Buick Roadmaster drive past the lot. It was the 1951 model. The car went on and disappeared down the road, out of sight.

Coincidence?

Maybe, but it was the third time I'd seen a black Buick Roadmaster in recent days. On the night Adamski was killed, the assassin had jumped into the passenger seat of a dark Buick Roadmaster. At the time, I was unable to determine the car's year or exact color since it was in the shadows. The second incidence, the other day on Centre Street, involved a Buick that was definitely black. Again, the lighting was too imperfect for me to identify the model year, but my CIA analytical senses were going haywire. It was the same car.

Shaken, I went inside and sat in a booth. Dora joined me in a few minutes, and then I excused myself to wash up, too. Not wanting to upset her, I steeled myself to shrug off my suspicions and act as normal as possible. When I returned, she had lit a cigarette and was looking at the menu. We both ordered hamburgers, fries, and Cokes. Very little was said as we ate.

The meal was refreshing and it was nice to give my shoulders a rest. Flexing the prosthesis did tax those muscles.

The afternoon's drive was more of the same. I took

Route 22 farther west and southwest through such communities as Allentown, Hamburg, Jonestown, and Harrisburg, where I turned onto U.S. Route 11 for the remainder of our journey toward Virginia. The radio provided some sporadic entertainment when we were close to towns, but we were more on the open road since leaving New Jersey. The scenery was gorgeous, there was less urban development, and more hills, trees, and the orange and red splashes of autumn leaves.

We went through a little sliver of Maryland, driving through Hagerstown, and then a shard of West Virginia before crossing the state line into Virginia in the late afternoon. We weren't far from Baltimore and my old stomping grounds, Washington, D.C., to the east.

"I could show you some Civil War battlefields if you want. They're all over the place around here."

She smiled at that. "No, thanks."

I did like her smile.

The sun was on its way to the horizon just as we approached the town of Harrisonburg. By then I was feeling fatigued. I figured we had gone close to four hundred miles. If I'd been able to pump up the speed, we'd have gone farther. Nevertheless, the leisurely pace was all right with me.

For the first night, I thought Dora would be more comfortable in a "nice" hotel rather than a cheap motel. I'd seen billboards for the Pure Village Cottages just south of Harrisonburg on Highway 11. Homey, with a bath, furnishings, a radio, and hot and cold water. The restaurant looked splendid, too.

Luckily, two cottages were available and we stopped for the night. We had made it through the first day of the trip.

However, Dora's reluctance to talk about the Centre Street event and my sighting of the black Buick had put me on edge. My training and experience had taught me that fate could turn on a dime.

12
October 25, 1952

VIRGINIA

The dinner at the Pure Village Cottages Restaurant had been so good that we ate breakfast there, too. Dora said she had loved being in the cottage since she had not slept well the previous night in New York. Her demeanor was now much less reserved and we seemed to be having a good rapport. It felt good.

Before leaving the restaurant, I used the pay phone to try to call Brinkley in New York. The operator told me how many nickels to put in the slot. I was a bit shocked. Long distance was expensive! I reached the CIA office and was surprised that Marion picked up on a Saturday. When I asked for the boss, she told me that he was out and she was catching up on work.

"He wants to know your progress, though," she said. I told her we were currently in Harrisonburg and were about to drive to Tennessee, likely stopping in Knoxville. She gave me another phone number and told me to call it before nine a.m. New York time on Sunday.

After filling up the Packard with Esso gasoline at

twenty-four cents a gallon, we finally pulled out of Harrisonburg around eleven.

"Dora, we're a little behind," I told her as we left the town's city limits. "I wanted to get to Nashville, Tennessee today, but I don't think we will now. It will likely be Knoxville."

"We'll make it to our destination before October thirty-first, right?" she asked.

"No question about it. Probably the twenty-eighth or twenty-ninth."

"Then that's fine. Let's take our time. I'm enjoying the countryside. Virginia is very beautiful."

"It is. Wait until you see the mountains in eastern Tennessee. They won't quite be the Great Smoky Mountain range, because that's farther southeast from where we're headed, but it's still hilly. You'll feel your ears pop a bit."

It was a gorgeous day, slightly overcast, with the temperature hovering around 65° Fahrenheit. Dora wore a light green sweater and was in another dress that accented her waistline and bust. I wore my usual trousers, button-down shirt, jacket, fedora, and the Iver secure at my side.

About fifty miles out of Harrisonburg, I noticed a black car behind us moving at the same speed. It was too far away for me to identify the model. If I were following someone, I would remain at a constant position behind my target, just as this vehicle was doing. Granted, that wasn't particularly unusual. We certainly weren't the only auto on the road. Cars and trucks passed us all the time, and we passed slower moving automobiles, too. It was the natural leapfrogging nature of driving on U.S. highways. The black car remained behind us for thirty miles or so until it eventually dropped back and out of sight. After a while I relaxed some, but that car was never out of my mind.

The radio once again provided sporadic entertainment. Out on the open road there was nothing but static, but as we approached and drove through towns, Dora found stations broadcasting music. In short bursts, we heard Eddie Fisher sing "Wish You Were Here," and Jo Stafford perform "You Belong to Me." When Vera Lynn belted out "*Auf Wiederseh'n*, Sweetheart," we both laughed. A little later we saw a sign that read, "You Are Leaving Staunton – Come Back Soon!" and Dora announced, "*Auf Wiederseh'n*, sweetheart!" That gave her the giggles.

As we approached Lexington, I noticed that the black car was back and had positioned itself a little closer behind us, still remaining at the same speed as the Packard. Wait—no, it wasn't black. The car was dark green. Not the same vehicle. Too far back to identify what kind. Just to see what the driver would do, I sped up a little. The green car didn't keep up; it diminished into the distance. *Good*, I thought. I drove on.

But after a few minutes it was back, matching our pace.

Was this a new guy following us?

Staring into the rearview mirror, I studied the vehicle and came to the conclusion that it was a Studebaker, possibly the Champion model. Maybe 1949 or '50.

I spotted a Gulf Oil station up ahead. "Dora, I'm

going to make a quick stop. Maybe you want to stretch your legs for a minute, too?"

"Oh, I'm glad you said that," she said. "I will take advantage of the ladies' room."

I pulled in to the station and parked at the side of the building since I didn't need gas. We both stepped out of the car. Dora went inside the station and I watched the highway.

Sure enough, a green Studebaker Champion sped past and kept going. From what I could tell, there was only the driver inside.

Was I being paranoid or were multiple vehicles following us?

Well, it was my job to be paranoid. Part of the profession, whether I was a spy for the CIA or a detective with Pinkerton's.

These thoughts put me on edge. I went inside the station, bought a pack of cigarettes, and went to the men's room to freshen up. After washing my hand, I looked at myself in the mirror. The scars on my face were indeed fading. My straw-colored hair perhaps needed cutting. The grey eyes didn't appear as tired as they had the previous night at the cottage. I was all right, but I told the guy in the mirror that he'd better pay more attention to what was going on. If the Buick earlier was indeed the car from New York ... if the Studebaker was following us ...

Whatcha gonna do? I heard my father say.

"Be goddamned careful," I said aloud to the mirror.

The trip continued through Lexington and onward to

Roanoke, where Dora and I decided to stop for lunch. By then it was nearly two in the afternoon.

It was perhaps the largest community we'd been through since leaving New Jersey. Highway 11 traversed the downtown area and the city felt sizable and alive. Not knowing exactly where to go, we drove slowly until Dora saw a billboard pointing to the Roanoker Restaurant, just off the highway.

It was a homey place in a Colonial style building that was full of a wide variety of people. Businessmen in suits, farmers in overalls, mothers with small children, and transients like us. The late hour made no difference. This was the American heartland on full display.

"This place is buzzing," I said as we entered. "Let's get a booth there by the window." I wanted to be able to view the parking lot.

As we were finishing the grilled T-bone steak, waffle potatoes, and vegetables, I noticed a green 1949 Studebaker Champion pull into a space outside. Was it the same one that I'd seen on the road?

"Beautiful car," I said aloud, standing to get a good look at it and the driver.

"Are you going to buy it?" Dora asked, teasing me.

"Actually I have an order in place for a *customized* Studebaker that will be ready at the end of the year." My attention went to a tall man wearing a tweed herringbone flat cap and a trench coat getting out of the car. I was still studying the vehicle when the hostess led him to the table next to ours.

Let's find out who he is. "Nice car, sir."

"Oh, thank you! Yes, it's a right gem," he said with a British accent. "Do you know cars?"

"I'm an enthusiast, yes."

"What are you driving?"

I pointed. "The Packard."

"Oh, that's a lovely one, too. Not the top of the line, though. I collect cars back home in England. It's an expensive hobby, I'm afraid."

"You and I are of like minds," I said, sticking out my left hand. "Jack Hatch."

He grasped my palm firmly. "Alec Whitehall."

I turned to Dora, who had remained sitting. "And this is Phyllis Davidson." I gave her a subtle wink. *Keep cool, Miss Wysocki.*

"How do you do?" Whitehall said, giving her a slight bow and removing his cap.

The man sat and we continued small talk for a little while.

"What brings you to this part of the United States, Mr. Whitehall?" I asked.

"Oh, call me Alec, we're already friends now. I'm on my way south. I'm an oil man working in the States. I have to inspect some oil fields and thought I'd see a little of the country first by driving across it." He smiled at Dora. "And where are you dear people headed?"

Dora started to reveal, "We're on our way to—"

"Kansas City," I interrupted before she could say "Texas." That would take us on a route completely opposite from the one we were on. "We have people to see there. And, who knows, Phyllis, didn't you say you wanted to go north to Minnesota? Minneapolis?" I nodded at her with raised eyebrows.

"Oh," she said, just barely catching on. "I ... yes, I think we talked about that."

"Ah, well you'll be seeing quite a bit of the country," Whitehall said. "I'd like to go to the southwest myself and see Arizona. Grand Canyon and all that. Not sure I have the time, though. My employers indulged me this road excursion, but I doubt they would let me do more. Perhaps next holiday."

I noted that Alec had a sophisticated, posh accent. He was obviously well educated. Perhaps an Eton man, like my good friend in the Secret Service over there.

We spoke of a number of trivial things such as the weather and the upcoming election. Alec was certain that Eisenhower would win, and I agreed with him.

"You know, we in the U.K. are more interested in American politics than you might imagine. Ever since the war ended, you Yanks are dictating world policy, whether you know it or not."

"The Soviets have a bit of influence, too," I countered.

Alec tilted his head and then nodded. "I grant you that. The Chinese are also making headway. A lot has changed since we beat the Germans and the Japanese. Did you serve?"

"I was a Marine in the Pacific."

"Good show, old man. I was in the army. European theater." He pointedly indicated my prosthesis. "I take it you saw some action?"

Not wanting to get into that story, I merely answered, "I did," which was truthful.

"Well, thank heavens you survived. Your sacrifice is noted and appreciated." He gave me a little bow of his head.

"Thank you."

"I was among the many crossing the Rhine in 'forty-five. Took a lot of fire, but I luckily avoided being wounded. Unlike many of my mates."

I was beginning to tire of the man. Glancing at my wristwatch, I turned to Dora and said, "My dear, we need to hit the road. We're running late."

She gave me a grin that indicated I had read her mind. Gathering her purse, she said goodbye to our new "friend" and excused herself to the ladies'. I paid the bill and then shook hands with Alec Whitehall once again. "Good luck on your travels, Alec. Take care of that car."

"Oh, I will. And you two be careful as well."

Outside, Dora and I got into the Packard. When I started the car, she asked, "Why did you lie back there about our names and where we were going?"

"Dora, I didn't want to tell you this, but I have a nagging suspicion that we're being followed."

This visibly alarmed her. "What?"

I held up my hand. "Don't worry. It's probably nothing. I've seen his car and another car a few times, but they could very well be going in the same direction as us. I just don't want to broadcast to any Tom, Dick, or Harry where we're going. And you shouldn't either. Okay?"

"All right."

I didn't want to say that something about Alec Whitehall activated my radar, but I didn't know what it was or why. "I should have asked you before, but does anyone else know that you were planning to go on this trip?"

"My sister, Ava. She's expecting me."

"That's all?"

"That I know of!"

"All right, then."

I pulled out of the parking lot, got back on Route 11, and we continued our journey toward Tennessee.

13

Virginia – Tennessee

I stayed on U.S. Route 11 moving southwest to the bottom of Virginia. While the scenery became lusher with greenery and the topography became craggy, the sky became dark with ominous clouds.

"I think we're going to get a storm," I said.

"Your car doesn't leak, I take it?" Dora asked.

"No, ma'am."

A crack of thunder was so loud it startled her. "Oh, my!" she exclaimed, and then the droplets began to fall. They were heavy, slow individual splotches on the windshield at first, but after a couple of minutes we were in a downpour. I turned on the wipers, of course, but they weren't doing much good. Visibility was kaput. Once you couldn't see where you were going, it was time to pull over to the side of the road and wait it out. I did so and parked on the shoulder. The Packard was at a slight tilt because the two passenger side tires sat in a shallow ditch.

"So, Miss Wysocki, did you bring a deck of cards?" I asked.

She laughed. "I think you can start calling me Dora, now, Mr. Leiter."

"Well, then, you'd better call me Felix. As soon as the rain lets up some and I can see the road in front of us, we'll head out. It shouldn't be long." I tried the car radio and just got static, but I didn't want to leave the engine running too long. I shut it off.

The storm battered the top of the car and it sounded like tommy guns. We sat there in an awkward silence, unable to see a thing outside because of the water streaming down the windows. We lit cigarettes. I cracked my window just a hair so that the smoke could escape. She followed my lead and did the same on her side.

"Tell me about Ava," I finally said.

Dora shrugged. "She's my older sister by two years."

"How did she come to live in Texas?"

"I'd first have to tell you how we came to live in New York."

"I have no place to go at the moment."

She grinned and said, "You are a captive audience then. I think I told you that our parents were Polish-Americans. They were born in America when both sets of grandparents immigrated in the late 1800s. Ava and I were born in Queens. My father had a job with DuPont and he was transferred to Warsaw to work at a subsidiary there. Ava and I were very young when we moved to Warsaw and we spent twelve years in Poland. But in September 1939, you know what happened. There was a mad scramble to leave and come back to America. My father had to bribe many officials to get us, first, on a plane. But I'm afraid I had a fit before we could board."

"You mentioned you were in a plane crash? What happened?"

"Oh. When I was eight, my father and I flew in a small single engine plane. It was just supposed to be a 'ride' for fun. My father had a pilot license, he had flown in the First World War. Anyway, it did not go well. We crashed. Luckily, neither of us were hurt but it frightened me so badly that I had nightmares for weeks. I really can't go near a plane now."

"Sorry to hear that."

"Maybe you can't go near water now."

I shook my head. "It's not the water that bothers me. Just the sharks. Please go on with your story."

"Well, there was yet another mad scramble and we finally got on a boat. It sailed first to Denmark, and then to England. We had passage on a different ocean liner to take us to America. I remember it took forever. We settled back in Queens."

"What happened to your parents?"

"My mother died of tuberculosis while the war was still going on. The disease was still going around New York at that time. My father passed away from a stroke six years ago. By then Ava and I were adults and on our own in the city. She worked in the garment district. I worked in the diamond district."

"You don't still work, do you?" I asked.

"There was a man ... my boss, actually ... who did not behave like a gentleman. I left my employment not long ago. I was about to begin searching for a new job when all *this*—" she gestured to the interior of the car around her—"happened." She gave me a little smile with that.

"I hope the Pinkerton's fee isn't putting you out too much."

She shook her head. "My mother had some valuable jewelry. My sister and I sold it and split the money. My father had a very nice pension from DuPont and my sister and I inherited it. I could probably live for a couple of years without working if I wanted to."

"That's not bad."

"No. Anyway, in 1949, Ava met a man at a nightclub. He was from Texas. His name was Don Spence and he worked for an oil company in Odessa. He and Ava had a whirlwind romance. At the end of one week, Don asked her to marry him. She accepted, and Ava went back to Texas with him. I haven't seen her in three years!"

"I take it she was happy doing that? She must have been a fish out of water."

"She was, but she did love Don. For some reason she didn't take to New York after returning from Poland. Sadly, Don had a heart attack. In 1950! They were together less than a year. But she inherited a large ranch property and a lot of money. So she's still there, alone. I'm sure there are suitors lining up at her door, and, knowing Ava, she is likely entertaining each and every one. So far, though, she has not remarried."

I decided to go for broke and ask the question. "Dora... has anything happened between you and Ava?"

She was a little startled. "Why do you ask?"

I certainly didn't want her to know I'd seen that torn up letter in her apartment. "No reason. I guess I'm curious as to why you feel the need to travel all the way to West Texas to see her in person when you could have picked up a phone."

Dora straightened in her seat a bit. "Mr. Leiter, I believe that falls under our agreement that there are 'no questions asked' regarding your assignment." She then focused her eyes straight ahead and clammed up.

So we were back to 'Mr. Leiter.'

The rain began to slack off, so I started the Packard and slowly pulled out of the ditch.

A couple of hours later, we went through Bristol and then crossed the state line between Virginia and Tennessee. Thoughts of the black Buick Roadmaster kept me on alert. There was a moment just as we entered Tennessee when I thought the car was behind us again. Up ahead, Route 11 split into east and west forks but they both ended up in Knoxville, our destination. Route 11W might have been shorter, but I chose 11E just to see what the black vehicle would do. I slowed a bit and kept vigilant. Sure enough, the car took the same road.

And then the rain decided that it wasn't finished. Another cloudburst dumped on us.

I slowed so much that the car had to tailgate me. Yes, it was a black Buick Roadmaster. Silhouettes of two men were in the front.

"Why are we going so slow?" Dora asked.

"Shh."

She started to look behind us and I snapped, "Don't! Keep facing forward."

"What's happening?"

"Stay calm."

I waited to see what the Buick would do. After maybe five minutes of following us with only a few yards between vehicles, it pulled into the oncoming lane and sped up. As it passed us, I tried to peer into the car to see the occupants' faces, but the rain made it impossible. The Buick swerved back into our lane ahead of us and went faster.

I floored the gas pedal.

Now it was *me* tailgating them.

"Felix! What are you doing?"

The alarm in her voice was palpable. I didn't answer her.

Our two vehicles stayed in this position for a full minute. Then the Buick shot ahead. Despite the downpour that made visibility a concern, I gave the Packard speed.

"Felix! Slow down!"

The speedometer told me we were at sixty miles per hour and climbing. Seventy.

The Buick went even faster.

Was this worth it? No, I decided.

I let off the pedal.

The Buick was now a dot in the distance and growing smaller. They'd lost us.

"Dora, that was the car following us. And I think it was the same one on Bleecker Street the night your friend was killed."

She said nothing to that and remained silent for several miles. The rain slacked off and the sun dared to break through the clouds.

"Please don't do that again," she finally said.

I didn't apologize. I had merely wanted to test the Buick's driver. Wasn't sure if I'd received any answers, but I now knew there was a serious game afoot.

The landscape had grown much hillier. The road continually ascended, descended, and curved this way and that as we traversed what was known as the Great Appalachian Valley, with the Cumberland Mountains to the west and the Great Smoky Mountains to the east. The sun eventually began to set as billboards and other landmarks indicated that we were only a few miles away from Knoxville. We passed a drive-in movie theater, crossed the Holston River, and then saw the Arrow Motel on the right of the highway. It looked fairly new and had a bright neon sign proclaiming that there were vacancies.

"How does this place look to you?" I asked. "You'd probably save some money out here than if we went into the city and stayed at a fancier place."

"It's not the cottages we had last night, but I'm sure it will do."

We checked into adjoining rooms. It was certainly a no-frills establishment, but there was air conditioning, heat, and a radio. We ate a few miles closer to the edge of town at a small pizzeria run by an Italian family who had come from New York. On the way back to the motel, I thought I'd try another attempt at breaking the ice and said, "It's still pretty early. There's that drive-in theater near the motel. You want to go to a movie?"

She smiled a little and said, "I don't know. I've never been to a drive-in."

"It's the new American way to see pictures, especially if you're teenagers like we are."

That made her laugh.

"*And* ... I have a nice little bottle of good Scotch whisky in the trunk."

Dora's eyes met mine with a spark and I knew we had a date.

The River Breeze theater was showing a double feature—*The Day the Earth Stood Still* and *The Thing From Another World*, both pictures from last year that neither of us had seen. Drive-ins were popping up all over the country. While they did appeal to the teen crowd, plenty of adults went to them, too. This one had spaces for about four hundred cars, and we were one of maybe a hundred that night. We settled in with the speaker attached to my window and passed the bottle of Haig & Haig back and forth as the short subjects played. Then, when the first feature began, my jaw dropped to my lap when I saw the lead actress. It was *her*! The one I thought Dora looked like! The same actress that was in *Operation Pacific*.

I turned to her and said, "Has anyone ever told you that you look like that actress?"

Dora wrinkled her brow and gave me a cockeyed glare. "What? Her?" She squinted her eyes and peered more intensely at the screen. "I do not. What's her name?"

"Patricia Neal."

She shook her head. "You're crazy, Felix. Pass me the bottle."

I laughed and did so. Maybe I *was* crazy.

The movie, about a space alien who comes to earth to save the planet, was pretty good if you go in for that sort of thing. Dora found the robot scary and she tried to memorize the nonsense words Patricia Neal had to repeat to stop the thing from wreaking havoc. We stayed for only half of the second feature, although it wasn't bad, either.

Back at the motel, Dora stopped before going into her room. She stood for a moment outside in the cool air gazing at the sky. An outline of a dark mountain range could be seen against the backdrop of stars. The earlier clouds had all dissipated and it was a gorgeous night. She lit a cigarette and leaned against a post.

"This place is beautiful," she said. I think she was a little tipsy.

"It is." I also lit a Chesterfield and stood beside her.

"*Klaatu Barada Nitko* . . ." she muttered.

"What?"

"It's what your actress girlfriend said to the robot. I can't get those words out of my head."

I chuckled. "Uh oh, you said it, now I can't blast you with my space beam."

I liked watching her laugh. Was she beginning to open up to me more?

We stood there for a moment in the quiet of the shadows until we both stubbed out the cigarettes on the pavement. Then she turned to me. Her face was perhaps a foot away from mine. In the moonlight, that pouty mouth beckoned to me.

She placed a hand on my left shoulder.

Holy mackerel, did she want me to kiss her?

"Thank you for the enjoyable evening, Felix," she said.

Do it! I commanded myself.

But before I could lean in, Dora turned away and adroitly unlocked the door to her room. "Good night. See you in the morning," she said.

The Earth had indeed stood still for an instant.

14
October 26, 1952

Tennessee

Before leaving the Arrow Motel on Sunday morning, I went to the pay phone in the lobby. I got a dollar's worth of change from the receptionist and then sat in the booth. I asked the operator to ring the number that Marion had given me. Brinkley promptly picked it up.

"Buddy," he said, "this won't be a secure line and I'll bet the friendly operator is listening in. You're in Tennessee?"

"Knoxville. About to drive to Nashville and then hopefully make Memphis by tonight."

"Be discreet, but do you have any news?"

"Someone's looking after us," I said. "Drives a black Buick Roadmaster. Could be the fellow you mentioned, starts with an M."

He would know from the coded message that we were being followed, possibly by Marko.

"My advice is to let him know you don't need help."

In other words, *lose him*.

"I'll see what I can do," I said, "but I have a hankering for Russian caviar." Meaning I'd like to shoot the guy.

"Felix, 'Russian caviar' and 'hankering' are words that don't go together in the same sentence."

"It's what we say in Texas, pal."

"Well, don't go messing with our competitors. Could have a bad outcome for business. You follow me?"

"Sure." He wanted me to see the mission through to the end without getting hurt.

"How's our girl?"

"Quiet. No word yet regarding her intentions. I haven't closed the deal."

"Well, stay the course. Evaluate her goals at your final destination. You can always call this number outside of office hours. If I'm here, I'll answer."

I hung up and thought about what he'd said. He didn't want me to engage the SMERSH agent. But if Marko was driving that Buick, I'd better keep my saddle oiled and my gun greased.

After filling up the tank with gas, Dora and I ate a quick breakfast and set off west on Highway 70. A road sign indicated a turnoff toward Kentucky.

"Dora, have you ever had authentic bourbon and branch water? Kentucky's the only state where you can get the real thing." I explained to her what that was. "I'm tempted to turn the car around and just go. To hell with Texas!"

She was only slightly amused. "I don't think so, Felix."

"Yeah, okay."

The first couple hours of driving was still on a winding, up-and-down road, but the landscape gradually smoothed out as we traveled away from the mountain ranges. The countryside was still picturesque but the sky was cloudy. I thought we might get more rain at some point.

Dora was rather subdued. There was an intangible tension in the air between us, but it was not an unpleasant one. We had bonded somewhat the night before by going to the drive-in, drinking the whisky, getting tipsy, and laughing a bit together. Then there was that face-to-face moment. I likely didn't act quickly enough. Or maybe if I had I would have blown it and made things *really* awkward for the remainder of the trip. It was difficult to know.

Her nervousness had lessened, though, that's for sure. She seemed to have warmed to me more since we left New York.

As if she were reading my mind, she asked, out of the blue, "Felix, have you ever been married?"

Okay, that was a topic that could reveal some things. "No. Have you?"

She shook her head. "That hasn't happened."

"Do you want it to?"

"I don't know. Yes, probably. Someday. To the right man."

"I take it Karl Adamski was not the right man."

Dora looked at me. "Karl was not my lover. We were just acquaintances. Friends."

"What kind of work did he do?"

"He told me he was a journalist. I don't know what he wrote, though. We met at Caffe Dante."

"That's a regular spot for you, it seems."

"It is. It's right on my street! Karl and another man were at a table speaking Polish. When the other man left, I said something to Karl in Polish. He asked me if I liked jazz. We didn't know each other very long. Not even two months."

Sure enough, it started to rain. I put on the wipers and kept going. It wasn't like the downpour of the day before.

"I imagine you have many suitors," I said.

"Why do you say that?"

"Because you look like Patricia Neal?" I looked at her and winked.

She smiled and shook her head. "Oh, stop it. But, yes, if you must know, there have been boyfriends. What about you, Felix? Why isn't there a girl in your life?"

"Oh, there was. Before The Mishap." I nodded at the hook on the gear shift.

"What happened?"

"Ah, Sandra. She's in D.C. We were dating there. I can't say it was anything serious but we had fun. I quite liked her. Then I was transferred to New York. It's not a long train ride from Penn Station to Washington, so we were probably going to still see each other when we could. But after that shark took away some souvenirs, Sandra didn't seem too keen on being with me anymore."

"That's terrible!"

"Why? You can't blame her, can you?"

"You are still a handsome man, Felix," Dora said.

That surprised me. I glanced at her. "Thank you. Still . . ."

"Felix, did you see that movie with the army veteran with no hands? He won an Oscar."

I knew exactly what she was talking about. "His name is Harold Russell. Actually he won *two* Oscars. *The Best Years of Our Lives*, right?"

"That's it, yes. It was a wonderful picture."

"Yes, it was."

"There is that scene that was so touching. The one where the girl he was engaged to tells him that she still wants to be with him and marry him."

"And he's flabbergasted," I said. "I remember it well." The conversation had quickly made me uncomfortable. I was ready to change the subject. "See if you can find something on the radio. We're getting close to Nashville. I'll bet there are stations we can pick up."

She turned it on and twirled the tuner knob. The voice of Kitty Wells filled the interior of the Packard as she sang "It Wasn't God Who Made Honky Tonk Angels."

"Oh, my," Dora said. "This is country music."

"That's what you're going to hear in Nashville, sweetheart," I said.

She sat back and listened with a smile on her face. "I kind of like it," she said.

We stayed on that station as the city grew nearer. Hank Williams came on next with his latest number, "Jambalaya (On the Bayou)." I'd never heard it before.

The lunch stop was at an enticing little joint called Varallo's, located in the center of downtown. Dora went for the fried catfish and fries. I got the fried chicken. The place was what might be called "down home" and colorful, attracting quite the crowd for lunchtime. Signs for the Grand Ole Opry adorned the place.

"You know, Dora," I said, "if we stayed here for the rest of the day and overnight, we could go hear some *real* country music at the Ryman Auditorium. I don't know who's performing tonight, but I'm sure the place would be kicking."

Dora laughed. "I swear your southern drawl was quite prominent when you said that."

"Ha! Wait until we're in Texas. Then I'll sound like Ragtime Cowboy Joe!"

I couldn't talk her into staying in the country music capital of the nation, so after we finished eating, we hit the road again and continued west toward Memphis with the radio broadcasting Hank Thompson singing "The Wild Side of Life." Radio reception was surprisingly good between the two cities. It faded in and out only when we were at the midway point. The closer we got to Memphis, though, Dora was able to switch stations and find a different, more mainstream genre of music. Al Martino crooned "Here in My Heart," Kay Starr sang "Wheel of Fortune," and we had a good laugh when Vera Lynn's "*Auf Wiederseh'n,* Sweetheart" made a reprise.

So far I hadn't seen the black Buick. I supposed that was a good thing. Brinkley's admonition to stay clear of it was still on my mind. And Dora Wysocki was indeed an enigma to me. I felt as if I had broken through some barriers that she'd erected around her, but I didn't believe I could have asked her what the purpose of her mission was. Not yet, anyway. "No questions asked," she had said, and she meant it. Dora tended to put up a wall as soon as I even danced around the subject.

I was going to have to let the thing play out.

As we drove into Memphis, once again the setting sun was hinting that we needed to find a place to stop for the day. Dora said, "Let's stay somewhere nice. After that motel last night, I want to go to a real hotel."

"It might be more expensive."

"I have the money."

Downtown Memphis was something to see. A southern metropolis had a completely different character than that of, say, New York or D.C. Even with newer skyscrapers, the town was something out of the past, an American icon representing a land and people quite foreign to New Yorkers. Not to me, so much, seeing that I was from Texas. But after living in Europe, in Washington, and New York, I was experiencing a transition shock.

We chose the legendary Peabody Hotel, located a couple blocks from the mighty Mississippi River that flowed through the city. As we checked in, Dora marveled at the fountain in the lobby where ducks swam freely.

The two of us dolled ourselves up a bit to go for dinner at Jim's Place across the street. She looked absolutely stunning in a red and black striped cocktail dress with a V-neckline that revealed a little more bosom than I had previously seen. I wore a clip-on tie. We had a drink of Haig & Haig in her room first—it was her suggestion!—and then left for dinner.

When we got back to the hotel, Dora gave me no indication that we were going to spend any more time together that evening. Despite our dressing to impress, she said goodnight to me, that she had enjoyed our dinner, and that she'd see me in the morning.

I went to my room down the hall and opened the Haig. I was more in the mood for bourbon, but the Scotch whisky was all I had. Glasses for water were provided in the room, so I poured myself a tumbler and downed it. It's a real man's whisky that assaults the taste buds with a 43% alcohol burn at first, but relaxes into a warm, smooth caramel malty taste tinged with oak. Eighty-six proof. I lit a cigarette and sat in the easy chair, not quite ready to hit the hay yet. For no reason at all that I could think of, I was suddenly reminded of a hotel I'd stayed in on the island of Guam at the end of '45. It was several months after we'd dropped the two bombs on Japan. The war was over. I was about to be demobilized and discharged, and I was going home. I don't remember why, but I stayed in a fleabag crummy hotel for civilians. It was god-awful and the mosquitoes and cockroaches were monsters. But I had cigarettes and a bottle of Haig & Haig, and I sat in an armchair almost the entire night drinking and smoking. By dawn I had decided to stay in the Marines.

That crappy hotel in Guam was nothing like the luxurious and elegant Peabody Hotel room, but the memory of it provided me with a foggy juxtaposition of where I was then and my current state of being. A lot had changed.

I wasn't the same me. But I was rebuilding.

Then came a knock on the door.

I got up and stood behind it. "Yeah? Who is it?"

"It's me, Felix."

Dora.

I opened the door and she was dressed in a robe. Underneath was a nightgown. *A nightgown and a robe!* It was all pink and frilly and downright gorgeous. She looked . . . spectacular.

"May I come in?"

"Sure." I closed the door behind her. "Is anything wrong?"

"I feel a little anxious and nervous. This trip is more stressful to me than you might think. Oh, I see you have your whisky. Might . . . might I have some?"

"Of course. Have a seat."

She sat on the edge of the bed while I poured a glass for her and refilled my own. I gave it to her and clinked it with mine. "Here's to ya."

I returned to my chair and pivoted it so I could look at her. She was a sight for tired eyes, let me tell you.

"You want a cigarette?"

"Please."

I tapped her one out of the pack, lit it, and handed it to her.

We sat there looking at each other for a long, long time, just drinking and smoking. Finally, she asked me. "Is it all right . . . if I stay here tonight?"

My God, yes.

I had to admit I was a little nervous myself. It would

be my first sexual experience since The Mishap. I had no idea how it would go. Prior to January 1952 I had the kind of confidence a man needed to please a woman. I'd had plenty of experience. Now? With only one hand? Was I supposed to take off the prosthesis or leave it on? They hadn't given me a manual for this situation back at the VA hospital.

As we both undressed, I made a move to take off the harness and prosthesis. Yes, at first it was awkward.

"I think I'll turn out the light," I said.

She could see I was uncomfortable.

"Felix, let's leave it on."

Dora approached me and was kind, considerate, and angelic. She had no problem with helping me discard the Above Elbow Upper Extremity appendage and then the Below the Knee Leg. It was only after we were together under the sheets that she reached over to the nightstand and turned out the light.

My self-confidence returned with a vengeance, and we didn't get to sleep until nearly two in the morning.

15
October 27, 1952

Tennessee – Arkansas – Texas
Monday morning. Six-thirty.

I got up and left Dora sleeping in my bed. As quietly as possible, I put on the harness of my prosthesis, attached the BK leg, and dressed. I needed some coffee in a big way. Dora rolled over once during all this but her breathing remained slow and heavy.

Ever so gently, I undid the latch on the door and opened it. The hallway was brightly lit, casting beams into the room. I quickly stepped out and carefully shut the door. On the way to the elevator, I paused to stretch my back and heard a few pops. The night had been quite the workout.

And it had been worth every ache and every ounce of fatigue I was going to feel for the rest of the day.

Down in the lobby, I bought a coffee. Before purchasing another cup for Dora, I thought I'd step outside and breathe some fresh air.

I dropped my coffee when I saw the black Buick Roadmaster idling at the curb right in front of the hotel entrance. A man was just getting into the passenger seat.

"Hey!" I shouted.

The Buick tore away, its tires burning rubber on the pavement. The screech was loud and jarring as the car bolted out into the road and ran a red light at Third Street, causing the few cross traffic drivers to slam on brakes and honk horns.

I went back to the hotel entrance and bought two more coffees inside. Stopping at the front desk, I asked the impeccably groomed hotel receptionist if anyone had been asking for me or if I had any messages. The receptionist informed me that a man had just a few minutes earlier asked if I had checked out yet.

"What did he look like?"

"Tall, bald ... I don't know ... He had a foreign accent."

"Did you tell him my room number?"

"No, sir. We don't do that. I asked him if he wanted to leave a message, and he said no. Then he left."

That clinched it. We were definitely being followed. Who were they? If they were SMERSH, then why weren't Dora and I already dead? What were they waiting for? Unless ... they wanted us to lead them to our destination.

Which brought me back to ... what was Dora's business in Odessa?

The elevator ascended to the fourth floor. When I stepped out I saw Dora leaving my room in her robe and nightgown.

"Psst, hey, lady!" I whispered loudly.

She whirled around, startled, and then exhaled and put a hand to her chest. "Felix! You frightened me!"

"Where are you going? I brought you coffee."

She stayed put as I went to her. "I woke up and you had disappeared. I decided to go back to my room," she said quietly.

I handed her the coffee and we went inside. She followed, sat on the bed, and gave me that nice smile of hers. I debated with myself whether I should tell her about the Buick, but I chose to keep that information to myself for now.

There was no mention of what had happened between us the night before. After some small talk over coffee and cigarettes, she stood and said, "I'm going to go bathe, get dressed, and pack. What time are we departing?"

It would have been smarter to get the hell out of Dodge, but we needed to eat and I didn't want to scare her. "I'd like to push all the way to Dallas today. A bit of a longer drive. I think we can do it."

She agreed and left the room.

At eight-thirty we were back on the road after filling up with gas and leaving Memphis behind. Highway 70 continued across the state line into Arkansas. The plan was to go beyond Little Rock and find a place to stop for lunch.

The terrain changed drastically on the highway to Little Rock. The landscape was flat and lacked the foliage we had seen in Tennessee. And yet, just to the north a ways were the mountains of the Ozarks, an outstandingly beautiful area of the state. I had been to the Ozarks and remembered them well. My father's family had been from somewhere in those hills and we had taken a trip to see them when I was six or seven. We were moving in a southwestern direction, though, too far away to see the range.

The radio had less reception as we got away from Memphis. The last thing Dora had picked up on the airwaves was news about the Korean War. Neither of us were in the mood for that, so we rode in silence for quite some time.

I was perplexed. The atmosphere in the car had definitely changed. She gave off no clues as to how she felt about last night. I didn't have any expectations that a romance would ensue. I wasn't about to put her on the spot and pretend she was my girlfriend now. No way. *I barely knew her.* What had happened was indeed enjoyable, but it probably wasn't a good idea to get involved with a client. Lord knows it's happened in the past. Those kinds of relationships become messy and uncomfortable. Did she feel the same way? Was that why she was ignoring the elephant in the room?

Fine. If she wants to pretend last night didn't happen, that's all right with me.

We went through Little Rock, switched highways to Route 67, and later had lunch at a whistle stop in Arkadelphia that was forgettable. The trek continued on to Texarkana and across the border into my home state of Texas.

After the few hours of the silent treatment, I finally attempted to break the spell.

"Is everything all right, Dora?" I asked.

She looked at me. "Yes. Why wouldn't it be?"

I shrugged. "Just asking."

After a pause, she went on. "I apologize for being quiet today. I've been thinking a lot about what will happen when I see Ava."

"And what *will* happen when you see Ava?"

"Felix, you're being paid not to ask questions."

I nodded. "Right."

The three hour trip across eastern Texas flew by as I was lost in my own thoughts. I had grown up in Dallas. Part of me wanted to drive by the old family home and see what it was like. Another side was telling me to let it be. There were some rather painful memories associated with my childhood.

The metropolis was upon us before we knew it, but the sun was indeed on its way down. I told Dora that it might be best to get on the other side of the city and find a place to stop for the night there and she was fine with that. Damn, the city had grown since the last time I was in it. Skyscrapers, crisscrossing highways, sprawling suburbs ... Dallas was proof of the adage that "everything was big in Texas."

By the time we had traversed downtown and turned onto Highway 1, it was night. Time to find lodging.

Then we hit a section of road that was under construction and the area was not well lit or marked. Road sawhorses blocked a lane of highway. As I slowed and pulled over to the lane where traffic was being rerouted, the noise of a loud engine alerted me to a car rapidly approaching from the rear. Its headlights blinded me in the rearview mirror. Voices of wild hooting and hollering. Teenage boys.

Sure enough, a shiny red late 40s model Cadillac Convertible doing maybe seventy miles per hour shot into my lane, forcing me off the road and crashing through the sawhorses. Before I could stop, the front end of the Packard hit a damned section of highway that simply wasn't there! There was a horrible *crunch* as we dipped into a shallow pit and came to an abrupt stop.

The passing car indeed contained five juvenile delinquents with cans of beer in their hands. They laughed and taunted us as the Cadillac driver broke all kinds of traffic laws. The convertible went zipping in and out of lanes and roaring like a hot-rodding speed demon away from the city.

"Jesus! Oh, for crying out loud!" I uttered a few extra curse words and quickly got out of the car to survey the damage. Dora did as well.

"You're not hurt?" I asked her.

"No."

"Well, the car is."

The front two wheels were hanging into the crevice. The under-chassis just behind the axle had smashed on the level pavement.

A pickup truck that had been behind me stopped. The driver was an old codger and a younger man was with him in the cab. They both got out to evaluate the situation, too. "You need help liftin' it, buddy?" the old man asked.

"Yeah, that might help. Maybe she'll still drive," I said.

The three of us positioned ourselves in front of the Packard and heaved it high enough to clear the hole and set the front end down on the road. Not easy with a prosthesis, so I was glad to have the assistance.

I got back in the car, started it, and lo and behold, the vehicle could move.

"Thanks, fellas. I think I'll try getting to where we're going."

They wished me luck and went on. Dora joined me in the car.

"We'll have to get this looked at in the morning. I doubt there'll be a mechanic open at this hour."

As soon as I navigated to Highway 80, the long, lonely road that would eventually lead us to Odessa, the Oil Pressure Indicator illuminated on the car dashboard. I could tell by the steering that the alignment was terribly off. I needed to shut off the car as soon as possible.

"We need to stop." I spotted the Alamo Plaza Hotel Courts up ahead. "And there're our beds for tonight."

Even though it was dark, the motel's neon street sign was bright and welcoming. The property was not the usual motel strip of identical doors, but instead there were separate small buildings in a U-shaped court, fronted by a façade that resembled San Antonio's Alamo Mission. I pulled in and asked Dora to go inside and get us some rooms while I checked out the car. The lighting wasn't great, but under the hood everything looked all right. But I checked the oil level and saw that it was nearly empty! I got down on my back to look under the chassis and could see a *drip . . . drip . . . drip* of the last dregs of oil. Either the oil pan had a huge hole in it or something else in the engine oiling system was faulty. Couldn't tell anything about the front axle.

I parked the car, went inside, and joined Dora at the front desk.

The receptionist, whose nametag read "George," was a man in his late twenties or early thirties. Thin, dark hair, and missing a front tooth.

"Hello, George. I've got some problems with the car. Where's the nearest garage?"

"The place I always send folks to is Freddie's, it's about a mile and a half down Highway Eighty. He has a tow truck if you need it."

"I might be able to get it to go a mile and a half on oil fumes," I said.

"He opens at seven-thirty."

George gave us keys to our respective "courts," and then he said, "Oh you might see my brother Billy cleaning out one of the rooms near yours. He's harmless."

Harmless? I didn't know what to think about that comment.

Sure enough, when Dora and I carried our bags to our adjacent rooms, we saw another tall, skinny man coming out of an open door. His overalls were quite greasy and even his shoes were leaving tracks of oily grime. A beat up 1945 blue Chevy pickup truck sat double-parked in front of the spot he was cleaning.

"Howdy, folks," he said. "You need help with anything?"

"You must be Billy?" I asked.

"Sure am! At your service!"

"Thanks, Billy, but I think we've got it." I stood with Dora as she unlocked her door and went inside. I told her I'd talk to her in a bit, and then I went to my room.

Billy approached me. His body odor about made me want to puke.

"Trouble with the missus?" he whispered.

"What? No, we're not married."

"Oh, I gotcha. Sorry. I was wondering, since, you know, you got separate rooms."

"We're just traveling together."

He leaned a little closer, much to my chagrin. "Well, if there's anything you want, I can get it for you."

"Excuse me?"

"You know ... booze of all kinds, narcotics, if you like that kind of thing ... if you need a piece I have a dealer that'll sell you a nice, unregistered handgun ... if you want, uhm, female companionship, I can arrange that, too ..."

I stared at the guy. "No, thanks." I unlocked my door. "Goodnight, Billy."

"Hey," he stopped me again. "Seriously, I need to get fifty bucks. If I can just get fifty dollars to bet on a rooster I've got my eye on, I'll be rich. I know he's going to win the cockfight tomorrow night. You interested? You staying long enough? Hell of a cockfight tomorrow night. You could make a whole hell of a lot of money! Lend me fifty and I'll pay you back, I promise. With interest, too!"

If it hadn't been so absurd, I would have laughed. "Good luck with that, Billy. Goodnight."

I went in and closed the door. It was a half hour later when I heard Billy's pickup leave the area. Dora and I had a late dinner at the sparsely populated Alamo Plaza Restaurant that was adjacent to the courts and then we retired to our separate rooms.

Once again, I pulled out the bottle of Haig & Haig and lit a cigarette. No sooner than I had poured a glass when there was a knock at the door.

"Yeah?"

"It's me."

This time she was still fully dressed.

"I thought we could share another glass of your Scotch whisky," she said. "If that's all right?"

"Sure."

And that's what we did. She also shared my bed for a second night. I didn't question it. With all the frustration and car trouble and second-guessing going on, I threw professional scruples out the window.

I figured that if I were sleeping with a Russian spy, then to hell with it.

16
October 28, 1952

DALLAS, TEXAS

On Tuesday morning I once again left Dora sleeping in my bed. I got up, did my routine of fitting my prostheses and dressing, and left her a note before heading out the door. I didn't like driving the Packard when the oil was likely completely depleted and the axle possibly damaged, but it was okay for the mile and a half down to Freddie's Auto Shop.

Freddie was a salt-of-the-earth stereotypical Texan mechanic who had a hell of a drawl, chewed tobacco and occasionally spit into an empty oil can. He was perhaps in his fifties. I explained the urgency of the situation and then waited in the small lobby that had two chairs and a radio in it, but there was a coin-operated newspaper bin with today's *Dallas Morning News*, so I bought a copy.

After a bit of a wait, Freddie walked in from the garage, wiping his greasy hands on a rag. "Well, sir. The front axle is bent. You'll need a replacement. You also need a new oil pan and oil pump. You had a hole as big as a golf ball. At first I thought it was too loose on the engine block or the pump cover gasket was too thick. I removed the thing and the pump gear is bent and the pump itself has a hole in it."

I shook my head in disbelief. "I'm hoping you can replace it all quickly."

"I don't have the parts. Have to order them from a dealer in town. The axle will be tricky. Probably won't get them until late today at best. Might be tomorrow or even the next day to get the axle."

"Is there any way to expedite this? We have to get to West Texas tomorrow, certainly by Thursday."

"Well, you could pay for special delivery. I'll have to see what it'll cost. If so, I can have the car ready for you tomorrow morning." He went back in his office to make a call, and then he returned in a few minutes. When he named the figure, I swallowed hard. I couldn't spare that much. I had it back in New York in the bank, sure, but not with me on the road. Hopefully Dora had the cash. No matter what, the car needed repairing. I told Freddie to order the parts. He offered for his son to give me a ride in his tow truck back to the Alamo Plaza, so I took him up on it.

I found Dora in her room, put my arm around her and told her the news. "Sorry about this. No one could have predicted it. I don't have the money. I mean, I do, but it would likely clean me out for the rest of the trip. Do you have that kind of money on you?"

She sighed. "Yes, I have it. It's in an envelope I hide in my luggage."

"At the very least, we're stuck here for a day."

"What are we going to do?"

"We'll think of something."

We ate breakfast at the restaurant and then sat for a little while by the outdoor swimming pool, smoking cigarettes. Finally, I said, "Let's take a taxi into town." Dora agreed. Her disappointment at being delayed seemed to have dissipated somewhat.

"Where are we going?"

"To the past."

The cab driver George called for us followed my directions and took us east into downtown Dallas. We eventually went a little farther north and onto Mockingbird, a major east-west street. When we reached the McMillan intersection, I saw that everything had changed from how I remembered it. I had the driver go east a little ways and then pull over to the curb. I pointed to some storefronts across the road.

"My father owned a men's clothing store right there. It was called Leiter and Sons, although I was the only son in the family and I was just a kid. I didn't work there. I guess he thought it sounded better with 'and Sons' added to it. My mother also worked there."

The place was now a five-and-dime store called TG&Y. That's a chain of small retail variety shops that had begun to appear during the Great Depression. They're all over the U.S., but the bulk of the stores are in the southern states.

I wasn't a person who dwelled much on yesteryear, at least not my *personal* past. It was not sensible in my line of work. If one worked in law enforcement or for the federal government, it was important to know and understand history, but you also had to have an eye toward the future. One's personal encumbrances had no place in the worlds of espionage or criminal detection. I knew that.

However ... I was in Dallas ... I might not ever be back ...

"Now take us to Delmar and Goodwin," I told the driver.

It wasn't far, maybe a mile and a half. It was an old residential neighborhood not far from a major north-south road called Greenville Avenue. I asked the driver to wait for us as Dora and I got out of the cab.

"Is this what I think it is?" Dora asked.

"If you're thinking it's where I grew up, you're right." We walked east on Goodwin past a few houses that had been built in the 1930s. We finally came to one halfway down the block and I stopped.

"This is it," I said, indicating a small red brick house. "It's been remodeled some, but I can still recognize our place there. My mother and father and I moved in when the house was new. I had a much older sister who married and left when I was seven. Before that we lived in a succession of spots I don't remember much. This is where I became a teenager and graduated from high school. Then I left home and joined the Marines."

Dora studied my face. "There is a sadness in your eyes. Something happened here."

I nodded. "My father's store was doing very well in the late twenties. He bought this house and we moved in.

Then, in 1931, the Depression was in its most destructive phase. My father had been hit badly by the Crash of '29, but he carried on. Times were tough, and we almost lost the house. One day I came home from school and found him on the floor of the bathroom. My mother was at the store. She later said he had gone home to get something, I don't know what. He didn't come back. I was used to coming home to an empty house after school. I've always wondered, though, why he thought it was a good idea to do what he did knowing full well it would be me who would come home to find him."

"My God, what happened?"

I had to pause before answering. "He'd taken his own life. Bullet in the head."

"I'm so sorry."

"Yeah. Me, too. It turned out he was flat broke. Was probably going to lose not only the house but the store, too. But you know what? My mother and I ... we pulled up our proverbial socks and kept the store going. She had a brother who came in and helped take over the business."

"What happened to your mother?" she asked.

"She passed away while I was with the Marines in the Pacific. Complications from pneumonia, so they told me. My uncle took care of everything because I was in the thick of it over there. This is the first time I've been back."

I then noticed that there were children's toys in the yard ... a ball, what looked like a toy fire truck, and a doll. The more I studied the house, I could see that it was well kept, had a nice flower bed in front, and a manicured lawn. A happy environment.

"Let's head back," I said.

"Are you all right?"

I nodded and forced a smile. "It was just something I needed to see. I'm confident that the place is something the inhabitants call 'home.'"

We walked back to the waiting taxi. The driver then took us back up to Mockingbird to a place called the Egyptian Restaurant, which incongruously served Italian cuisine.

Another cab drove us back to the Alamo Plaza and we went to our separate rooms. I unlocked the door, opened it . . . and saw that the place had been ransacked. My suitcase had been emptied, the clothes were strewn about, the dresser drawers were open, and the mattress was overturned.

"Felix!" I heard her yell.

I limped-ran to her room. The door was open and Dora stood in the middle of the same kind of chaos. The suitcase, the mattress, clothing, dresser drawers . . . Someone had had a field day going through our things.

She held an envelope in her hand and tears were in her eyes. My stomach lurched before she said the words.

"Felix, the money I hid in the suitcase is gone! All of it!"

17

DALLAS, TEXAS AND ENVIRONS

I stood there looking at Dora. "How much money was in there?"

She lowered her head. "Six hundred dollars."

"*Six hun*—! Jesus, Dora, that's nearly eight months of my rent in New York. That's a third of the cost of a new car. You were traveling with that much dough?"

"I didn't know how much we'd need! I thought it would be safe." She showed me a compartment in her suitcase behind the lining. "Look, see?"

A quick inspection of the door lock told me some things. "This wasn't a break in. Someone used a key."

Then I saw the linoleum floor. Faint traces of greasy shoeprints were all over the room.

"I know who did this," I said.

Dora followed me to the main office, where George was listening to a dramatic program on the radio. I pulled out my wallet and displayed my Pinkerton's identification card.

"Turn off the radio, George."

He switched off the show and asked, "Is there a problem?"

"We were robbed. Both of our rooms. My friend here is missing a nice bundle of cash. We know Billy did it. His greasy footprints are all over the rooms. Where is he?"

"Oh, come on, now, Billy wouldn't—"

I cross-drew the Iver and slammed it on the counter next to my ID. "Where is he? Can we settle this between ourselves, or do I have to call the cops?"

George's eyes darted back and forth. He knew he was in a corner. "Aw, hell. Yeah, Billy's a real screw-up sometimes. Always has been. I'm sorry, he ain't here. He went to a goddamn cockfight."

"Where is it?"

"It's at a campsite outside of Dallas, off of Farm Road 157." He gave me the directions. "You'll see a sign with a sombrero on it, says something about tamales."

"Great," I said. "Now, what are you going to let me drive there?"

"What?"

"Your car or truck. I need to borrow it."

"I can't let—"

"Yes you can." I picked up my Iver and broke it open enough to display the cartridges. I pretended to count them, and then shut the gun with another wrist snap. The sharp crack of the metal clicking in place made George flinch.

"I have a Ford pickup out back," he said.

"Better give me the key, then."

George reached into his trouser pocket, pulled it out, and laid it on the counter.

Dora and I left the office. I turned to her and said, "Go back to your room and straighten everything up. I'll be back in—"

"I'm going with you!"

"That's not a good idea."

"Felix, it's *my* money! I'm going with you!"

I sighed. "Dora. This will not be a safe place."

"I don't care. I'm coming," she practically barked.

This was a very different Dora. What happened to the nervous and timid Dora who didn't like to travel?

"Are you sure about this? I don't have a plan here. This will be an improvisation. It may not even work. We could get hurt—or worse."

"Two heads are better than one. I'm ready to go. Let's get in the truck."

I rolled my eyes. *Whatcha gonna do?*

The vehicle was a 1948 Ford F-1 half ton that had once been red. Now it was a kind of maroon-grey-green. The thing was a heap of junk. I did a walkaround, though, and the tires looked sound. I got in the cab, stepped on the clutch, and started the engine. The engine sounded as if it had whooping cough, but there was a full tank of gas and ... *oh no*. The transmission gear shift was a manual three-speed on the floor. How would I operate that?

"Well, Dora," I said as she got in on the passenger side, "it looks like you can be of use. You're going to have to work the gear shift."

"What? I don't drive."

"You don't have to. When I say so, all you have to do

is pull this handle down to the next gear. You only do it when I say to, when I step on the clutch. Let's practice."

I instructed her how to put it in reverse as I gently pedaled the gas and backed the truck out of its space. I braked, depressed the clutch, and told her to put the shift in first. I quickly explained how she could tell when it was in first, second, and third. Then the engine stalled.

"Try again," I said.

I started the engine, depressed the clutch ... Engine stalled.

"I'm sorry," she said.

"Let me try it myself." The engine kicked on and I attempted to manipulate the shift with my hook. The sequence of locking and unlocking the elbow got me all fouled up. Too difficult.

Damn it. It was times like this when the reality of my disability hit home.

"I'll try again," she said.

The engine started, I depressed the clutch, and she put it in first. The truck moved forward as I gently stepped on the gas.

"Now go to second."

Clutch. Shift. Gas.

"Third."

The truck shot out of the motel lot and I made the right onto Highway 80. She got the hang of it. We were in business.

In a couple of minutes we passed Freddie's Auto Shop. Moving on, there came a few instances of the clutch and gears grinding as we slowed for traffic lights and such, but pretty soon Dora was doing quite well. I instinctively wanted to reach for the gear shift with my right arm, which of course wasn't there. There were indeed times when I thought I could "feel" my right arm and hand, but as the docs explained to me in Florida, those were "phantom sensations."

I followed the directions to Farm Road 157 and made a left. We traveled quite a ways before the urban sprawl of Dallas thinned out into undeveloped areas under construction, which gave way to farmland and pure countryside. Thirty minutes later we were on a two-lane paved road in what seemed to be the middle of nowhere. In the dark.

After nearly an hour of driving, I thought George might have given us a bum steer. Then the headlights caught the sign with the big green sombrero on it. HOT TAMALES - 1 MILE! An arrow pointed left to a dirt road.

"Here we go," I said, making the turn.

We soon came to an area brightly illuminated with outdoor string lights. They were hung on poles that bordered and crisscrossed a space nearly the size of a football field. The largest structure was a tin-roofed, open-sided "arena." The rest of the grounds were filled with numerous shacks and smaller lean-to booths where vendors sold all kinds of goods. A small fenced-off area contained kiddie rides such as a thirty-foot high Ferris wheel and a small carousel with maybe fourteen bobbing horses. A "petting zoo" with a sickly-looking donkey, a sheep, and two uncooperative goats attracted the smaller children.

It was a goddamn carnival sideshow.

A young Mexican kid directed incoming traffic to a

dirt lot that was occupied by trucks, cars, motorcycles, and even horses hitched to posts.

As we got out of the Ford, I spotted Billy's blue Chevy pickup. "Well, he's here. At least we know we're in the right place."

Entering the grounds was an assault on the senses. Several booths featured food of diverse fare. Women and men of various races cooked and sold grilled and barbecued meats and vegetables. There were indeed hot tamales for sale. One woman was cooking carne asada and fajitas over an open fire. Another hawked tacos. Fried chicken. Hot dogs and burgers. At several booths you could buy beer, whisky, and tequila. Only one vendor offered Coke and Nehi grape soda, demonstrating the true supply and demand of the outpost. One man was selling live snakes and lizards. There were confidence games at which patrons could lose plenty of money. A fortune teller wanted to predict your future, for a price, of course. Across the way was a vendor grilling rattlesnake meat. I remember it tasted like chicken. There was even a tent where one could buy "souvenirs" consisting of piñatas, fireworks, cheap toys, and black velvet paintings of Jesus. Several desperado-types were selling assuredly illegal guns in a tent that was heavily guarded by armed men who could have been extras from *The Treasure of the Sierra Madre*.

"I've never been any place like this," Dora whispered.

There must have been two hundred people at the site, mostly men, but also a few women and even some families with children. All races were represented, but

Hispanics seemed to be the majority. Kids of all ages were riding the Ferris wheel, gawking at the snakes and lizards, and congregating around a booth that sold funnel cakes, deep-fried churro sticks, and cotton candy.

A few women were dressed provocatively. They stopped single men and spoke quietly, obviously selling their own kind of merchandise.

The place reminded me of carnivals and fairs that were prominent in small towns during the Depression. It was seedy and grotesque, and yet it was colorful, noisy, and full of life. Rural, southern Americana on full display.

"Have you been to one of these before?" Dora asked.

"A cockfight? Yes. I was a teenager. I went with some high school buddies. Believe me, I regretted it."

"How is it legal?"

"It's not! Every state has different laws about it, though. In Texas, it was declared illegal in the early 1900s."

"Then how do they get away with it here?"

"Dora, this is the south. They make their own rules here, and rules are not to be confused with laws."

I led her to the big tin-roofed structure, which was the home of the main event. I used my own funds to pay the pricey three dollar entry fee for each of us—highway robbery, in my opinion. The cockfights—yes, there were three in a row—were scheduled to begin at eight-thirty, which was in ten minutes. At three tables inside one could bet on the various roosters who were the combatants in the evening's festivities. Betting wasn't a requirement to watch, thank goodness. I noted that men were wagering as much as a hundred dollars on the birds. Madness.

In the center of the arena was an enclosure twenty feet in diameter formed by a three-foot-high wall of canvas. Bleachers surrounded the ring and in some spots—apparently "VIP" areas—had folding chairs. These were imprinted with ads and logos for Coca-Cola, Carta Blanca, and the like. There were already seventy-five to a hundred people in attendance, ninety percent men.

Dora and I took seats and I scanned the place. Billy was nowhere to be seen.

At eight-forty-five, men dressed in Mariachi uniforms and carrying musical instruments paraded into the ring. They began to play ranchera music and the crowd went wild with applause and cheers. A woman dressed in the style of a flamenco dancer leaped into the ring on cue and sang in passionate Spanish. She was apparently a popular personality at these events, because the audience was vocally and physically very appreciative. She played to the catcalls and whistles with happily seductive abandon.

Still no Billy. The music went on for twenty minutes. The spectacle was lively and, admittedly, entertaining, but I was anxious for the main attraction to begin.

Then, as soon as the band left the ring, Billy entered the arena and sat in the bleachers across from us.

Cockfight time.

18

Dallas Environs

The first fight paired a little red rooster against a pinto cock. The latter was a brown-and-white speckled bird. I overheard two men in front of us speaking in Spanish. My own Spanish wasn't great, but I could speak a little, and I overheard one of the men say that a pinto is a mix of German and Spanish breeding. The guy then called it a "headhunter" in English.

Sometimes the roosters are armed with steel gaffs attached to the natural spurs of the feet. Other times they are fitted with sword-like slashers or short, blunted spurs. Or, if the breeders agree, no "weapons" are attached to the fowls. For this first bout, the two combatants were young roosters likely participating in their first cockfight. Therefore, no extra accoutrements were utilized. That didn't mean it wouldn't be bloody and disgusting.

The referee called out "*¡Arriba!*" for the handlers to bring their birds forward, and the two men holding the roosters squat-walked to the middle of the ring. Each handler grasped the bodies of their respective fowls and held them a few inches above the ground.

Most of the crowd shouted, "*¡Pelea, pelea!*" while others simply yelled, "*Fight, fight!*"

The two birds struggled in the handlers' hands, eager to get at each other.

The referee held up both arms, held them high for a moment, and then brought them down. The handlers released the cocks and stepped back.

A flurry of screeching and feather flying commenced as the two roosters simultaneously attacked each other. Dora, beside me, gasped, but she didn't look away. The crowd called out for their favorite bird to do all kinds of horrible things to the other one. The handlers themselves shouted at their charges as if they were human boxers who could understand commands. Maybe the birds *could* comprehend the orders! Who knew ...

The pinto had a way of jumping in the air and slashing at the little red one. The smaller bird aimed for its opponent's legs, hoping to bite and snap a limb in two.

Suddenly, though, it was all over! The pinto had landed on the red cock with its spurs and claws out and proceeded to dig and slash at the poor thing's head and body. The red bird went flat as the pinto kept at it until it was a mass of blood and feathers. The referee called it off and declared the pinto the winner. Its handler grabbed it and pulled the bird away and held it high for the crowd. The audience, however, booed. They had been cheated out of a good, long fight. Still, the pinto had won, and whoever had bet on it was due some money. The dead bird's handler looked as if he'd lost a child. He slowly picked up the rooster's corpse and cradled it as he slowly walked out of the ring.

"That was sickening," Dora said.

"That bird was too young to fight and the handler pushed it into the ring too soon. It didn't have a chance."

I glanced across to the other side of the bleachers and noted that Billy was unmoved. This wasn't his fight. He likely bet all the money on the third, main event of the evening.

Two Mexican teenagers came out with brooms and dustpans and cleaned up the ring as best they could while two guitarists from the Mariachi band strummed high tempo rhythmic tunes.

The second fight featured two experienced "champions" from previous bouts held at the arena or at other cockfighting rings in the state or elsewhere. I knew that Mexico hosted the majority of them, but many of the southern states managed to hold these events, too. It was typical of the criminal element—if the demand was high enough, ways could be found to circumvent the law. Maybe the county sheriff was paid off to stay away. An organization of this size and visibility—when one knew where to look—had to have been on the radar of law enforcement. Still ... there were no cops in sight. Plenty of men with unconcealed weapons were present, though! It was a highly volatile environment.

The birds were introduced as Pedro and Thomas. *Thomas?* Okay, whatever. I didn't know what kind of roosters they were, but the hackles on one were bright orange and the other had blue main tail feathers and black sickle feathers in the back. Pretty soon they would be covered in red.

This time, the cocks were outfitted with razor-sharp gaffs, which resembled ice picks that were maybe two or three inches long, tied to the legs just above the feet. I had heard that handlers could suffer serious injuries from the gaffs and other weapons attached to their own birds. It was not a "sport" for the squeamish.

"¡*Arriba!*"

The two handlers brought forth their fighters. Pedro and Thomas squawked at each other, likely insulting one another in chicken-speak. Unlike the earlier inexperienced fowls, these two were relatively calm and didn't thrash about in their owners' hands.

The unruly crowd started up again: "¡*Pelea, pelea!*"

The referee's arms raised ... and went down.

The two cocks leapt at each other and actually swung their legs as if they knew very well that the deadly sharp weapons were a part of their appendages. They repeatedly jumped and lashed out. More blood, more feathers, more squawking. They danced around each other and then attacked again. They actually reminded me of sumo wrestlers I had seen in Japan when I was overseas after the war. While bulky and heavy, the wrestlers moved with lightning speed and ferocious strength. These roosters were much the same.

The crowd was going nuts. The men, especially, were overexcited as they shouted obscenities at the birds and handlers. Children in the audience were also enthusiastically participating in the spectacle. I remembered that

I had been disturbed when I saw a cockfight as a teenager. How damaged would these kids be? Or had they already seen so many that it was nothing to them? *Then* what would life mean to them as they grew older? Was it a healthy thing? I doubted it.

Thomas appeared to have the upper hand, so to speak. He kept jabbing at Pedro with the gaffs, one-two "punches," just as a boxer would punish an opponent. Finally, Pedro collapsed and lay on the ground, twitching. The referee called it, and the handlers went to collect their prizefighters. Thomas' owner held him high in the air and the audience cheered. Poor Pedro was taken away to be buried or cremated. I knew that the owners of these combat birds considered the fowl to be family.

Winning bettors left their seats to collect their money at the tables near the entrance. The Mariachi players returned to the ring to present more music while the ground was cleaned up once again. There was quite a buzz in the air as men—and women—called out to each other, laughing and taunting one another. The energy level in the arena rose to a peak. An argument broke out at one of the betting tables and one of the guards had to pull a gun and threaten the troublemaker. After hands were raised and apologies were given, the man was allowed to leave—probably without his earnings. The whole thing was crooked, I was sure about that.

"Where do these roosters come from?" Dora asked.

I shrugged. "They're bred to fight. Those handlers you see, this is their livelihood in most cases. They travel around the country and Mexico entering their birds in these cockfights. Winners take home a good size of the pot, and even the losers get a little something, just like in boxing. Some of the champion roosters become famous. Well, in *these* circles, they do."

The musicians filed out of the ring as the third set of handlers entered. The referee introduced the main event roosters as Diego and Salty. Diego was a big pinto, already straining in his handler's grasp. He was red and dark blue, with bright yellow hackles. His crimson comb was the longest and spikiest I'd ever seen. From what I could gather from the talk around us, Diego was a five-time champ that was favored to win. Salty was a brown and orange "liege fighter" with a super-long neck and long legs. Salty towered over Diego by three or four inches, but they were both very large birds. Both handlers held the roosters up and displayed to the crowd the dangerously sharp slashers attached to the spurs on the backs of their feet. Each blade was perhaps three inches long, curved upward like sickles. These things would do a lot of destruction. In fact—

"Agh!" Salty's handler yelped as he dropped the cock. The bird had struggled so fiercely in the man's hands that the slashers sliced his bare forearms. He was *spurting* blood, as if the man had taken a razor and attempted to commit suicide. Another guy who was the handler's assistant chased Salty around the ring, trying to catch the fowl. Many in the audience laughed at the grotesque comedy of the situation, while others were naturally horrified.

Workers rushed the wounded handler out of the arena after wrapping his arms with towels. There was a bit of a delay before the assistant finally caught Salty and verbally chastised the rooster for hurting his master. I was sure Salty didn't give a damn. He wanted to get at Diego as soon as possible.

Finally, they were ready to begin.

"*¡Arriba!*"

"*¡Pelea, pelea!*"

Arms raised. Arms down.

Diego *vaulted* at Salty and leapt over the bird's very tall crown, back-slashed the fowl in the neck, and then landed on its feet behind his opponent. Not to be outdone, Salty kicked behind him, jabbing Diego with the blades. Both birds were already bleeding profusely, but they didn't seem to be hurting. They went at each other ferociously as the crowd screamed and hollered at them.

Billy was now standing and calling for Salty to "bite his head off!" Apparently he had bet against the cock favored to win.

Diego, though, quickly landed more blows. He also violently pecked at Salty, using the beak as a formidable weapon. The pecking was at such a rapid pace that the rooster's head was a blur. Salty squealed in pain now as Diego jumped and landed on his opponents back. The slashers doubled down and jabbed at Salty's long neck, truly attempting to sever the bird's head.

But suddenly Salty kicked out and managed to swing one of his slashers across Diego's breast. Those yellow hackles were now streaming with blood.

"I can't watch," Dora said, turning her head and resting it on my left shoulder.

Billy jumped up and down, crying, "Yes! Yes! Go! Go!"

Salty had apparently delivered a serious blow to Diego. Wounded and wobbling, Diego attempted to keep up a valiant fight, but now Salty's bulk and height gave him the advantage. With almost calculated precision, Salty hacked and punched with the blades until Diego dropped to his side, unmoving.

Billy shouted, "Yaaay!"

The crowd roared with hoots, whistles, and cries of either anger or joy. Diego, the champion, had been bested. His handler was crying as he got to his knees beside his prize rooster. He picked up the bloody thing and held it to his chest, mouthing a prayer in Spanish as tears streamed down his face. Meanwhile, Salty's original handler, his arms now wrapped in gauze bandages, returned to the ring, picked up his new champion and held him high.

Billy bolted for the steps down the bleachers and headed for the betting tables.

"Let's go," I said to Dora.

We got to the ground and moved with the crowd out of the arena past the tables. I saw Billy in line, rubbing his hands with glee, a huge grin on his face. Many of the more inebriated attendees went outside, drew pistols, and fired them at the sky as they whooped and howled like revelers at a New Year's Eve party in hell.

Billy finally emerged into the night air and made a beeline to the parking area. Dora and I followed him. Luckily, not too many people were as anxious to leave as Billy. It was only ten o'clock and there was still food to eat, booze to drink, and money to spend. Leaving the campsite for the dirt lot considerably lowered the decibels of noise.

I pulled out my Pinkerton's ID and approached Billy as the man opened his pickup truck door, ready to step up inside.

"Hold it, Billy."

He turned. "What?" Then he recognized us and his eyes went wide.

"Get down, now! Raise your hands."

He did so and eyed my ID. "What ... what is that?"

"I'm an agent with Pinkerton's Detective Agency. You're in big trouble, my friend."

"What are you talking about?"

"You robbed us back at the motel. We want our money back. *Now*."

"You're crazy! I didn't rob you!"

"Your greasy shoeprints were all over our rooms! Don't lie to us. You know how many years you'll spend behind bars for robbing your own customers at the motel? What's your brother, George, going to think? It could put him out of business!"

And then Billy sucker-punched me, swiftly raising a fist and clobbering me in the face. I fell back and landed on my rear. The guy then quickly climbed into his truck and started the engine.

"Hey!" Dora shouted. "Felix, he's getting away!"

The truck started to pull forward.

Still on the ground, I cross-drew my handgun, which had been neatly concealed beneath my jacket. Extending my left arm, I aimed at one of the back tires and squeezed the trigger.

I missed. AGAIN.

Just as I was about to fire a second time, *Dora* grasped my forearm with one hand and placed her other on the top of the Iver. "Give it to me!" she snapped. She then pulled the piece right out of my hand, stood in an experienced shooter's stance, aimed at the back of the truck, and neatly shot a hole in the driver's side back tire. The truck continued to move, picking up speed. Dora aimed at the other back tire and fired again. *Pop!* went the passenger side wheel.

The woman had blown out both back tires like a pro. I stared at the damage with my lower jaw so far down that it might as well have been in my lap, and my pride was somewhere back at the cockfight arena in a pile of blood and feathers with the other losers of the evening.

I managed to stand and together we walked to the truck as Billy jumped out to look at the flat tires.

"Give it to me," I said to Dora, holding out my hand. She gave me the gun and I pointed it at the thief.

"All right, Billy. How much did you win back there?"

This time he raised his hands voluntarily. "Don't shoot!"

"I asked you a question."

"Uh . . . five hundred dollars."

"*How much?*"

He looked at the ground. "Uh . . . one thousand, eight hundred dollars."

"Jesus, Billy, you can buy a brand new car with that

kind of money. Well, look, I'll go easy on you. Give us back the six hundred you stole from my friend here. Now!"

The man reached into his grimy overalls pocket and pulled out a wad of bills. He counted out six hundred and handed them over. Dora took them from him.

"Now," I said, "as a Pinkerton's officer, you know I could arrest you, charge you with robbery, and you'd not only go to jail, but also have to pay a hefty fine."

"Please don't!"

"All right, then, the alternative is that I have to charge you interest. This will be a personal fine for assaulting an officer like you did back there and for committing the crime of robbery in your own place of business. So you owe us another two hundred dollars. Fork it over."

"Two hundred!?"

"Yes."

"That's not fair!"

"Of course it is. Unless you think going to jail is a better idea."

The man looked like he might cry. Finally, he counted out two hundred bucks and gave it to Dora.

"Look at it this way, Billy," I said. "You still have a thousand dollars. That's a *hell of a lot of money*. You're still ahead with more than you started with tonight. *Right?*"

"Uh ... I guess."

"Okay. We're going now. Be happy you're not in jail." I holstered my weapon and then wrapped my prosthetic arm around Dora's shoulders. We turned and walked toward George's pickup.

"Wait! I don't have spare tires!" Billy called.

"Good night, Billy!" I called.

"Are you going to leave him stranded?" she asked.

"What, you want to give him a ride?"

"Not really."

"Okay, then. Maybe he's learned a lesson."

We drove out of the parking lot, got back on Farm Road 157, and headed back to Dallas and our motel rooms.

"Could you really arrest him?"

"Hell, no," I said. "Pinkerton's detectives have no law enforcement power. He was too stupid to realize it. That works sometimes." I was still flabbergasted about what I had witnessed. "And what about *you*? Dora, what did I just see you do?"

"I spent some time with Ava at a gun range before she moved to Texas. There's one in Queens we used to go to. She thought she should learn how to shoot, so I did, too."

We said no more until we reached the Alamo Plaza.

She was lying to me. I knew that Ava allegedly met her Texas husband in 1949 and had moved from New York that year. If I'd read those letters correctly, the two sisters were not speaking to each other at that time.

I had just seen a side of Dora that made me question everything I thought I knew about her.

19
October 29, 1952

DALLAS, TEXAS – ODESSA, TEXAS

When I woke up early Wednesday morning, Dora wasn't in bed with me. I was surprised that I had not heard her get up and leave my room, for I was usually a light sleeper. I was trained to become alert to any kind of movement or disturbance in the air around me when I slept. It was a self-defense mechanism that many in law enforcement, especially government agencies, possessed.

I quickly harnessed, dressed, and left the room. Perhaps she had gone back to her own bed for some alone-time before I picked up the car—there had been word at the front desk that the Packard was ready. I went to the lobby to buy coffee. George said nothing to me about Billy or the previous night. I told him we'd be checking out in a little while.

And then I saw Dora in the phone booth, talking animatedly to someone. I stood and watched for a moment and then she hung up. She sat in the booth, staring at the telephone for a few seconds, then gathered herself and exited.

"Felix!" she said.

"Good morning." I moved closer to her. "I, uh, was wondering where you went."

"I needed to go to my room for a while."

"And make a phone call."

"Yes."

We walked outside and back toward our courts.

"Who were you talking to?"

"Ava. I let her know we would arrive today."

Oh, really? Was that the truth?

"Okay." When we got to her room, I said, "Look, why don't you get ready and pack. I'm going up the road to get the car. I'll drive it back, we'll have breakfast, check out, and go. All right?"

"Sounds good."

We were off by mid-morning. The last leg of the journey felt longer than it really was. Highway 80 all the way to Odessa was a straight, dull, monotonous trek across approximately 350 miles of nothing. After going through nearby Fort Worth, the landscape gradually flattened and the kind of foliage and beauty that had made previous travel days interesting became sparse. The closer we got to West Texas, the environment turned barren and the horizon was a flat line that stretched across our vision. We were on a lost highway to the edge of the world.

Lunch was in Abilene at a roadside diner. It felt as if we'd been driving six hours, but it had been only a little over three. There was another stretch of three hours to reach our destination in the afternoon.

A different dynamic floated between us in the car. The

night before had been puzzling because she had come to my room not to make love but simply to sleep in the same bed. I figured that was all right, but her demeanor had changed since our arrival in Dallas. Something was quietly bothering her and she wasn't about to say what it was. Perhaps she was worried about seeing her sister, but I thought her mood might have something to do with me. I'd long ago stopped trying to understand women. Seeing her in the phone booth, however, triggered a red flag. Unless she had previously snuck off to use the phone when I didn't know it, it was the only time during the last several days that she had done so. It didn't feel right.

We drove nearer to West Texas, passing through such whistle stops as Big Spring, Stanton, and finally Midland, the "sister" city of Odessa. The terrain could easily be called the desert. Yellow and brown earth, hardly any trees other than short, ugly mesquite, and a bright blue sky over an astonishing 180° plane that seemed to go off to infinity in all directions. The topography was at first occasionally, then more frequently, dotted with oil rigs and pumpjacks. The region had become oil company paradise in the last couple of decades.

When we finally reached Odessa, the sun was merely a golden sliver behind the horizon and would disappear very soon, plunging us into darkness. I had to admit that the sunsets in Odessa were truly gorgeous—the sky was streaked with red, orange, yellow, blue, and black, all reflected on the clouds in a painterly fashion.

Dora said, "I can't believe it's so flat here. And the streets are so wide!"

"Welcome to West Texas, the armpit of the state. If you look at the map, the shape suggests it. We're at the bottom of the Panhandle and we're also at the corner of the section that protrudes west toward El Paso. Odessa sits at that right angle, not far from New Mexico."

"You've been here before?"

"Once, as a kid. Just passed through. Believe me, this is Small-Town Texas, Dora. Don't be surprised if we're looked at as 'Yankee strangers.' In many ways, it's still the wild west. Now, I'm going to stop at a gas station, buy a city map, and fill up. Give me Ava's address, and we'll go straight to see her. How's that sound?"

Highway 80 turned into 2nd Street as we drove into the city. Ava Spence lived on the northwest side of town, outside the city limits on a ranch road off Highway 302, which took one to the tiny town of Kermit. The address wasn't on the city map, so I had to ask the gas station attendant where I'd find it. The young man's answer was only a guess, but he thought it was near an itsy-bitsy community serving the oil fields called—I kid you not—Notrees. "That's because there ain't no trees," he explained.

We drove north through the quaint downtown on Grant Avenue. An old hotel called the Elliott; pawn shops; liquor stores; the Do Drop Inn Café; F. W. Woolworth and Wacker's variety stores; a handful of banks; women's clothing boutiques with names like The Model Shop, MayFair Women's Smart Apparel, and more. It was Main Street USA, Texas-style, a snapshot of 1930s-40s small town America undergoing growing pains as more modern establishments were moving in and replacing the old.

Night enveloped the landscape as Highway 302 took us in a westerly direction into the oil fields and eventually to the farm road that was our destination. Ava's home was a substantial status symbol of a wealthy, albeit deceased, husband. The ranch house was large, perhaps 3,800-4,000 square feet, and it sat on at least five hundred acres of, well, nothing but sagebrush, mesquite, and dirt. Neighbors were far away. A freshly-cut grass lawn bordered by a short stone fence surrounded all four sides of the home.

We parked the Packard on the gravel drive in front. A 1949 blue and white Cadillac sat on the gravel drive, another badge of prestige for the Spence family. The place was still and quiet. No exterior lights were on.

"Is she home?" I asked.

"She's supposed to be," Dora said.

We got out of the car and went to the front door. Dora looked tense, more cautious than eager to see her sister. She rang the doorbell. Nothing.

"She must be out," Dora said. "Do you think she's all right?"

"How should I know?"

Then Dora knocked on the door ... and it swung open with a creak. It had been slightly ajar. I pushed it farther so that we could step inside. The lights were on.

"Ava?" Dora called.

"Hello?" I shouted a bit louder.

As we moved deeper into the house, we saw that the living room was in shambles. The furniture had been overturned and the cushions of what once was a lovely antique sofa had been ripped to shreds.

"Ava!" Dora called again.

I drew my handgun. "Dora, go back to the front door and wait there. I'm going to have a look around." She did as she was told and I took a sweep of the house as I was trained to do. The kitchen appeared untouched, but a room that was an office was also ransacked. Filing cabinets were open and papers were all over the oak desk and the floor.

My senses somehow told me that all this had happened very recently, within the last few hours.

Moving on, I looked in one bedroom that was untouched, and then found the large master bedroom. Sitting on a table was a Hallicrafters HT-20 shortwave radio, just like the one Adamski had in New York. The only difference was this one was smashed to pieces.

"Holy mackerel," I said aloud to myself.

An open suitcase lay on the bed and its contents—clothes and things—had been dumped out. Had Ava been packing and interrupted by someone?

A throw rug decorated with Navajo designs occupied most of the room. It was blemished by several spots of blood. Still wet.

I backed out of the room and continued the search. No one was in the house.

Returning to the front where Dora was waiting, she asked, "What's happened? Where's Ava?"

"I don't know. Stay put." I went back to my car, opened the trunk, foraged for my bag of tools, and removed a flashlight. I flicked it on and cast a bright beam into the darkness around the front of the house.

"Dora, get in the car and wait for me."

"No. I'm coming with you."

I figured she'd say that. "Suit yourself."

Following the white radiance of the flashlight, we moved to the right side of the house. Nothing there, so we continued to the back.

A splash of something white and frilly lay on the dirt about thirty feet from the rear of the house, just beyond the grass yard and short stone fence. The back door to the house was open, leading inside to an apparent utility room containing a washer and dryer, and beyond that, the kitchen.

As I moved closer to the object on the ground, the light beam revealed a woman's body wearing a white dress. She lay on her back. Three splotches of red covered her chest. I recognized them to be exit wounds. My first impression was that she had been running from the house and had been shot in the back, and then either she had managed to roll over before dying, or the killer had turned her to make sure she was dead. The blood was still quite wet.

"Ava," Dora whispered.

20

Odessa, Texas

Bloody lesions on Ava's face indicated that she had been hit a few times. I knelt to get a closer look at her wrists. Red rings around them.

"Dora, this happened just a little while ago," I said.

She whirled around and marched into the house through the back door.

"Dora! Wait!" I went after her and found her standing in the kitchen, her hands on the counter, breathing rapidly.

"I'm so sorry," I said. "We'd better call the police."

She shook her head. "No."

"What do you mean, 'no?' Hell, we need to call not only the cops but the FBI! Dora, your sister had spy communication equipment in one of the rooms. I saw it, it was all smashed up. This is an espionage case! The killer or killers were here searching for something." She wasn't listening. I grabbed her by the shoulders and turned her to face me. "I've seen this kind of thing before! Ava returned home and caught them in the act. Or she was here, they came, and she wouldn't give them what they wanted. She was handcuffed and interrogated. There's blood on the rug in her bedroom. She tried to run away. I believe the killer removed the cuffs after she was shot."

Dora's eyes were wild. "Felix, we cannot alert the authorities. It would ruin *everything*."

"What in blazes are you talking about, Dora?"

"You are not to ask questions!"

"To hell with that, Dora! Your sister was *murdered*! Doesn't that mean anything to you?"

"Of course it does! But this is . . . This is bigger than you or I. There is . . . oh, God, I can't tell you, Felix. I'm sorry. I just can't."

Her rapid breathing approached hyperventilation as her eyes darted around.

I knew the feeling. It had happened to me long ago at my home in Dallas.

"I need to call Pinkerton's and check in. This is serious, Dora. I don't know what game you've been playing, but you're right. It *is* bigger than you or me!"

A phone was mounted on the wall of the kitchen. I picked up the receiver, but the thing was silent. I jiggled the receiver's cradle several times. No operator. Dead. Cut.

I slammed my fist on the counter and shouted, "Goddammit, Dora, tell me what the hell is going on! If you won't, then I'm walking out the door, getting in the car, and going to the police myself."

She left the kitchen, stormed through the living room, and back to Ava's bedroom.

I took a deep breath, followed her, and stood in the doorway. She was searching the table around the smashed shortwave. I watched as she frantically looked underneath it and then went to the dresser. She opened each drawer and rummaged through clothing and other items, before going back to the suitcase on the bed and rifling through the spilled contents—printed documents and hand-written pieces of paper. She sat on the bed and began to go through them.

Three small, framed photos were among the piles of clothes. One was the same picture I'd seen in Dora's New York apartment of her younger teenage self in front of the *biblioteka* that had been torn in half. The difference was that this print was complete. The other person in the photo was another teen girl. Perhaps even prettier than Dora.

Displaying the photo, I asked as gently as I could, "Is that Ava?"

She shot a glance at it, paused, and nodded. Then she went back to what she was doing.

Another picture revealed an adult Ava and a man wearing a cowboy hat cutting a wedding cake. Don Spence and his new bride. Dora was attractive, to be sure, but Ava was downright gorgeous. I wondered if this might be one of the issues Dora had with her sister.

The third framed photo was of Ava with a different, younger, slightly chubby man who was also wearing a cowboy hat. They stood in front of the exterior of a bar called The Oil Patch.

"Dora, do you know this man with your sister?" I asked, holding the picture up for her to see.

"That must be Bork," she answered. "Her new boyfriend. I've never met him."

The name rang a bell. Ava had mentioned him in one of her letters to Dora. "Bork" had proposed to her. I remembered she'd said he was a bartender. At The Oil Patch, perhaps?

I dropped the frames on the bed and then stood behind her. She quickly skimmed the papers, which were a lot of the same things I'd seen in Titov's and Adamski's apartments. Notes written in Polish.

A page torn from a brochure or magazine displayed text and a black and white photo of a man in his forties, dark hair, Slavic features. The header proclaimed him as RURIK BABANIN. The text, the man's bio, was in English. He was apparently a Soviet diplomat to the West.

I had never heard of Rurik Babanin. Currently the Soviet Union did not have a consulate-general presence in the United States, at least not in New York. There was still a Soviet ambassador and Soviet Embassy in D.C. As the U.S.S.R. was a founding member of the United Nations, the Soviet Mission to the U.N. still operated on Park Avenue at E. 68th Street.

A U.S. passport was among the items on the bed. I opened it to see Ava's face and name. Inside was an envelope containing two airline tickets. One was in her name, the other in the name of Jerome Borkowski. Bork. They were flying on November 1 from El Paso, Texas to Dallas, connecting to Chicago, Illinois, and then boarding another flight to New York. On November 3 they were flying to London, and then, two days later, finally to

Paris. I showed the tickets to Dora. She examined them briefly—and then *tore them up*.

"Dora!" I was so surprised by her angry demeanor that I wanted to shake her! Instead, I sat on the edge of the bed and once again attempted to break through to her. "Damn it, Dora, I can help you but not unless you tell me what all this is about. Why did we make this journey? What are you looking for?"

Dora exhaled with frustration and swiveled to look at me. "I need to interfere with a job that Karl Adamski was supposed to do, but he was killed."

"And . . . ?"

"Damn," she said.

"Jesus, Dora. Don't you trust me? After what we've . . . Come on."

"All right. I am undercover. I am FBI."

"*What?*"

"I am an undercover FBI agent working to expose a Soviet spy group that is attempting to steal nuclear secrets from the U.S. Karl was supposed to courier those secrets, which are being smuggled from Los Alamos."

"So was this why you were, uh, *friendly* with Karl Adamski in New York? You were spying on him?"

"Yes."

"And do you know what the smuggling plan is?"

"There is a Soviet spy employed right there in Los Alamos. He is a high level assistant to scientists working on the hydrogen bomb. They have completed the research, and a test of the hydrogen bomb is imminent. No one outside the government knows this! It's top secret."

"He's Russian?"

"No, he's Polish-American! His name is Stanley Masters. But he anglicized it. Changed it from Stanimir Masternak."

"Why doesn't the FBI arrest him?"

"Because they want the proof that Masters is indeed attempting to smuggle the plans and deliver them to a Soviet diplomat in New York this coming Sunday." She pointed to the printout I'd laid on the bed. "Him."

I picked up the page again. "Babanin? Is he the ringleader?"

"We think so."

"And what was Ava's role in this? Was she part of the spy network?"

"Yes, she was coordinating the handoff from Los Alamos to the next link in the pipeline. That was supposed to be Karl. But since he's dead, Ava changed the operation."

"So it was Karl that Ava was talking to on the short-wave and vice versa."

"Yes. Would you believe they used a crazy coded system in Polish that sounded like it was nothing but food recipes? That's how they went undiscovered all this time. Anyway, all we know is that Ava got her boyfriend, Jerry Bork, to replace Karl. He and Ava were going to meet with Masters and receive the plans." She indicated the torn airline tickets on the floor. "And then they would have taken them to New York. Now it will be only Bork. He lives here, in Odessa."

"Do you know where and when this handoff is supposed to be?"

"We have only a date—October thirty-first."

"That's the day after tomorrow. Halloween."

"But we don't know *where* it's going to be. Somewhere in New Mexico. Originally it was supposed to be Santa Fe, but that changed when Karl was killed. That's why I'm looking through all this. For clues! I *must* find where and when the handoff will be."

"How is Masters delivering such a complex set of plans? I'm assuming you mean the bomb's design and technical specifications, the whole damn recipe?"

"No, no, not all of it." She gave a little chuckle. "Well, yes, you're right that it's a recipe of sorts. It's a summary. A *Reader's Digest* version of the essential 'ingredients.' And it all fits on a microdot. And unless they've changed the original plan when Karl was supposed to be the courier, that microdot will be stuck on a plain U.S. quarter."

I stood and began to pace the room. "A twenty-five cent coin can be dropped into a pocket, hidden and mixed with other change."

"Exactly. The year on the coin is what will identify it. Unfortunately, we don't know that date."

"And what were you hoping to do when you got here to Odessa?"

"I was to intercept the coin from either Ava or Bork and deliver it to the FBI myself. And then the FBI would arrest everyone."

My head was spinning. One sister was a Soviet spy. The other sister was an FBI agent. How could that be? "Wait, wait, wait. Why did you need me to escort you all the way from New York?" I couldn't help the sarcasm. "Seeing that *you're the goddamn FBI!*"

"Felix, it was part of my cover. I'm an innocent Polish-American traveling to see my sister. You are a non-governmental detective-for-hire whose *bodyguard* services were required. At least that was for appearances."

"Appearances for whom?"

"Look around you! My sister was murdered! The place is ransacked! Someone else is after the same information! The Soviets are not the only ones after the secrets of the hydrogen bomb. We know that there are other dangerous agents here in the country that want those secrets, too. But if they can't get them, then they will make sure *no one* gets them. Ava was murdered by a foreign agent who didn't want her to succeed. Likely the same assassin that killed Karl Adamski."

And Gregory Titov. Dora didn't know I was aware of him.

She caught her breath and continued. "I will tell you something else. That motorcycle down at City Hall Park. The man shooting at us?"

"Jan Bartosz. He was Karl's former roommate."

"He was after *me*. He was working for Ava and her team! To stop me from making this journey."

"Well, who killed *him*?" I growled.

"I don't know!"

She went back to the desk and continued to look through the stuff as I tried to get my head around it all. Taking a leap, I asked, "Dora, was Ava a Prometheist?"

She blinked rapidly and visibly shivered. "What?"

"You know what I'm talking about."

"Felix, the Promethean Movement died during World War Two. They were all wiped out by the Nazis. No, she wasn't. She was working for the Soviets. Come on, help me look at these papers. We must find clues about the handoff. And Jerry Bork."

My brain hurt. Michael Brinkley had told me a SMERSH operative was in the States. Was he in the black Buick that had been following us? Marko? If Ava and her team were Soviet spies, then Marko had seemingly killed his own people—Titov, Adamski, Bartosz, and, likely, now Ava. So I asked myself again—why hadn't he tried to kill *us*?

"Don't you want to get the police out here, Dora? Your sister is lying in the dirt outside."

"We will, Felix. But we'll do it anonymously. I know you probably think that is cold of me. I'm FBI. I'm sure you understand that my job must override personal feelings. I will grieve later. Besides . . ."

"What?"

"Ava and I were not exactly on good speaking terms lately."

"And why is that?"

"I knew about her treacherous activities! I knew she was a traitor!" She practically groaned. "Oh, Felix. Ava was not really my sister."

"*What?*"

"I was an orphan. The Wysocki family took me in when I was four, just as they were about to move to Warsaw from the States. I was never formally adopted.

Ava and I grew up as sisters but we were like oil and water. We never got along."

I examined the photo of Ava Spence and Jerry Bork. The bar called The Oil Patch. "Well, I hope Bork isn't already dead, too." I went to the kitchen and found the address of the bar in the directory by the phone. But there was no listing for a J. Bork or a J. Borkowski.

Returning to the bedroom, I said, "I know where Bork might be. Let's go."

Dora finally gave up in the bedroom. She gathered herself, told me to wait a moment, and then went back outside to the back. She took a few minutes to stand over Ava's body. I kept a distance so that she could be alone. What was she really feeling? I had no idea. Finally, she turned and strode around the house to the drive and climbed into the Packard.

"Ava knew she was playing with fire," she said with a mixture of sadness and anger. "Start the car, please."

Right. We were leaving a crime scene and a corpse, off to hunt for a man who might be another dead body, and then attempt to intercept a handoff of government secrets somewhere in New Mexico in less than two days.

And what about Dora? She had become a completely different person.

I *thought* we had grown close. Hell, I didn't know what it was between us now.

But my gut told me one thing—I did not believe she was FBI. She was lying through her teeth.

21

Odessa, Texas

We drove back to town. I stopped at another gas station and made the emergency call. The operator connected me with the police. I told them there was a body at Ava's address. I hung up before they could ask me to identify myself. Dora and I could not get involved in a police investigation. Not then. If what she told me about the October 31 smuggling operation was true, then we had to stay clear of anything that might hinder us.

Dora took a change of clothes from her suitcase into the ladies' room, so I knew she'd be a few minutes. I took the opportunity to phone Michael Brinkley.

"How's West Texas, cowboy?" Brinkley answered.

"We had a delay in Dallas by one day, but we got here today."

"And . . . ?"

Thinking about the operator and the unsecure phone line, I said, "The sales conference isn't going too well. We found that the client we needed to see here had canceled with no possibility of a reschedule."

After a beat, he said, "That's too bad. How did your business partner take that?"

"Not as bad as I might have thought."

"Why is that, do you know?"

"She claims to be working for our sister organization."

Brinkley was silent.

"Michael?"

"Yeah, I'm here. Felix. Don't believe a word that woman tells you. I hope she hasn't got under your skin or anything like that. Do you follow?"

Hell. What was I supposed to say to that? *Gee, Michael, I admit we've been sleeping together a little bit, just a little bit.*

"I understand," was all I said.

"Felix, you need to keep doing the sales rounds with her. Make sure she completes her sales goals. Got it?"

He wanted me to keep "protecting" her.

"Got it."

"Now, tell me more about the big sales conference coming up."

"The designs of our New Mexico product are being shared without a proper license by an employee whose loyalty is in question. We believe he will pass the designs to another employee with the same loyalty issues. That employee lives here in Odessa, and supposedly he will courier the designs to our competitor in New York."

"Our biggest competitor?"

"That's correct."

"That second courier is a man?"

"Yes."

"Felix, is there a possibility that this courier will also cancel sales meetings and refuse to reschedule?"

"It's very possible, sir."

"In that case, Felix, you may need to replace him."

Was he saying what I thought he was saying?

"Sir?"

"You heard me. You will personally have to take over that courier job and get those plans, not to our competitor, but to *me*. That's an order."

Wait a minute. If Jerry Bork happened to die, then I should take his place? Become the courier meeting Stanley Masters in New Mexico?

"That's crazy, Michael, I don't know if that's possible."

"It has to be possible, Felix. Find a way to be that courier. Think of it this way—you're supposed to be in costume on Halloween! If you pull this off, I can guarantee that you'll be reinstalled in your former position on our sales force. Could be a very big bonus in it for you as well."

Hm. As much as I wanted to rejoin the CIA and receive a pot of gold at the end of the rainbow, I sure didn't want to impersonate Jerry Bork and pretend to be a Soviet spy. I thought it'd be better for everyone just to make sure Jerry Bork stayed alive.

"Felix, I'm coming out that way," Brinkley said, "so don't be surprised if you see me soon. Leave messages of your whereabouts at the office."

We hung up and I pondered what I'd just heard. Even though Brinkley wouldn't like it, I thought I'd better call Steve Sandlin. Surely he could confirm if Dora was truly an FBI agent. But I also felt that the FBI should know about the smuggling plot. The rivalry between the CIA and FBI was often tiresome.

Unfortunately, the night desk operator at the New York FBI field office said Steve was out until the weekend.

Dora was back. Time to go.

It was nearly ten o'clock when we arrived at The Oil Patch, which was located on Highway 51, otherwise known as "Andrews Highway." It, too, was way out of city limits near some other honkytonk nightclubs.

My first impression of the bar was that it was a dreary place. A real dive. A juke box on one side of the joint was playing "Shotgun Boogie" by Tennessee Ernie Ford at a high volume. The room was big enough to hold seventy, but at the moment only six men sat on stools at the bar. Eight booths were on either side and eight square tables with chairs occupied the floor. A Texas flag was draped on the wall behind the bar.

The bartender was a tall man who was in his fifties. He wasn't the figure in Ava Spence's photograph. All six customers, four in cowboy hats and all of them dressed in grimy oil field work clothes, swiveled on their stools to look at us when we entered. They stared as we sat in one of the booths.

"Well, this is awkward," I spoke into Dora's ear. The music was extremely loud. "I'll get some drinks."

The six men decided that I must not be a threat since I had a disability and had come in with an attractive woman. They turned back to their booze and continued to imbibe. Thankfully, the juke box record ended and the place was plunged into deafening silence.

"What'll you have, sir?" the bartender asked as I approached.

"Two Jim Beams, neat."

As he began to prepare the drinks, the patron nearest me turned on his stool and asked, "Europe or Pacific?"

I didn't miss a beat. "Pacific."

"The bastards got your arm, huh."

Not wanting to engage the guy, I made a gesture with my left hand and hook that was the mime equivalent of *Whatcha gonna do?*

The bartender set the drinks on the counter and said, "One dollar. You get the veterans' discount."

I gave him a buck and a quarter. "Is Jerry Bork around?"

"Bork? He doesn't work here anymore. You know Bork?" The bartender began to wipe the counter with a rag. "I ain't seen you in here before."

"I don't live here. I'm from Dallas."

"How do you know Bork?"

"I knew him back before the war when we were younger. You got a way I can contact him? Do you know where he lives?"

"Are you a bill collector, mister?"

"No, why do you ask that?"

The man shook his head. "Never mind."

The customer closest to me said, "Because Bork owes bill collectors, big time!" He started to laugh and the fellow next to him joined in and added, "Bork owes *everyone*, big time!" More laughter.

The bartender frowned at his customers and walked to the other end of the bar without answering my query. I took one drink to the booth and gave it to Dora, and then returned to the counter to pick up mine.

"If you're looking for Bork, he's not in town," said the patron who had asked about my service record. "He was here two nights ago and quit his job as bartender. Now Sammy's got his job." He indicated the bartender, who was serving a drink to a guy at the end of the counter. "I heard Bork say he was leaving today for New Mexico with that dame he's been seeing."

I took a shot. "Oh, you mean Ava?"

The fellow cocked his head at me. "You *do* know Bork. Yeah, that's her name."

"I need to find him. Do you know where he lives?" I asked.

"Not really, it's way out Andrews Highway, but he's probably gone for good."

I merely nodded, said, "Hm," and then took my drink back to the booth.

"What's up?" Dora asked.

Sipping the bourbon, I answered, "Jerry Bork is betraying his country for money. Would he be getting a big payoff for meeting with that guy Masters?"

"I have no idea. It's possible, I suppose."

"Which leads me to the question, what about Ava? Was she being paid to do this?"

Dora kept her voice down. "The Russians have their

ways to recruit operatives. Ava didn't need money, her ex-husband left her a huge estate. I'm afraid it was ideology that drove her. I don't know why."

"You'd think she would hate the Soviets after what's happened to Poland." *Maybe Sandlin was right. Ava could be a Prometheist.* "We need to find where Jerry Bork lives. If he didn't go on to New Mexico without Ava, then he might be at home."

I just hoped he wasn't dead.

People were starting to drift in. A middle-aged couple came through the front door and sat at a booth on the other side of the room. I turned to get my bearings of the place. Directly behind me, to the side of the bar, was a corridor leading to restrooms and a door with an "Employees Only" sign.

"Dora, do you have any change?" She nodded. "Go to the juke box and play something raucous. The noise will cover what I'm about to do."

"I don't know anything raucous."

"Play anything. I'll be back." We both stood. The bartender was busy serving the new couple ... and then a group of four men entered. That would keep Sammy busy. She went over to the juke box while I moved into the corridor as if I were headed for the men's room.

Of course, the Employees Only door was locked. No one could see me in that hallway, so I extracted the lockpicks from my belt buckle and used the one I thought would fit the standard keyed entry doorknob. Nope. The tools were still a challenge. I cursed under my breath and tried another pick.

Concentrate, Felix!

The juke box suddenly began blaring "Salty Dog Rag" by Red Foley. It was raucous enough.

Exploring the tension of the tumblers through the metal pick with my left hand was still alien to me. The therapist in Florida had mentioned something about using the other side of my brain for tasks like this. Sure, doc. Whatever that meant.

Aw, hell. The music was loud enough. I lifted my BK leg and kicked the door as hard as I could. It had the effect of a battering ram. The lock broke.

I'd done it. I was inside the office in a flash. I flicked on the light and was met with a messy desk covered in papers, an adding machine, and a phone. Adorning the wall above it was a calendar illustrated with a Gil Elvgren pinup girl that was hard not to miss. A two-drawer metal filing cabinet sat next to the desk.

I rummaged through the papers and found nothing of interest. Tried the desk drawer. Nothing but pens, pencils, and a stapler. I opened the top drawer of the filing cabinet. Folders marked as tax records, sales records, and other business related junk were empty. But a manila folder marked "Employees" contained a single piece of paper with "20-3-14" written on it.

A safe combination.

But where was the safe?

I did a full turnaround in the little office and saw no safe.

The music ended out in the bar. I willed Dora to play another tune, and she did. "Indian Love Call" by Slim Whitman filled the place. Not as raucous, but it would do.

Come on, Felix, think. Where's the safe?

I looked under the desk. I studied the floor for an indentation.

Then I eyed the saucy pinup calendar. The half-dressed woman was winking at me.

Okay, darlin'.

I lifted the entire calendar. The safe was behind it, firmly planted in the wall.

Its door opened easily with the combination. Right in front were the folders of tax records, ledgers, and a binder of employee stuff, including a contact sheet. Crossed out with a single line in ink, was Jerry Bork, followed by an address on Hillmont Road and a phone number. I grabbed a pen and stray piece of paper and jotted down the info. Then I turned off the light and slipped out the door.

I went out into the bar and saw that several more people had entered and were grabbing tables. By then, the music had ended and the joint was quiet again.

"Find anything?" she asked.

I laid the piece of paper on the table. "Bork's place."

"Oh, my. Shall we go?"

I held up my glass. "One minute. We can't leave good bourbon un-drunk!" She actually smiled at that—the booze had somewhat taken the edge off her earlier manic conduct.

At that moment, though, a tall man with a tweed herringbone flat cap entered the dive. He looked awfully familiar. I watched as he walked across the floor to the counter, and then I recognized him.

He wasn't wearing the trench coat. Just a short-sleeve button down dress shirt and trousers. A cigarette hung out of his mouth. A cool customer. Too cool for my taste at this juncture.

"Dora . . ." I gestured with my head at the guy, who was now speaking to the bartender.

Her eyes went wide. "What's *he* doing here?"

"I have no earthly idea."

"What if he sees us?"

"I want him to see us. I'd like to hear what he has to say, don't you?"

Alec Whitehall turned away from the counter holding a large glass of beer. When he did so, his eyes met ours and he stopped in his tracks. The look of confusion on his face might have been genuine, but he could have also been a good actor.

"Roanoke, Virginia?" he asked, coming closer to our booth. "Is that really you?"

"Mr. Whitehall, isn't it?" I asked.

"Alec Whitehall, at your service," he said in his inimitable British accent. "What on earth are you two doing here?"

"I could ask you the same question."

"I thought you were on your way to, what was it . . . oh, Kansas City! My dear fellow and madam, you are nowhere *near* Kansas City." Jovially, he asked, "Are you following me?"

"No," I answered, "but I think you might be following *us*. Have a seat. Let's talk."

Dora scooted over and Alec sat beside her. He held the beer up and said, "Cheers."

Both Dora and I clinked our bourbons against his beer.

He squinted his eyes and pointed at us, back and forth. "Jack ... Hatch. And Felicia ..."

"Phyllis," she corrected.

"Phyllis, pardon me. Phyllis ... I'm sorry, I can't recall the last name." When she didn't offer it, he switched gears and said, "Well, I must say, this is a surprise."

"Is it?"

"Oh, come, come, Mr. Hatch, surely you don't really think I'm following you? This is an amazing coincidence. Why are you both here? Do tell!"

"You first. Please."

"Mr. Hatch, I work for British American Oil Company out of Toronto. I'm in West Texas scoping out the oil fields here in which Gulf Oil has an interest. There's a merger coming soon. Gulf is going to swallow us up. I'm here to evaluate what's going on in this godforsaken corner of the earth. Have you ever seen a landscape so bloody flat? My word!"

His story was possible. It was good cover. I didn't believe in coincidences, though. Fate, yes. Two different things. My gut was telling me that running into Alec Whitehall again was the latter.

"And what about you two? Why are you in Odessa, Texas, of all places?"

I hesitated just long enough for Dora to answer, "We're here because my sister died."

"Oh, dear," Alec said with believable earnestness. "My deepest condolences. I shall buy the next round of drinks, then!"

I held a hand up. "I'm afraid we must decline. So sorry, we were just leaving."

"That's quite all right, old chap." He stood to let Dora out of the booth. "Well, where shall we meet next? San Diego? San Francisco?"

I gave him the best authentic grin I could muster. "Good luck with your scoping of oil fields."

We both said good night and quickly vacated the premises.

Outside, we got in the Packard and Dora asked, "What do you think?"

"I don't know, but my radar is going haywire."

22

ODESSA, TEXAS

It was just after eleven as we drove south back to Odessa. Hillmont Road was the northern border of a small air field called Schlemeyer. The area was sparsely populated, being the last vestiges of civilization on that side of the city limits. Jerry Bork lived in an old brick house that sat alone on Hillmont two miles west of Andrews Highway, which was pretty much the boondocks. It must have once been an outpost for the oil fields. Like Ava's house, it was isolated and far away from its nearest neighbor.

A newer model of a white Ford pickup truck sat in the driveway in front of the house, and a somewhat chubby man wearing a cowboy hat was loading the bed with boxes and a suitcase. When my headlights caught him, he looked at us with wide-eyed fright. I recognized him from Ava's framed photo. Probably in his late forties, starting to bald. Bit of a paunch.

I stopped the Packard at the curb and he immediately ran to the front door. A porch light illuminated him. We got out and I hollered, "Wait! Jerry Bork! Hold on!"

"What do you want? Stay back!"

"Where are you going, Bork?" I asked as we approached him. He froze with the front door partially open.

"Who are you?"

"This is Dora, Ava's sister. My name is Leiter. I'm a detective with Pinkerton's. What's happening in New Mexico, Bork? Is that where you're headed?"

Bork's face registered terror. "I didn't do anything! I have to go." He pointed at Dora and said, "You! You stay away, you traitor! Shame on you!"

With that, Bork panicked and slipped into the house. He attempted to slam the door, but I stuck my BK leg in, blocking it. He exhibited an expression of great surprise to see that I wasn't hurt. Another useful feature my peg-leg provided. When Bork saw that he couldn't keep us out, he disappeared into his dwelling. I cross-drew my weapon and called out, "We're coming in. Don't do anything stupid!"

We traversed a small living room and through an archway to find him in the kitchen, fumbling with a Smith & Wesson Chiefs Special. I pointed the Iver at him and said, "Drop it, Bork."

"Yes, drop it and raise your hands."

I looked over to see Dora holding and aiming a Colt M1911A1 semi-automatic pistol.

Where the hell did she get that?

Trembling, Bork laid the revolver on the counter and stuck his hands in the air.

"We just want to talk to you," I said. "Do you know about Ava?"

At that point, Bork broke down. He began to sob. He

turned and plopped into a wooden chair next to a small dining table with a Formica top. He nodded. "Ava ... oh, Ava ... I went to her house when I hadn't heard from her."

"When was that?" Dora asked.

"Forty-five minutes ago. Sheriff cars everywhere. I couldn't get near ... I couldn't ... get involved ..." With tears in his eyes he looked at us. "Do you know what happened to her?"

"She's dead," Dora answered coldly. "Murdered." Then, as an afterthought, she added, "I'm sorry."

Bork barked at Dora, "What do *you* care? You tore out Ava's heart! You betrayed her with Don! She—"

Dora aimed her pistol at his face. "*Stop*! You know nothing about Ava and me."

I gestured at Dora to lower her gun. "Calm down, calm down." I filed away what Bork had just said, and then I commanded, "Tell us about New Mexico."

His eyes darted between us like a cornered rat. "You have to let me go! The police will blame me because Ava was my girlfriend. But I didn't do it! I have to get out of town!"

"Where do you plan to go?" I asked.

"I'm not sure. Canada, I think."

"You're not going to Paris, Bork? By way of New York and London? You and Ava had airline tickets from El Paso."

His eyes grew wide again. "I know who you are! You're here to kill me!"

"We're not here to kill you. But you'd better tell us everything. We can protect you."

"The hell we will," Dora muttered, the gun still aimed at his face.

I ignored her bizarre behavior and continued. "We need to know all the details about what's going down in New Mexico. We know you're supposed to meet a man named Masters."

Bork squeezed his eyes shut as if he were in pain. He nodded. "How did you know that?"

"Where and when are you meeting him?"

"No . . . I promised Ava . . ."

"Answer me, Jerry!" I snapped.

He groaned, realizing he was trapped. "The meeting is Friday, the thirty-first. I'm expecting a phone call tonight at midnight. That's when I'm supposed to find out where the meeting is and what time." Bork winced and shook his head. "We were planning to do it together. But she . . . She said if something happened to her, then I'd have to go alone . . . I promised I would, but I don't want to . . ." He sobbed again.

"Was Ava giving you money to do it? To pay off your bills?" Dora asked.

He narrowed his eyes at her. "We know all about you! Ava said you might show up! If you try—"

We heard the sound of tires on the gravel out front.

"Who's here?" Bork gasped.

"I'll take a look. Watch him, Dora."

I went to a picture window in the living room that faced the street and peered outside. My Packard was parked on Hillmont at the curb. Bork's truck was on the gravel drive.

Behind it, half on the drive and half in the street, was the black Buick Roadmaster.

Three men armed with handguns emerged from the car.

"We've got trouble!" I shouted. I got away from the window and noted a gun case against the wall containing a shotgun. The door on the cabinet was locked, so I used the butt of the Iver to break the glass. By then, Dora and Bork were in the front room with me.

"What are you doing?" Bork cried.

I pulled out the shotgun and broke it over a knee. It was loaded with two shells. I snapped the gun back and tossed it to him. "Now's your chance to avenge your girlfriend. There are men outside who want to kill us. That means, you, too."

Bullets smashed the front picture window and perforated the door. Bork screamed in terror. "Get down!" I yelled. Dora and I hit the floor but Bork was frozen in horror. Dora grabbed his left arm and pulled him down.

"Bork," I said, "crawl to the window. I'll take the right side, you take the left."

Dora barked, "Felix we should leave! Out the back! Let him be!"

"You go on!" I called to her.

"Come with me!"

"Go, Dora!"

She finally moved to the rear of the house.

I inched to the wall beneath the window as the gunfire subsided for a bit. Rising to my feet, I stood at the right side of the window and used the wall for cover. I peeked out. The three of them stood in the front yard, pistols aimed right at us. The middle guy was tall and bald. A cigarette hung loosely out the corner of his mouth. He was the same man I'd seen twice in New York—once after the murder of Gregory Titov, and again after the murder of Karl Adamski. Was he really the SMERSH agent, Marko? If so, why did he want to eliminate Jerry Bork, assuming that disappointing specimen of a man was the target?

Despite my deprecating opinion of him, Bork stood, aimed the shotgun out the window, and pulled the trigger. The noise of the blast was louder than sin, but to my amazement, the man to the left of Marko jerked, stumbled, and *fell dead*!

That, of course, immediately prompted another barrage of gunfire from the remaining two men. Bork and I ducked as bullets whizzed overhead, shattering more of the remaining glass in the window.

A few seconds later the shooters had to reload. I stood, aimed the Iver out the window at Marko, and fired.

And missed. *Goddammit...!*

Marko said something in Russian to the remaining guy. They ignored their dead partner and ran back to the Buick. The second man leaned into the car and Marko went around its rear. The trunk lid opened and Marko pulled out a couple of sticks of dynamite.

Right, the guy was a pyromaniac.

The Russian plunged one stick in his trouser pocket and held on to the other one.

"Come out or I blow you up!" he shouted in English.

Bork rose again, pointed the shotgun, and fired the last shell way too wildly to hit anything. Not good.

Dora appeared again. "What's going on? Why aren't you coming?"

"They have dynamite," I answered. "Bork, we have to leave!"

"Dynamite?" Her eyes went wide. "What's *wrong* with him? He's *insane*!"

"Not coming?" Marko called. "Okay, I blow you up!" He walked purposefully toward the house, holding his cigarette to the fuse.

Dora bolted back through the kitchen and to the rear of the house.

"We need to get out of here, Bork!" I shouted as I followed her. But when I reached the back of the kitchen next to the rear door, he wasn't behind me. Then I heard Bork scream . . .

The explosion was immense and deafening. I hit the kitchen floor. Debris, dirt, and smoke enveloped the space, blinding me and cutting off air. Time stood still. The air was thick with fumes and all kinds of crap. My ears were ringing. At first I thought I might have died . . . but I took stock of my body and realized, *yeah, okay, I'm still here and I didn't lose my only good arm.* I didn't know what had happened to Bork. Had he made it?

I had the wherewithal to crawl to the rear door. With the Iver still in my left hand, I made it out, rolled into the dirt at the back of the house, and gasped lovely, sweet oxygen. I coughed hard for a nearly a minute and couldn't see a thing. It took a few seconds to shake off the shock, and then I looked up to see a pistol pointing at my face.

"Hold it," Marko's pal said in English. My first thought was that he was terribly ugly. He had a flat, pug nose.

I froze.

"Drop your weapon and stand up."

I left the Iver on the ground, stood, and raised my arm and prosthesis.

Through the back door, I saw the damage that the dynamite had done to the front of the house. The living room was almost gone, some of it in flames, wide open to the street and the night air. What was left of Jerry Bork lay in the rubble, obviously no longer indebted to his various collectors.

"You stupid idiot! You're crazy! Why did you do that? You could have killed us all!"

Dora's voice. At the side of the house. A man shouted back at her, but I couldn't understand him. Russian or Polish. I heard her grunt and cry out, and then the man I presumed to be Marko appeared from the back corner of the house with Dora. He had her in an arm lock. She did her best to struggle, but he was too tall, too strong, and too experienced. He threw her to the ground at my feet. Her gun was gone. She was no longer the timid, nervous woman who had ridden with me in the Packard all the way from New York. Tough, rebellious, and angry, she cursed at the man in Polish.

Marko redrew his weapon from a holster at his side. I thought it might be a Tokarev, but it was difficult to say in the dark. He pointed it at me and said, "Mr. Pirate

Hand! Very nice to meet you at last." He laughed a little and nodded at my hook. "A SMERSH shark did that, eh? We train all our sharks to bite the arms off CIA agents."

Dora sat up and looked at me. "CIA? What?"

I just said, "Long story, Dora."

Marko gestured with the Tokarev. "Let's go."

"Where are we going?"

"For a ride."

He and Pug Nose got Dora on her feet, but she broke away and moved close to me.

"Felix," she desperately whispered, "you must go meet Masters in Bork's place! You have to do this for me! You—"

Before I could help her, Marko's long arms reached around her neck and torso from behind and pulled her away.

"Shut up, you!" he snarled.

They then marched us around the side of the house to the front. The structure was in shambles. The door and façade were completely gone.

Why weren't the police on the way? Hadn't someone heard the explosion and gunfire? Or were we too far out from the city? Was Odessa that much of the wild west that neighbors thought nothing of gunfights going on just a few blocks away?

Wait a second . . .

Another car was parked across Hillmont Street. It was completely in the shadows, but I could see its outline. The two shooters didn't seem to be aware of it.

Marko and Pug Nose forced us to walk to the Buick. The trunk was still open. Pug Nose took me around the rear of the car. With all the strength I could muster, I elbowed him and thrust my hook into his face.

The guy punched me hard and I fell over halfway into the trunk, stunned. Pug Nose grabbed me by the shoulders and stood me up. It was then that I could see the trunk's contents. My eyes focused on a box full of dynamite sticks. They appeared wet, as if water had splashed all over them.

Pug Nose slammed the trunk shut, forced me to move to the passenger side of the Buick, opened the back door, and spat, "Get in."

My mind was still processing what I'd seen. That dynamite was sweating! It was old! Didn't they realize how volatile those sticks were? An accidental collision in the street and it could all blow.

A gunshot resounded from the car across the street. The round blew a hole in the Buick's back windshield, causing the glass to spider-web.

Yes! Someone was on our side! But, Christ, don't shoot the trunk! Don't hit the dynamite!

I took advantage of the distraction to dive into Pug Nose's belly as if I were tackling him on the forty yard line, simultaneously grasping his gun arm with my left hand. We fell to the gravel and wrestled for the weapon.

Marko shot blindly at the dark car, but then he shoved Dora into the Buick, climbed in beside her, and started the engine.

Pug Nose dropped his weapon and rolled on top of

me. He punched me hard in the face and was ready to do it again when a spurt of blood erupted from the man's brow. A round had entered the back of his skull and exited between the eyes. He stiffened, looked blankly at me, and fell to the side.

The Buick's tires screeched loudly as it backed into the street.

"Felix!" I heard Dora scream from the interior of the car.

It tore away and sped down Hillmont Street into blackness.

I attempted to stand but was too dazed from the blows. Everything was spinning. I thought I might vomit. I reached to draw my Iver but it wasn't in the holster...

The shooter from across the street was walking toward me.

"Are you all right, old chap?"

I knew that voice. A familiar British accent.

My head...

The world turned upside down and I toppled over face first onto the gravel drive.

23

Odessa, Texas

The smell of burnt wood and metal was what brought me around.

My eyes opened. The night sky above. I felt cool dirt underneath my body. My head hurt like the dickens.

"How are you feeling, old chap?" The British accent again. "Mr. Hatch?"

I managed to sit up a bit. "Where am I?"

"You're behind Mr. Bork's house. I carried you back here. More comfortable than the gravel drive."

Turning my head, I saw that Alec Whitehall stood against the back wall of the house by the door, smoking a cigarette.

Then I remembered. *Dora* . . .

I jerked up to a sitting position and tried to stand, but I was wobbly.

"Take it easy, Hatch. She's long gone. You'll never catch them. They drove away. If you're able, I think we should go inside what's left of the house and talk before the police get here. There are two dead bodies in the front of the house and one inside in the rubble. But the fires are out. We have a few minutes. Your piece is right there on the ground where you left it."

Sure enough, the Iver was next to me. I picked it up and holstered it. By then I could stand all right.

We went through the back door. The kitchen was still smoky and without power. Two-thirds of the house was surprisingly still intact. Only the front living room and façade had sustained damage from the blast.

Then I remembered. "What time is it?" My vision was blurry and I couldn't read my watch.

"A little before midnight."

"We should call law enforcement," I said, but what I really wanted was to make damn sure the telephone worked. If that call from New Mexico didn't come through, I didn't know what I'd do.

He shook his head. "We can contact the authorities when we're ready to leave. Trust me, you don't want to get involved in a police investigation here."

I picked up the phone anyway. An operator's voice asked how to direct my call. I hung it up and said to Alec, "No, you're right. The thing works, though."

We both took seats at the Formica table. He placed a flashlight on the surface pointing upwards to better illuminate the space.

"All right, Alec, let's make this quick. Who are you working for? Are you British Secret Service?"

"How perceptive of you!" He offered me a cigarette from a gunmetal case. I didn't know the brand, but I took it. He lit it with a lighter he pulled from his trouser pocket, and then did the same for himself. It wasn't bad tobacco, but I preferred my Chesterfields.

"Are you ... a Double O?" I asked.

Alec laughed. "What? No, no, not at all. I'm not *that* good. Just an ordinary low-level agent. No license to kill, I'm afraid, although I've been known to ignore that rule, as you have seen. Mr. Leiter, I do know who you are."

That figured.

"Jack Hatch indeed. You are known to us. Felix Leiter, former CIA. Now you're working for a two-bit gumshoe agency. Pity. And the woman is not Phyllis Davidson. She is Dora Wysocki. Now, what am I going to do with you?"

The nicotine did wonders for my head. The fuzziness was rapidly dissipating. "Call me Felix. Mr. Leiter was my father. Look, Alec, what is your game here? You helped me out earlier. Saved my life, I reckon, your shooting at those men. Now you're making subtle threats. Aren't we supposed to be allies?"

The man sighed. "Not when it comes to nuclear weapons. Your government closed the door on us. You're not playing nice. You're not sharing. You're familiar with the Atomic Energy Act of 1946, the so-called McMahon Act? That shut out Britain. We had to go and build our own atomic bomb, which we successfully tested at the beginning of this month."

"Operation Hurricane."

"Yes. Would you believe that the United States is about to test a thermonuclear device? A *hydrogen* bomb? It's a thousand times more powerful than an atomic bomb. That's serious stuff, old chap."

"I agree with you, and please don't call me 'old chap.'"

"Felix, the point is that our government has had to resort to good, old-fashioned back alley espionage to get nuclear secrets, just like the Soviets and everyone else on the planet. We have our own very capable physicists, thank you very much, but I doubt Hurricane would have happened without a little help from international spies buying and selling information under the table."

"I have a feeling that you, Dora and I, are after the same thing," I said.

"We are. How astute of you."

"You've been following us since Virginia."

"Felix, I've been following you since New York. You spotted me on the road in Virginia, so I went ahead and made contact in Roanoke. I know all about your car trouble in Dallas. That was an annoying delay, but I didn't want to interfere. I was hoping you and the lady would lead me here, to this very spot, to that very man." He pointed to Bork's corpse. "There was a lot we didn't know. You and Dora Wysocki have been very helpful. The problem is, what did Mr. Bork here know about a certain handoff of privileged information that is supposed to occur in a couple of days? Is that something you can tell me?"

My thoughts went back to what Brinkley had ordered me to do. With Jerry Bork dead, was I now supposed to *be* Bork? Even Dora had pushed it.

Alec smiled. "Your hesitation tells me that you do know something. Look, Felix, our countries are indeed allies. Why don't we work together?"

Ha. What were we going to do? Split the microdot down the middle? "I'd like to help Dora," I said. "Can you do that?"

His face dropped. "The individual who has her wants to eliminate the possibility of anyone but the Soviets obtaining those secrets."

"His name, or his code name, is possibly Marko."

"It is."

"And he's SMERSH."

Alec shook his head. "We suspected as such, but I'm beginning to think he is some kind of rogue agent whose motivations I don't understand yet. He has been following you since New York as well, hoping that you and Dora would lead him here. But why has he murdered every member of the smuggling pipeline *before* the transaction has occurred? SMERSH wouldn't do that, would they?"

"That's a good question," I said.

"Felix, seeing that Marko now has Dora, I'm afraid it is very doubtful that she will be able to complete her task. I'm sorry to say this, but it's likely that her body will be discovered somewhere in the oil fields in the near future."

Those words struck me in the chest like a sledgehammer. It was the godawful truth.

"What do you know about her, Felix? I mean, *really* know. In our line of work, personal attachments can be heartbreaking. They can be fatal."

"I'm well aware of that. You know about Ava?"

He grimly nodded. "You beat me to her house. And apparently Marko beat us both there. I arrived shortly before the sheriff and his men did, just a while ago. Looked like Marko was pretty rough with her. I don't know if she talked or not."

The phone rang. I glanced at my watch. My vision was clear. Midnight on the dot.

"I have to get this." I stood, went to the receiver, and picked it up. The operator told me it was long distance from Los Alamos, New Mexico. I accepted the charges.

There were clicks and static sounds and then a voice. "Bork?"

Was I really going to do this? I figured I had no choice. "Yeah, it's me. Masters?"

"Yes."

"Well?"

"As you know, the Santa Fe visit is canceled."

"Obviously."

"Yeah. Blown. But a handful of colleagues and I aren't needed for the big—well, we have Friday and Saturday off. We're going to make a casual trip to Carlsbad Caverns National Park. You know it?"

"I can find it." I knew the caverns were located in the southeast corner of New Mexico, not too far from Odessa.

"It's perfect for us. It's a public place and easy for me to get away from the lab with a small group this way. Go to the park. Take the nine-thirty tour on Friday morning. We'll meet in the underground Lunch Room, the halfway and resting point of the tour, between eleven and noon. My colleagues won't suspect anything if they see me innocently conversing with a fellow park visitor."

"I'll be there," I said.

"Ava never shared your picture. How will I know you?"

I wasn't about to wear a cowboy hat. "I have a prosthesis for a right hand. Blond hair."

"You have a what for a right hand?"

"A prosthesis. A hook!"

"Oh. Ava never mentioned that. I'll have on a Santa Fe sweatshirt. Glasses. I look forward to meeting Ava in person, too."

Uh oh. Tell him the truth? Yeah, I probably should. "Sorry, but Ava is dead."

I heard him audibly gasp. "Oh, no. Does that mean ... uhm, you haven't seen ... Dora?"

I didn't know what to say. "Why would you think that?" I asked.

"Just tell me if you've heard anything from Dora, Ava's sister."

Well, now. "Dora is not here," was all I could say.

"Okay then. Plan B is enacted. Much more ideal. See you Friday." With that, he hung up.

Plan B? What in blazes was Plan B?

I replaced the receiver and Alec said, "You were expecting that call, Felix. I take it you just learned something."

"Alec, bring your flashlight. I want to look in Mr. Bork's bedroom and make sure he didn't leave anything behind that might help us."

Together we searched as much of the house as we could and also Bork's truck out on the driveway. There was nothing. One detail struck me, though—I didn't find

Dora's Colt M1911A1 anywhere. Perhaps Marko had confiscated it from her.

It was apparent now that Bork was not a committed member of the spy team. Ava had likely convinced him to step in and do Adamski's job because there was no one else, and he only agreed to do it for a payoff... and for Ava.

"You know, I think you could use my help," Alec said. "Are we going to work together or not? I did save your life tonight, you know."

Could I trust this guy? Probably not, but I figured the old adage was apt. *Keep your friends close but keep your enemies closer.* "All right," I said. "We have to go to New Mexico tomorrow."

"Let me guess. You're taking Mr. Bork's place? The guy on the phone thought you were Bork?"

I nodded.

"Where's the handoff going to be?"

"I'll tell you tomorrow. Where are you staying?"

"The Lincoln Hotel."

"Let's meet at your hotel at eight in the morning." I held out my left hand. "Deal?"

"How do I know you won't just take off without me?"

"How do I know you're not lying to me and you won't kill me the first chance you get when we have what we're after?"

Alec grinned. "Touché. All right. I give you my word of honor."

"As an English gentleman?"

"Is there any other kind?" He grasped the hand. "Deal."

We returned to the kitchen. Alec picked up the phone and asked the operator to give him the police. Once connected, he proceeded to tell him that there had been an explosion and gunfire at the Bork address. He refused to identify himself and hung up.

"We had better go," he said.

Exiting the house through the back, we hurried to our cars and drove off in opposite directions. I heard the police and fire sirens growing nearer and eventually the vehicles passed me, going north as I headed south.

24
October 30, 1952

ODESSA, TEXAS – WHITE'S CITY, NEW MEXICO
Dora and I had never checked into a hotel upon arriving in Odessa. After leaving the wreckage of Bork's house, I drove to the establishment I'd seen downtown, the Elliott Hotel, and checked in around two in the morning. Naturally, I wasn't able to relax.

The past twelve hours had revealed some things. Pieces of the puzzle were falling into place. Tidbits I had picked up here and there from Dora, Brinkley, Bork, and Alec—these things were buzzing through my brain. A picture was forming out of the muck.

From the bank of phone booths in the Elliott's lobby, I attempted a call to New York. I tried Michael Brinkley's personal number and no one answered. I then phoned his office and got a night desk operator. I left a message that I was going to New Mexico and revealed where and when the "event" would be on Friday.

After that, I went through Dora's belongings that I'd brought from the car to my hotel room. She had shown me the hidden compartment in the suitcase, so I looked inside. The envelope of money we had acquired in Dallas was not there. I did find an empty holster for a Colt M1911A1 among her clothing. It had been a shock to see her with a gun.

Part of me had wanted to get back into the Packard and drive all over Odessa to look for that damned black Buick and for Dora. But I knew that would be a futile exercise. If Dora wasn't already dead, as Alec Whitehall suspected, then her abductors could very well be taking her to New Mexico. Perhaps Dora might be able to get a jump on Marko and escape.

But my gut told me she was gone.

The whole thing made me frustrated and angry. The professional thing to do would be to let go of her in my heart and mind, but I couldn't stop thinking about the woman. I already missed her voice with that sultry Eastern European accent, the way she wore her hair, the pouty lips . . .

Stop it!

I was being ridiculous. It was time to leave and move on.

I had to keep telling myself that.

With those anxious thoughts swirling in my head, I threw myself on the bed and finally drifted away.

*

I got maybe three hours of sleep.

After checking out of the Elliott, I drove the short distance to the newer and larger Lincoln Hotel to meet up with Alec. He was standing beside his Studebaker

Champion. I pulled up alongside and lowered the driver's side window.

"Right on time," he said. "Are you going to tell me where in New Mexico we're going?"

"To a little nothing of a place called White's City. It's a three to four hour drive. They have two motels. I plan on establishing base there, as it sits right on the outskirts of Carlsbad Caverns National Park."

"Are we going into the park?"

"Just follow me."

We set out, leaving Odessa behind. Through the little town of Andrews, and then west across the border into New Mexico to tiny Eunice. A shortcut took us to Carlsbad, a city not connected to the national park except by name, and then thirty miles down to White's City.

The southeast corner of New Mexico is much the same as West Texas. Desert. Dirt. Rocks. Mesquite. Wide open spaces. A bright sun that blinds you if you aren't wearing sunglasses, even at the end of October. The closer we got, the land became hillier. The park was up a gradually ascending, winding road to a higher elevation in a range of the Guadalupe Mountains.

White's City was indeed a pitstop. It was early afternoon when Alec and I checked in to different rooms at the Pueblo Motel. Alec told the clerk we preferred rooms at the far end of the complex.

Alec and I agreed to meet for dinner and he went to his room. I asked the clerk if a Stanley Masters had checked in. She told me that no one by that name was registered. While Alec was in his room, I went over to the only other motel, the older White's City Cavern Camp, and inquired there as well. Again, no luck.

It was driving me crazy that I had to wait until the following morning. The clock was ticking! What was I supposed to do?

I got in the Packard and drove around the White's City community to see if I could spot the Buick Roadmaster. It was wishful thinking. It only took me five minutes. There wasn't much to search in the little strip of town. At the very edge was an impressive giant billboard with a color painting of the caverns. It stood at the side of the road with "Carlsbad Caverns – 7 Miles" emblazoned at the top.

Stopping by the billboard and exiting the car, I raised my only fist to the sky. I had the urge to scream curse words at the wide open spaces, but my father's voice somehow penetrated the anxiety and near-overwhelming powerlessness.

Patience, Felix ...

I took a deep breath.

Sometimes the best course of action is to let the clock run out and go into overtime, because that's when something unexpected will happen.

My eyes closed. The hot sun baked my skin.

Dad's words were true. In fact, they reflected my CIA training. Sometimes an agent had to wait endlessly for something meaningful to occur. Surveillance was nothing but ticking minutes, hours, and days. Anticipating handoffs or defections might take *months*.

By this time tomorrow, it should all be over.

Maybe.
Patience, Felix . . .

*

After sunset, Alec and I had Mexican food together at a joint simply called "Café."

"So are you going to tell me what is happening tomorrow?" Alec asked me. When I didn't answer, he continued. "Come on, Felix. I'm British Secret Service. It's my job to know things. I know the broad strokes of this thing, but not everything. Apparently, you are going to meet a man and pretend to be Jerry Bork. I heard it all, remember? The purpose of the meeting is for him to hand over smuggled technical specifications for the new hydrogen bomb. Do you have any idea what you're going to do with them after that?"

"I do," I said, even though I really didn't. Take them back to New York, I supposed, unless Brinkley showed up in New Mexico. That would make things easier.

"What would you like me to do, Felix? How can I assist you?"

"Alec, are you going to try and take the specs away from me?"

"My government does want them. They will pay you handsomely, you know."

I laughed a little. "So would the Soviets. So would the Chinese. So would, I don't know, the French? The Japanese? The Lithuanians?"

Alec made a face. "The Lithuanians?"

"That was a joke."

"Hmpf. Well, there's got to be something in this for me and my country," he said, "or else why am I here?"

"I'll have to talk to my superiors."

"Where? At Pinkerton's Detective Agency? Do they have any influence at the White House or Pentagon?"

"Alec, how about you just keep a lookout for this Marko fellow or anyone else who could be a threat."

"Where exactly are you meeting this man from Los Alamos?"

"I'll tell you tomorrow."

Alec slapped his hand on the table. "Bloody hell, Felix! You know I could get rid of you and impersonate Jerry Bork myself."

"Aha! You can't because now he's looking for a man with a prosthesis." I held up the hook and opened and closed the pincers a few times. It was the equivalent of wiggling my eyebrows.

"Bloody hell," he said again, this time under his breath.

We finished the meal in silence.

Later, after we'd separated, I thought I'd try making phone calls to New York again. I went to the lobby where I'd seen a couple of phone booths side by side. I was just about to go through the ritual with an operator again when I heard a man's voice in the cubicle next to mine. The phone booths didn't offer much privacy, as the partition between the two was quite thin.

The man was speaking Russian.

People from all over the world visited Carlsbad Caverns National Park, but what were the chances that a Russian man was in town on that particular day? I doubted that White's City was home to many Russian-speakers, especially since the population of the town was less than twenty souls.

Then I clearly heard him say, mixed in with the Russian, the words "Los Alamos" and "Carlsbad Caverns."

Remaining quiet and still, I waited in the booth. The man's conversation went on a few minutes longer, and then he finally hung up. I shrank into the small space, not wanting to be seen when the guy emerged.

He opened the folding door, walked out, crossed the lobby, and exited.

Alec Whitehall.

25

WHITE'S CITY, NEW MEXICO

I knew I was no match against Alec physically due to my disabilities. My initial instincts about the guy were correct, though, even way back in Roanoke. There was something about him that was off. It was almost as if he was trying too hard to be "British."

Alec Whitehall was an imposter.

Back in my room, I sat, lit a cigarette, and pondered what to do. It was getting late, not quite midnight. I was miles from any significant civilization other than the national park, and it was closed now. Dora's predicament worried me. Had I failed her? I thought back to what had happened at Bork's place. She was ready to kill Jerry Bork herself. Why? She had been unusually aggressive and threatening. She had a gun. Where she had got it and how long she'd had it, I had no idea. A few minutes later, she was in Marko's control. Dora seemed to be putting up a good struggle, and then she was gone with her captor. What could I have done differently?

Nothing.

I had to put it out of my mind and do what Brinkley

wanted me to do—meet Masters at the caverns in a little over twelve hours. Even Dora had implored me to do that very thing. But there was Alec Whitehall, or whoever he was, to deal with. Should I leave the motel, drive to one of White's City's campgrounds and sleep in my car?

No. I had a better idea.

First, I went out to the Packard, opened the trunk, and took the bag of tools that I had brought. The last bottle of Haig & Haig was in there, too, so I grabbed that and carried it under my prosthesis arm. Returning to my room, I stashed what I needed.

Next, I called the front desk on the phone in the room and asked to be connected to Alec.

He answered promptly. "Yes?"

"Alec, it's Felix."

"Felix, you're still up, too?" The cheery British accent was back.

"I am. Hey, I'm a little restless. I have a nice bottle of Haig & Haig here with me. Would you like to come over for a nightcap?"

"Why, that's awfully sporting of you! I would love a nightcap. Be there in a jiffy."

Finally, after hanging up, I placed the whisky and two glasses provided by the motel on the small table in the room. There was only one chair, but that was all right. I was still dressed, of course, but I had removed my jacket. My Iver was on full display.

The knock on the door soon came, so I went and opened it. Alec stood there without his trench coat and flat cap.

"Very decent of you to invite me over, Felix," he said with a smile.

"Come in, Alec." He did and looked around the room, wondering where he would sit. "Please, take the chair. I can sit on the bed. In fact, I want to take my BK leg off. The stump gets sore after too many hours of wearing the damn thing. But first, let me pour you a glass of this nectar."

"Thank you very much!"

I poured two glasses, picked up one of them, and held it out. "Cheers."

"Cheers." He clinked my glass with his and we both had long sips. The burn was wonderful, and it prepared me for what I was about to do next.

"What *is* that gun you're carrying?" he asked. "I noticed you had it at Bork's house."

"Iver Johnson. It suits my left hand."

"Oh, right, I've heard about them. Never fired one, though."

I went to the bed and set my drink on the nightstand. "I'm glad you're here, Alec. It will be good to have backup tomorrow."

"Are you now going to tell me what the plan is?"

"I am. First, let me remove this." I rolled up my trouser leg to my thigh, revealing the artificial replacement. I unlaced the harness that attached to my upper leg and pulled off the wooden appendage with the shoe still on. The stocking came off next, revealing the stump to be red and calloused, as it always was at night when I removed the prosthesis. I then laid the BK beside me on the bed.

"That must be quite the annoyance," Alec said.

I shrugged. "I'm already pretty used to it." I took another drink, and so did he.

"How long ago did you say the attack was? Last January?"

"Uh huh." I picked up the wooden leg and stood on my one good leg. It was a good thing I had excellent balance, a result of my physical therapy. "I need to wash out the attachment, excuse me a second," I said, pointing to the other side of the room where the bathroom was. I then hopped behind him as I crossed the floor.

He took another drink, still sitting and facing the other way.

Keeping the bathroom door open so he wouldn't get suspicious, I ran water in the sink.

"This will only take a sec," I said.

He continued to sip the whisky.

The sound of the water masked me hopping away from the bathroom the few feet to the back of his chair. I held up the leg with the shoe at the end. "You know, Alec," I said, "when we last spoke about my injuries, you thought I'd gotten them in the war." I slammed the shoe down on the back of his head as hard as my left arm and right prosthesis could do. He fell over the table, spilling his drink. "How in the world did you know about my 'attack in January'?"

Alec groaned and tried to lift himself to a standing position.

I swung the leg and shoe again, this time clobbering him on the side of the head. He fell to the floor. Lights out.

"Lying bastard," I said.

Hopping back to the bed, I kept an eye on him to make

sure he wasn't faking. I sat, reattached the leg, and laced it up. When I could properly walk again, I went to the bag of tools I had stashed in the corner and removed the coils of rope I'd brought. I got on the floor and tied his hands behind his back. Then I bound his ankles together. The knots were good and taut. Once he was secured, I went through his pockets. He had a Canadian passport with his name and photo, a wallet with a couple hundred dollars cash, his motel room key, the Studebaker key, and an old, loaded Remington Model 95 double-barreled derringer. Since that piece was produced twenty years earlier or more, I had to take a moment to admire its condition and quality.

"Not bad, Alec," I said. "Sneaky." His Sauer handgun was probably in his room.

The derringer went into my bag of tools. I then sat in the single chair with my Iver in hand and waited. In about five minutes Alec moaned and began to move. He quickly realized he was trussed and became more alert. He uttered a string of curse words and insults.

"Leave my mother out of this, Alec, she's not here to defend herself," I said. "Now. Don't bother yelling for help. We're at the far end of the motel, remember? You requested that. Were you planning to bump me off or something? Doesn't matter now. If you scream I'll only knock you out again. So tell me. How long have you been working for the Soviets?"

He groaned again. "What?"

"I know you're a Soviet spy. You want to tell me about it?"

"I am *not* a Soviet spy, old chap! I don't know what you're talking about. Seriously, I can't even speak Russian."

"Liar. I heard you speaking Russian on the phone in the lobby earlier. Don't try to deny it." His eyes gave away that he knew he'd been caught. "Confess, Alec. I want to hear you say it."

"Go to hell." The British accent was decidedly missing on that one.

Since I wasn't the kind of guy who tortured people to get them to talk, I simply sighed and said, "Have it your way, Alec."

I grabbed the Studebaker key, stood, and went to the door.

"You're not leaving me here like this!" he growled through his teeth.

"Be right back."

Outside, I shut the door behind me and found his car parked in front of his room. I got in, started it, backed out, and pulled it up next to the Packard in front of my room. I shut off the engine, got out, and opened the trunk. It was empty. Then, I returned to my room.

"Look, Felix," Alec said, "I can pay you a hell of a lot of money. Just let me go."

"Not interested, Alec." I went to my bed, picked up the pillow, and removed the slip. I got on the floor again beside his head. "Open wide," I said, but he wouldn't cooperate. I used my hook to pinch his lower lip ... *hard* ... until he yelped. I got the pillow slip in his mouth and wrapped it tightly around his head. Another good knot and he was gagged as well as could be.

"You're a tall man, Alec," I said, "but thank heavens you're not overweight." I lifted his shoulders until he was sitting. He attempted to writhe out of my control, but it was no use. I bent forward and hoisted him over my left shoulder. I then carried him out the door to the open trunk of his car. I didn't mean to drop him so hard, but he fell into it with a loud *thunk*.

"Ummfmmf!" he cried through the gag.

"Sorry, old chap," I said. "Have a nice sleep."

I shut the trunk, went around to the side, and got into the driver's seat. *It is a nice car*, I thought as I started it up and drove it out of the motel lot.

The Carlsbad Caverns painted billboard I'd seen earlier was built so that it was mounted on a solid structure affixed to the ground. A few yards behind the billboard was a dilapidated, abandoned building made of adobe. I drove the Studebaker in between the billboard and the building and then cut the engine. The vehicle was neatly hidden from the road in both directions. One would have to do what I had done—drive off the road and around to the back side of the sign—to find the Studebaker. Alec Whitehall was concealed until further notice.

I got out of the car and removed the knuckle-duster dagger from my BK leg, and then I stabbed all four tires. I made sure they were completely deflated. After returning the knife to my leg, it was a short walk back to the motel in the dark. Just to cross all the Ts and dot the Is, I went to Alec's room, unlocked it, and stepped inside. Went through his things. Found the Sauer and holster, some more money in an envelope that I left alone, a few road maps. And ...

A pair of handcuffs in a zipped liner on one side of his suitcase. A couple spots of dried blood dotted them, too.

That son of a bitch.

I ejected all but one cartridge from the Sauer, pocketed the gun, exited, locked his door, and walked all the way back to the billboard. Alec was kicking up a storm inside the trunk of his car, making as much noise as possible. Unlocking it, I opened the trunk.

I loosened the gag from his mouth. "You killed Ava Spence. Why?"

He narrowed his eyes and spat the words, "*Smyert Shpionam.*"

SMERSH. *Death to Spies.*

I didn't bother replacing the gag. "This is for being an enemy operative, a liar, and an all-around shit," I said, and then I shot the bastard.

The kicking stopped.

I threw the empty Sauer into the trunk and slammed the lid.

A half hour later I was back in my own room.

It was time for a good night's sleep before things got really interesting in the morning. Knowing I had finally achieved revenge against SMERSH helped ease me into dreamland.

26
October 31, 1952

CARLSBAD CAVERNS NATIONAL PARK, NEW MEXICO
After checking out of the Pueblo, I drove the Packard up the winding road from White's City to the national park entrance. Literature about the caverns that I'd picked up in the motel lobby informed me that I should wear a sweater and my jacket. The temperature underground dropped to about 56° Fahrenheit year-round. What about my gun? In the end, I decided that my jacket, if I kept it buttoned, would conceal it. Better to be prepared than not.

There was no visitor center, only a ticket booth and an elevator lobby. Signs and diagrams had been posted indicating that a brand new visitor center on the surface was in the planning stages and was hoped to be completed by 1958. Visitors could elect to take the elevator down to the Lunch Room, which was really the halfway point in the tour. From there one could simply see what was called the Big Room, the main attraction of the caverns that was apparently quite huge and full of spectacular formations. This was recommended for the elderly or families with small children who might find it strenuous to walk down into the caverns from the natural entrance, which was what most folks elected to do. The incline on the path down could be rather steep. At first I wondered if I'd be able to do it with my bum leg, but the Marine in me told me that I could manage. I chose to join the line of visitors waiting along the natural entrance switchbacks for the nine-thirty a.m. tour to begin.

There were perhaps thirty-five adults and maybe twenty children in line. The kids were elementary school age, probably fourth or fifth graders. I didn't see a man wearing a Santa Fe sweatshirt. Was Masters going to show up?

At nine-twenty I was beginning to get nervous that he might not.

A park ranger whose badge name read "Mark Joop" walked along the line toward the front. He then loudly introduced himself and said that the tour would commence shortly. We were to follow him along the winding switchbacks down the incline to the mouth of the cave, which was impressive in and of itself. The trail down was a little over a mile, descending to 829 feet below the surface for some of the cave rooms, and then up to approximately 750 feet to the Lunch Room. The ranger said it was the equivalent of walking down a seventy-five-story building. It would take a little over an hour to reach the midway point, and along the way Joop promised that we would see some amazing sights.

There was a profound mystery inherent in caves, especially in big ones like Carlsbad. I had been to Mammoth Cave in Kentucky, and it was mighty extraordinary, but I'd always heard that Carlsbad was prettier. The Big

Room was the largest single chamber cave by volume in the United States.

Just as the group began to walk forward, three men and one woman joined the end of the line, rushing to catch up to us. A middle-aged fellow wearing glasses and a Santa Fe sweatshirt was among them. A second park ranger took up the rear of the tour.

As we approached the mouth of the cave, every few seconds birds and a few bats would fly in or out. Ranger Joop told everyone that at dusk in the summer we could sit on the rocks or stand along the entrance trail and witness hundreds, maybe thousands, of bats emerge from the caverns to hunt for nightly meals. Sometimes the sight resembled smoke billowing out. The park had plans to one day build an amphitheater specifically for viewing the bat flights.

The group walked down into the mouth toward what the ranger called the Main Corridor. We were told that the paved trail had been completed only a year earlier. Prior to that, visitors walked on packed clay paths throughout the caverns. In the early days of the park's existence, the ranger told us, people had to climb down wooden staircases, but those were long gone.

As fascinating as all this was, I was *itching* to talk to Masters.

Patience, Felix . . .

As we descended, the light from the natural entrance receded. Artificial lighting had been placed strategically in the cave so that everything could be viewed in a somewhat darkened but beautifully lit tableaux. We passed the so-called Bat Cave where multitudes of the creatures were sleeping upside down on the ceiling. There was a rather long descent after that until the ranger pointed out a massive hill of boulders that were the remnants caused by explosives when the national park service opened up the space directly beneath the natural entrance, expanding the original surface hole discovered by explorer Jim White.

After a half hour, we stopped at a spot containing man-made stone benches. The two rangers had us all sit and rest while each man spoke about the history of the caverns, White's discovery of them, and what it was like for him when he first descended alone from the surface.

"It was dark," Joop said. "Very dark. To show you how dark it was, with no natural light from the sun anywhere, we're going to turn out the lights for ten seconds to give you an idea of what Mr. White would have experienced if his little oil lantern had gone out."

He counted down from three and the lights extinguished.

Everyone ooh'd and ah'd, and the kids giggled and made spooky noises. It was the *blackest dark*. Downright chilling.

The lights returned and it was time to continue the descent. As we got up and filed back into line, the group from Los Alamos happened to exit a row of seats to merge into the line right behind me. As we walked, the man wearing the Santa Fe shirt came close.

"Mr. Bork?" he whispered. The man had an Eastern European accent, just like Dora.

"Masters?"

"We'll talk more in the Lunch Room."

I nodded and he rejoined his colleagues, who had moved ahead a bit.

We began to pass unusual formations like the Whale's Mouth before coming to the Devil's Den, a cavern room that appeared sinister and foreboding with its oddly shaped walls and lighting design. Eventually we got to what was called the Iceberg, the largest known rock that fell during the collapse phase of the cave's development.

The incline had leveled out and we were finally on flatter ground. As I gazed at the jaw-dropping beauty of the Green Lake Room with its stalactites and stalagmites, I also pondered what the mission had in store for me in the next hour.

Masters believed I was Bork, so that was good. Assuming the handoff of the coin went smoothly, then what? I'd simply go back to New York and hand it over to Brinkley? Or would he really show up in New Mexico?

Visions of Dora haunted me. She could be suffering! Was it even possible to find her? Or would some hapless hiker stumble upon her corpse in the Texas or New Mexico wilderness?

There was also Marko the Pyromaniac to deal with. Alec Whitehall might not have been the only SMERSH agent in the country. He had said that Marko was working for someone else. Was that the truth? If so, who was the thug's employer?

Once more, the many pieces of this infuriating puzzle began to come together in my head. My CIA-trained analytical abilities examined each and every step I had taken since the whole thing began.

THE HOOK AND THE EYE

The tour group went through the King's Room, the Queen's Chamber, and the Papoose Room, a succession of otherworldly scenic wonders, before ascending a bit and entering the Lunch Room, 750 feet below the surface. It was just after eleven o'clock. We passed the bank of two elevators and the restrooms to get to it.

I held back as others in the group went past me, for I wanted to scan the space to see who might already be in there. Curved concrete counters and picnic tables in groups occupied its floor. Cold sandwiches and fried chicken in white boxes were apparently prepared on the surface, brought down by elevator, and sold to visitors along with coffee and sodas.

There might have been fifty people in the Lunch Room. Some may have been there from a previous tour or could have come down the elevators to join only the Big Room Tour, which would begin in an hour. The school children sat together at the far end. Masters and his three companions took a table midway. The echo of the visitors chattering in the craggy cavity was simultaneously calming and unnerving. People were far, far underground and eating a meal!

And then I spotted them.

It was a good thing I hadn't walked right in and revealed myself.

About thirty feet away, Marko sat at one of the picnic tables with another man who was scowling and resembled a wrestler.

There was no way I could enter the Lunch Room without them seeing me.

27

CARLSBAD CAVERNS NATIONAL PARK, NEW MEXICO
I stepped back from the Lunch Room entrance. How was I going to get Masters' attention and talk to him without Marko and his goon noticing?

At that moment, Ranger Joop emerged from the men's washroom and I got an idea.

"Hello, sir," I said.

"You doing all right?" he asked.

"I am. But I was wondering if you'd do me a favor. I need a little help with the harness on my prosthesis. My friend knows how to do it. Could you possibly ask him to meet me here?"

"Sure, who is it?"

We stood in the entrance to the Lunch Room but I kept well behind the park ranger. I pointed. "See the man with glasses and the Santa Fe sweatshirt? That's him. Just tell him I need to talk to him. Be discreet, please, it's kind of embarrassing."

"Okay, I understand."

Joop left me there and I went back to stand in front of the restrooms. A minute later, Masters appeared.

"Bork?" he whispered. "I was all prepared to get away from my friends and sit at a table in there and talk."

"Stanley, the opposition is inside."

He blinked. "What do we do?"

Too many visitors were going in and out of the men's room, so that wouldn't work. We needed to get into an area that afforded privacy. I spotted the access to the second half of the tour, the Big Room, on the other side of the Lunch Room.

"Walk with me but stay on my left side. We're going to the Big Room."

I unbuttoned my jacket and did my best to hide my prosthetic arm underneath it. As I was a bit taller than Masters, I hunched over and turned my head to face the lunch counters rather than the picnic tables. We then walked into the Lunch Room together and moved naturally at an even pace. It was apparent that Marko and his pal didn't know what Masters looked like. Their eyes were focused elsewhere, probably searching for *me*. When we made it to the sign that indicated the direction to the Big Room, I glanced back. Marko and his man hadn't budged. We'd made it.

"Don't we have to wait for a park ranger to lead us?" Masters asked.

"No one's looking. Come on."

We went through the rocky tunnel and emerged into an absolutely breathtaking stadium-sized wonderland with three gigantic stalagmite domes in the background. For a second we both had to stop and take in what we were looking at.

"I don't believe this," Masters said.

The two of us then walked quickly into the darkened but artistically lit Hall of Giants, which consisted of the sixty-two foot high Giant Dome and the remarkably uniform and extremely phallic Twin Domes. Above us was an over 200-foot-high ceiling of stalactites that went on and on.

When I thought we were a safe distance from the Lunch Room, I kept my voice down and said, "All right, Masters, let's make it fast. You have the coin?"

"Ah," he answered quietly. "It's a good thing Dora didn't beat you here. Ava warned me about her. She broke Ava's heart. I've known them since the late thirties. In Warsaw, before the war."

That throw away statement was something important. "Go on."

"The New York contingent—may they rest in peace—and Ava and I have been working on this for some time, but our communications were short and strictly business. My radio was in a rented apartment in Santa Fe. On my day off I'd go into town, and she and I had prearranged transmissions at night. Ava kept things on a need to know basis. She only revealed after Karl died that she and you would be the ones picking up the goods."

He expected some kind of response from me. With just enough sorrowful inflection, I said, "And now she's gone."

Masters sighed. He put a hand on my shoulder. "I know you meant a lot to her. I must say I was wary when you joined the team so late in the game, but Ava vouched for you." He reached into his pocket and took out a handful of coins. "It's so dark in here, it's difficult to see the dates." He stopped walking forward and moved closer to one of the light fixtures at the side of the path. "Ah. Here it is. You have to give me the password first."

What? Oh for God's sake, what's the goddamned password?

I'd have to take a stab at it. A wild guess.

Think, Leiter, think!

What had I seen during this journey that could possibly give me a hint? I thought back to anything Dora might have said and came up with nothing. Had there been anything in Ava's house? Likely not. Then I went back further to New York and the notes and materials I'd seen at the apartments of Titov and Adamski. But they were all written in Polish, weren't they? I didn't know the language! How the hell was I supposed to ...

Wait. There had been a couple of words in English.

Adamski had written the word "Hurricane" on his calendar on the date of October 3. And, sure enough, the British had tested their atomic bomb, code named "Hurricane," on that very day. The other word I'd seen was on the date November 1.

That was tomorrow!

"Stanley," I asked, "is the nuclear test tomorrow?"

There was a glint in his eyes and a hint of a smile. "Well?"

"The password is ..."

He raised his eyebrows, waiting for it.

"... *Ivy.*"

He exhaled and nodded. "Ah, for a second there, I thought maybe Ava hadn't told you."

"For a second there, I thought maybe I had forgotten it."

He handed over a quarter. One twenty-five cent piece. "Here you go. This has the special microdot. Just in case. You know, Babanin has his press conference at the United Nations on Sunday. It's the only time he'll be in public."

Press conference? Sunday? Was Ava or Bork supposed to deliver the coin to Babanin at his press conference? And the nuclear test was *tomorrow?*

I took the coin and examined it. The date was 1937. Perhaps in better light I might have been able to spot the microdot, but it was well hidden.

"Just keep it in your pocket with other change. No one will know," Masters said. "I'm surprised they let my colleagues and I off this weekend, seeing that the test is tomorrow. But here I am."

I dropped the quarter in my trousers. Masters seemed to be a nice guy—too bad he was a damned traitor. Certainly not a professional spy. Los Alamos truly was a leaky faucet and had been since its inception. I was beginning to think that Ava and her team, including Masters, were all a bunch of amateurs. They were playing a game that was far more insecure and dangerous than they realized. Microdots were still being widely used in the spy business, but they were yesterday-technology.

Masters then looked around to make sure no one was near. "Now, listen! Here's the other thing ... and it's *vitally important*." He took my left hand and placed another small object in it.

"What is this?"

"Plan B! Bork! Didn't she tell you?"

"I'm afraid not." More improvisation. "She was supposed to tell me yesterday, but she . . ."

"Right. Give me your ear," he said, so I leaned in for him to whisper. What he told me was surprising . . . and terrifying. He gave me some instructions that I barely comprehended because of the shock, but I concentrated and listened to what he had to say.

When he finished, I saw them coming over his shoulder. Marko and the other guy.

"We need to run!" I said. He jerked his head back and practically yelped in fear. I pulled him along. "Come on!"

We hurried down the path deeper into the Big Room with Marko and his goon not far behind.

28

Carlsbad Caverns National Park, New Mexico
"Running" was not exactly what I'd call my awkward gait of moving quickly down dimly lit paved pathways in an underground cavern. I considered drawing the Iver, turning, and shooting at our pursuers. But then I thought—*wait*, can I fire a *gun* inside a cavern like this? Would it cause a *cave-in*? I had no idea. I hoped that Marko wasn't crazy enough to bring *dynamite* into the caverns.

The two of us kept moving as the path kept winding through the enormous space past magnificent formations. The Big Room certainly lived up to its name. It could take an hour and a half to make the circular route around the cave's perimeter, over a mile, back to the Lunch Room. Were we going to *run* through the second half of the national park tour? Or should we go back, stand our ground, and fight those guys? Looking at Masters, though, I realized he was not built for combat. He was an office worker and assuredly had no training in self-defense. Before The Mishap, I could possibly have taken on Marko and his goon and done some damage, even if they were to eventually overpower me. Now, though, with a bum leg and an artificial arm? Not likely.

"You're holding me back," Masters said, breathlessly. "Sorry!" With that, he picked up speed and actually ran ahead of me. Fine. I didn't want him hurt, even if he was an enemy spy. I looked back and saw the two thugs perhaps thirty yards behind ... I could barely see them, but every second or two the light would catch their moving figures. It wouldn't be long before they caught up to me, because, dammit, *I wasn't fast.*

I kept going and eventually came to a crossroad to the left. The sign said that this was a shortcut to the other side of the Big Room and the return trail to the Lunch Room for any visitors who had become tired and didn't want to complete the entire circle of the tour.

The shortcut sounded good to me and I began to cut across. Masters had gone on. Would the goons split up, one of them following Masters and the other behind me? Was there a place to hide? The tour group had been warned by the ranger at the beginning to never touch a formation, for the oils in our skin could forever damage the beauty and possibly disrupt the creation of still-active growths.

But our lives were at stake.

I stepped off the path onto hard, limestone rock, and squatted behind a boulder-like outcropping.

Then there were voices. Russian. Two men stood at the intersection of the main trail and the shortcut. Then ... they split up, too. Marko took the shortcut and briskly walked past the boulder behind which I was hiding. He went on to the other side of the Big Room, likely thinking I was headed back to the Lunch Room. The other man went ahead toward the far end of the cave in pursuit of Masters.

I rolled up my trouser leg and opened the compartment on the BK. With the index finger of my left hand, I pulled out the trench dagger by the loop cord. If I couldn't fire a handgun in the caverns, then, by golly, I could be armed with a silent, deadly weapon of choice.

Ever so slowly, I raised my head to look around. I saw neither Marko nor the other man. It wouldn't be long before my tour group would finish lunch and be on their way into the Big Room for the second half of their caverns experience. I needed to get to the surface *pronto*.

Then I heard a scream in the near distance. It sounded like Masters. Moving swiftly back to the main trail, I debated whether I should go help him or retreat back to the Lunch Room.

Marko might be waiting for me if I chose the latter. Going forward and maybe helping the traitor could buy some time. Neither choice was particularly solid.

Aw, hell.

There was nothing to do but proceed forward as quickly as I could, my BK prosthesis be damned. My stump wasn't yet in agony, but that joy was not long in the future. The path curved and twisted and switched back, but for the most part it remained level. Finally, I came to the end of the Big Room, where the Bottomless Pit took up a large section of the space. Guard rails wrapped around the monstrous, gaping black hole, but those would not have kept a person from slipping through the bars. The park administration likely figured that no one would want to tempt fate by stepping beyond the rails to get a closer look at the pit. I had read that this huge, scary abyss was not really bottomless, but rather a whopping 138 feet to its floor. The complete blackness of the thing spoke of infinite, blind, and silent hell.

Stanley Masters lay on the trail in front of it.

I squatted to examine him and saw that he had been stabbed several times. Blood puddled around his body. The trouser pockets had been pulled out. A wallet drooped on the ground surrounded by some change. None of the coins were quarters. The killer must have known about the special twenty-five cent piece and had taken any that Masters had.

A blow like a battering ram hit me from the side, knocking me to the trail. Stunned, I rolled and had the presence of mind to deflect a fist punch with my left arm. It wasn't Marko, but the other guy, Scowling Wrestler. Unfortunately, my prosthesis wasn't built to be a defensive appendage. Wrestler slugged me with the other fist and stars exploded in my skull. I thought I might lose consciousness as the man dived for my right trouser pocket to empty it—but he found the Iver strapped to my waist.

"Oh, ho!" he hooted.

He pulled the gun out of the holster and, momentarily distracted from his mission, examined it as if he'd found an abandoned toy. Wrestler then pointed the barrel at my face.

"Do you have it?" he asked in heavily accented English.

All I could do was groan. Apparently he wasn't afraid of a loud noise triggering a collapse.

His left land grasped my throat and began to squeeze, tightening by the second. My own gun barrel was against my forehead and my voice box was about to be crushed.

But then I remembered my left hand. The object it held was still there in my palm.

With all the strength I could muster, I swung my arm up and jabbed the dagger into the side of Wrestler's neck.

His roar sounded more like that of a wild beast than a human. The man immediately released my neck, dropped the gun on my chest, and clawed at the knife with both hands. My grip was still on the hilt, so I pulled the thing out myself. Blood spurted everywhere, all over me, him, and the path we lay on.

Wrestler sat straight on my belly, clutching his neck and staring at me in horror.

I then vigorously plunged the knife into his sternum. Even though the blade wasn't very long, it did the trick. He stiffened momentarily and then became dead weight, slumping over to the right. I pushed his body off mine.

I had to lay there for a second, catching my breath. Finally, I rose to a sitting position and then managed to stand. I leaned against the rails in front of the Bottomless Pit and breathed, my back to the two corpses on the ground. I had to get out of the caverns and make it to the elevators without causing too much attention, but the blood on my jacket would certainly give the park rangers pause.

Just as I was about to gather my strength and begin

trekking back toward the Lunch Room, I heard a heavy, scraping noise behind me.

Wrestler was stirring, still alive, attempting to get up.

I tried to jerk away from him, but his thick hand grabbed my left leg to keep me from stepping further. Of course, my left leg is made of wood. If he dug his fingers and nails into it, I wouldn't feel a thing.

Holding on to the rails, I kicked him in the face with my right foot. But the man would not let go of my prosthesis. Instead, he twisted it, causing great pain to my stump. I had to rotate my torso with the leg, otherwise it would have chafed my skin so badly it would have bled. This caused me to fall onto the trail.

Wrestler stood, wavering on his feet. He breathed heavily, obviously in great distress. The knife was still in his sternum. I know he wanted to leap at me, attack me, kill me . . . but he couldn't gather the wherewithal to move. His eyes were demon red, boring holes in me.

Move! Now!

The Marine in me injected a boost of adrenaline into my system. I managed to scramble, twist, and stand. Wrestler stared at me, his brain cells malfunctioning. He desperately wanted to strike, but his muscles weren't responding.

I reached out with my prosthesis. Opening the hook, I clasped the dagger and yanked it out of his chest. Wrestler yelped in pain and wobbled backwards against the guardrail.

Should I?
Yeah. I should.

Folding my left arm and right prosthesis inward to my own chest as if I were about to block a linebacker, I rushed and rammed him as hard as possible.

Wrestler's upper body bent backward over the rail. It took only a little more heaving on my part to hoist him over. He landed on the other side of the rail with a thud ... and then he began to roll, slowly at first. His heavy body picked up speed on the rocky incline as it trundled toward the black pit. He screamed ... and then dropped into the darkness. His cry of horror echoed from the hole, diminishing in volume until it was nothing.

I had to catch my breath once again. My gun and knife lay at my feet. I retrieved them both, holstered the weapon and replaced the dagger in the BK compartment.

But what had happened to his partner, Marko? Was he going to attack me at some point on my way back? I trekked the second half of the Big Room trail at a brisk pace, my eyes scanning the stalagmites and rocky protrusions as I moved on. Anything could happen. But after passing the final attractions of the Crystal Spring Dome and the Rock of Ages, I finally approached the Lunch Room.

The path took me directly to the elevator banks. My old tour group was just getting started on the other side. Ranger Joop led them forward. They were, unfortunately, going to discover a surprise at the far end of the cave.

I ducked into the men's room and went into a stall. I removed the bloody jacket and examined my sweater. There were only a few drops of blood on it, but the jacket was ruined. I couldn't go out among the public with it on. Without it, though, my gun and holster were exposed. I had no choice but to remove the holster and Iver from the belt and wrap the jacket around them, inside out so that the blood couldn't be seen, and then carry the bundle under my arm.

After a few minutes at the sink washing off traces of blood on my face and hand, I was ready. I stepped out and joined four other people waiting for the elevator. I stood with them and watched the counter at the top of the doors.

Something poked me in the small of my back, and it was a sensation with which I was very familiar. You never forget what the barrel of a gun feels like against your body.

A woman's voice whispered, "Be silent, Felix. Act naturally."

I turned my head and my heart nearly stopped.

Dora Wysocki stood behind me. A jacket was draped over her arm and she held the Colt M1911A1 in her hand. There was just a bit of a smile on the corner of her pouty mouth. "Hello," she said.

"What are you doing?"

"Taking you to the surface."

"You won't use that here," I continued to whisper.

"Try me."

The elevator arrived and the doors opened. A few people emerged and then Dora prodded me with the gun to step forward with the other visitors who were leaving. There were six of us in the car when the doors closed. The speedy ascension was disorienting. One person said, "Oh, my ears just popped!"

The car finally stopped, the doors opened, and we stepped outside. The other folks laughed and one man commented that it had been like an amusement park ride.

"Where's your car?" Dora asked.

"Over there. In the lot. How did you get here?"

"Marko drove me."

What did that mean? Was she on Marko's side? What was going on?

Was she SMERSH?

"Aren't we going to wait for him?" I asked with blatant sarcasm.

"He has his own escape route. Let's go."

We walked to the parking lot, past a park ranger who nodded at us and said, "Hope you enjoyed your visit! Come back soon!"

When we were in the car, she took my bundle of jacket and gun and dropped it on the passenger floorboard.

"I know you have the coin," she said.

"What makes you say that?"

"Shut up, Felix. Drive."

"Where are we going?"

"Felix, I *will* shoot you if you don't do as I say. I *can* drive. I'll dump your body in the trunk and drive the car myself after I've gone through your pockets and retrieved the coin. But we're going to get out of the park before we get down to business. Drive."

I started the engine and pulled out of the lot.

29

WHITE'S CITY, NEW MEXICO

"Where are we going now?" I asked once we were on the main highway.

"Go through White's City and all the way to the town of Carlsbad. From there we'll go to Roswell. I have a motel room there," Dora answered. "We can finish our business."

My response couldn't hide the scorn. "Oh, are we going to bed again, or was that all an act, too?"

She glared at me for a moment while I kept my eyes on the road. She then turned away and said nothing.

It would be an hour-and-a-half trek to Roswell, much of it in silence.

As the winding road went through White's City, I asked, "You really think shooting me will solve anything for you?"

She sighed heavily. "Felix, you did the job I hired you for. And I'm prepared to pay the rest of your fee as soon as you hand over the quarter. We'll take care of that business in my room. Then, I'll go. A ride is waiting for me in Roswell. And you can leave and return to New York on your own."

Right. I wanted to laugh. No doubt a hapless maid would find my corpse in that motel room a few days from now.

"What if I don't have the quarter?" I asked.

"You do, Felix. It's what we came all this way to get."

"What, are you and SMERSH going to make me give it to you?"

She turned her head to me and said with coldness, "Something like that."

Okay. It was clear where I stood. "So, the other night at Bork's house ... your abduction was fake? You were in league with this Marko character all along?"

"Stop talking, Felix. Just drive."

We eventually reached Carlsbad and turned off toward Roswell. As we shot forward along the surprisingly deserted road, though, the clues that had been gestating for days were coming into focus.

"I get it now," I said. "What this whole thing is about."

"What are you saying?"

I kept my eyes on my driving, but it all spilled out.

"This is the story, Dora. You tell me if I'm right. In 1939, you and Ava were in Warsaw. You were both part of the Promethean movement. You were young. Teenagers. You found it exciting. Romantic. The movement was centered around the University of Warsaw and you thought you were big shots, hanging around with older boys. They were intellectuals, artists, scientists. Interesting people. Even Stanley Masters was there, under his real name. How am I doing?"

She just blinked.

I went on. "Ava got a lot of attention from the boys. She was, well, very pretty. Maybe you were a little jealous. Then *you* met someone. A Russian soldier named Bogdan Apalkov."

Her head jerked. "How do you know that?"

"I'm a goddamned Pinkerton *detective*, Dora." Her open jaw told me that I was exactly on the right track. "Bogdan was older than you, but still young. And he was in Warsaw. And you were in love with him."

She sighed.

I went on. "And the Prometheists hated the Soviets. They found out you were seeing him. And I'll bet it was Ava who ratted on you."

After a beat, she said it. "Yes."

"The Prometheists killed him."

She nodded. "One night they ... surrounded him in an alley."

The memories were getting to her. She was starting to open up.

A sign indicated that Roswell was ten miles away. "That was in August 1939. And we all know what happened in September. You had to flee."

"My adoptive parents forced me to come with them. I wanted to stay in Poland, but I ended up coming to America. But I never, *never* forgave Ava."

I prompted her. "Go on."

"She stayed in touch with her Polish friends. Eventually she made contact with other Prometheists in New York. It was a tiny but tight-knit network of people who hated the Soviet Union for what they had done—and became—after the war. In the meantime, Ava met Don Spence, moved to Texas, and married him."

"Ah, and that's the other part of the story," I said. "Why Ava was upset with you. You did something that hurt her. Something to do with her marriage. Bork said you 'betrayed her with *Don*.'"

Her eyes welled a little, but she spoke with venom. "At the end of 1949, Don was back in New York on business. Without Ava. We had dinner together. To put it bluntly, I seduced him. We spent the night together. He went home to Texas. And I . . . I wrote to Ava and told her what had happened. It was my revenge for what she had done in Poland."

"And he had a heart attack."

Dora nodded. "Ava blamed me for *that*, too. She claimed that he felt so terrible about his infidelity that the stress killed him. Fat chance. He had a bad heart. Now shut up and drive."

Would she use the gun? Did she really have the gumption to shoot me? She could be hurt or even killed if I crashed. Surely she was bluffing. No, she wanted to get me to that motel room in Roswell so that *someone else* could do the dirty work. Marko? Probably. They'd make me hand over the quarter, and then . . .

The temptation to steer the car off the road and wreck it in the ditch was overpowering.

And yet, the detective in me wanted to see how all this would play out. I was determined to hold on to the coin until I couldn't. If pain and sorrow awaited me in her motel room, then so be it. I would then know that at least I had acted honorably and with integrity to my profession.

"Dora, if you're being forced to do this, blackmailed or something, I can help you. We can get out of this together."

Again, no response to that.

As soon as we passed a billboard indicating that we were one mile away from Roswell, a New Mexico State Trooper's Ford pulled out from behind the sign and began to follow us. Dora didn't seem to be aware of it. Her eyes were focused on the road and the upcoming town in the distance.

The closer we got, though, flashing lights were visible in the distance. She saw them, too, and this caused her to sit up straighter and lean forward. She quietly gasped. Very quickly the tableau became clearer.

The road was blocked by several State Trooper cars and one black governmental Chevy sedan.

"Oh, my God," Dora muttered. "Felix, stop. Turn around!"

"I can't," I said, noting that the trooper's car behind us had flicked on his lights as well as the siren.

She turned around to look and then panicked. "Let me out!"

"How am I going to do that? If I stop, that cop will be right on top of us. And where are you going to go if I let you out? You're going to run into the desert? They'll catch you in five minutes!"

There was no escape. Were the cops after me, Dora, or both of us? Did they know I had in my pocket secrets smuggled out of Los Alamos? Or was it about what had happened at the national park? Had Masters' body been discovered? Were the cops going to pin his murder on me?

My forehead was suddenly damp with sweat.

Dora bowed her head and placed her free hand over her eyes. Was she weeping?

"This wasn't supposed to happen," she said.

There was nothing else to do but drive right up to the blockade and stop. Several state troopers with guns drawn surrounded the Packard and ordered us out of the car. I opened the door, got out, and held my hand and hook high. Dora did the same, and they confiscated her weapon. Then one officer told us to face the side of the Packard and submit to being frisked. They didn't find the knife in my wooden leg. My handgun was still wrapped in my bloody jacket on the floor of the Packard.

The passenger door of the black sedan opened and, boy, was I glad to see the face attached to the man who appeared.

"Felix, buddy boy!" Michael Brinkley hooted. "Fellas, let him go, he's one of us."

My heart leaped. "Michael! Is that really you?"

"I told you I was coming out your way. I got your message and here I am." He turned to two other men wearing trademark government suits and sunglasses who had also emerged from the sedan. Pointing at Dora, he ordered, "Take that woman into custody. She's a traitor to the United States!"

Her eyes shot daggers at me. I just looked at her and shrugged my shoulders. *Hey, I didn't do this.*

One of the suits handcuffed her wrists in front and marched her past the blockade to a black Chevrolet sedan delivery vehicle. He opened the back door so that Dora could climb inside.

But the CIA had no authority to arrest anyone. They weren't a law enforcement agency! "Michael, what's going on? You can't do this . . . can you?"

"Felix," Brinkley said, "I'll be turning her over to the FBI. Note that I never said she was 'under arrest.'" He put a hand on my shoulder. "We discovered the SMERSH agent's Studebaker this morning where you'd left it. Congratulations, Felix, you did the CIA proud."

"Whitehall also murdered Ava Spence."

He nodded. "Dora Wysocki will be going away for a long time."

My head was spinning again. A lot was happening too quickly. I said, "There's still someone missing. That assassin, the one who killed the two men in New York is running free. He was back at the caverns and—"

"You mean the psychopath known as Marko? Dynamite boy?" Brinkley smiled again. "He's in police custody at the park. I understand there was some trouble there a little while ago. One of my colleagues will pick him up and ship him back to New York. Don't you worry, Felix, you're in the clear. Sometimes the U.S. government can smooth the rough edges of bureaucracy the way we want."

He then leaned in and whispered to me, "You have the goods from Los Alamos, right?"

I nodded. "Yeah."

"Okay, not here."

Brinkley clapped me on the left arm and stepped back. "Felix, I need you to get in your Packard and follow us to Walker Air Force Base. I need to debrief you. It's not far. From there the woman and I will be flying back to New York for some due processing. Follow us. You'll see signs for it. Stay behind us."

He turned to the New Mexico State Troopers and waved. "Thanks a lot, boys! We'll take it from here!"

They all muttered an acknowledgement and got in their own vehicles. Brinkley returned to the black sedan and got in. His two suited agents locked up the doors on the sedan delivery. The last thing I saw of the interior before the door slammed shut was Dora's face.

Oddly, she was smiling.

Setting off behind them in the Packard, we formed a caravan. My stomach, though, was lurching. The whole thing was very disturbing. It wasn't sitting right. I was missing part of the big picture.

Once again . . . *Patience, Felix . . .!*

30

ROSWELL, NEW MEXICO

Walker Air Force Base was located south of the city of Roswell. It was used for training purposes during the war, but afterwards the Army Air Force took it over. Apparently, since my former boss at the CIA had access, it served as a governmental depot when necessary.

The caravan of vehicles was allowed through the security gates and I followed the other two cars to a hangar where armed MPs were stationed at attention. A Northrop YC-125 Raider sat on the runway nearby, and I guessed this might be Brinkley's ride back to New York.

After reattaching my belt, holster, and Iver Johnson, I donned my jacket and got out of the Packard. The blood had dried, eliciting the appearance that I was a walking dead man. To be on the safe side, I pulled out my Pinkerton's ID to show it to the MP. He gave me the up-and-down blinking eye gawk when I approached the hangar, but he didn't stop me. I stuck the ID in my jacket pocket and went on in. When Brinkley saw me, though, he said, "Heavens, Felix, you need a dry cleaner."

I ignored the quip and said, "Michael, I think we need to talk."

"We do. Come inside." He led me into a small office up a flight of steps in the hangar.

Brinkley offered a cigarette from his Camels. I still had a partial pack of Chesterfields in my jacket pocket, but I chose to save them. We lit up and then he spoke.

"Felix, tell me everything that's happened from the moment you arrived in White's City yesterday."

"I'm going to back up to the night before." I proceeded to relate the tale of how Marko showed up at Bork's house, killed Bork, and abducted Dora when Alec Whitehall showed up. At least I'd thought Marko had abducted Dora. I went through how I discovered that Alec was crooked and how I'd neutralized him. Then I related everything that happened in the caverns, even copping to killing Marko's partner in self-defense.

"We were wondering what happened to him," Brinkley said. "We'll have to tell the park authorities to go down into the pit and bring the body up."

"Yeah."

"Did this fellow Masters tell you anything we need to know?"

My gut tightened. The little nagging gremlin inside me was telling me to be quiet. Call it instinct, call it fear ... whatever it was, I thought it best to hold off telling all.

"Not really," I answered. "Now you tell me your side of the story."

"Right. The man who called himself Alec Whitehall was indeed a Canadian working for SMERSH. He was out to steal the nuclear secrets. He likely would have killed you once he had what he wanted from you. So, Felix, you did the right thing by leaving him for us to find."

"How *did* you find him?"

"Some Mexican kid saw the Studebaker behind the billboard. The police came and opened it up. By that time I was in that little town looking for you. I liaised with the local cops, of course, and they told me they'd found him. I knew who he was by then. So, good job."

I shrugged. "Thanks."

"Now. About Dora Wysocki..."

"Yeah, what *about* Dora Wysocki?"

"She is not an FBI agent."

"I figured that."

"She is also not a Russian agent."

"No?"

"She is what they call a Prometheist. Have you ever heard that term?"

The only thing I could do was tell the truth, but I did not want to involve Steve Sandlin and the FBI. "I know about Prometheism," I answered. "But I thought the Promethean Movement was defunct."

"Nope. The whole network of spies we've been dealing with, the folks smuggling the hydrogen bomb specs out of Los Alamos, was a gang of Prometheists. Their handlers are members of an underground group in Warsaw, the remains of the Promethean Movement from before the war. They have their own agenda, working against the U.S. government. What they were attempting to do . . . well, they were not working for the Soviets, but rather against them. Apparently in their little cabal in Warsaw is a collection of physicists. They want to make their own bomb. We can only guess what they would do with it. Blackmail the Soviets into letting Poland go free? Hurt *us* for not standing up for them after the war? Probably they just want to destabilize the balance of power and give themselves a standing in world politics. That still makes them enemies of the USA, and Dora is a member of their team."

I stared down at the table top and shook my head. "I don't believe it . . . Michael, I think she was working for someone else. She wasn't part of the team that included Ava Spence, Adamski, Titov, or Jan Bartosz. Or Bork, for that matter. He was a stooge that Ava recruited at the last minute. Hell, Bartosz tried to kill Dora in New York. Dora and Ava were on the outs. That team didn't want Dora near them."

"I'm sorry, Felix. I told you she was a liar. I know you're fond of her."

"What's going to happen to her?"

"I'm taking Miss Wysocki back to New York, where she will be properly interrogated, handed over to the FBI, and charged with various crimes. She's in a lot of trouble."

"I feel terrible about it."

"I know. But, Felix . . . you did what you had to do. You did what I *told* you to do. You *became* Mr. Bork!"

"She had the same idea."

"That's because she was using you. The whole time!

She thought you'd be the perfect patsy to 'accompany' her across the U.S. from New York. She knew all along that a SMERSH assassin would eventually kill her sister and that Bork fellow."

"But she thought that was Marko. Like you did. He didn't kill Ava Spence. Alec Whitehall did. And Whitehall told me that Marko was working for some rogue outfit. You really have Marko in custody?"

"We do. There is much we don't know about him. He will soon go through some intense interrogation, too. Maybe Marko wasn't SMERSH at all and was indeed working for someone else. It's pretty clear, though, that he also wanted to intercept the nuclear plans, but his first priority was to make sure the Prometheists didn't get it. Felix, you were the ace up Dora's sleeve. Ava's ham radio communications were carelessly intercepted. We knew, they knew, *everyone* knew that the traitor from Los Alamos was only going to give the goods to either Ava or Bork, so Dora chose you to step in and replace him." Brinkley looked at his watch. "Oh, look at the time. It's nearly four o'clock. Now. I have something to tell you that's classified."

"What's that?"

"A couple of hours ago or so, way over in the Pacific Ocean, on the island of Elugelab in the Eniwetok Atoll, the United States government successfully tested the first thermonuclear weapon. A hydrogen bomb. Over there the date is November first. They're what, seventeen, eighteen hours ahead, I can't recall which."

I played dumb, since Masters had already told me.

"No kidding." But only now did the thought fill me with dread. How powerful did a nuclear device really have to be for us to flaunt our superiority?

"No one knows about it except, well, the White House, the Pentagon, the FBI, and the CIA. I'm sure news is going to leak to the media, but I'm betting that Truman won't say anything about it. He'll leave that job to our next president. Eisenhower. You know what the code name for the nuclear testing project was?"

It didn't matter much to me, but then he just said it.

"Operation Ivy."

Well. Of course it was. November 1. Ivy. The password in the caves. All written on Adamski's calendar. That made some kind of ironic sense.

"As I understand it," he continued, "the secondary code for this first test was 'Mike.' I think there's going to be another test in a couple of weeks. They're calling that 'King.' And that brings me to the other business at hand," he said. "I need you to give me that twenty-five cent coin. I'll make sure it gets into the right hands, you know, the folks with pay grades above mine. They'll know what to do with it."

He held out his hand.

Something bothered me. My loyalty to Brinkley and to the CIA was strong, but...

I knew what I had to do.

Taking a breath, I stood and reached into my trouser pocket. Pulling out all the change, I sorted through it and found three quarters. There was only one with the date 1937. It was the one Masters had given me. I plucked it out of my palm with my hook and dropped it into Brinkley's hand.

"It's all yours," I said. "I'm actually very happy to be rid of it." That was the truth.

"Thank you, Felix. Your work on this assignment has been exemplary. I'll be in touch about you getting your old job back. If we can't make you a field agent again, then it'll be the Reserves. But I'm telling you, the way you handled yourself here will go a long way to underline your integrity."

"Thanks. What now?"

Brinkley stood and produced a little purple felt jewel box that would ordinarily contain a wedding ring. He opened it and dropped the coin inside. After putting the box in his pocket, he stuck out his left hand and I shook it.

"You're welcome to ride with us in the plane, Felix. You'd have to dump your car here, though."

"I'm not doing that."

"I didn't think you would. Go on, drive back to New York. Take your time. I'll fix it with Pinkerton. Try to enjoy the road trip. See America."

"When are you taking off?"

"In a few minutes. We'll make a stop at Malden Air Force Base in Missouri to refuel, and hopefully make it to Idlewild before midnight, but that's doubtful."

We walked out of the office and into the hangar. When we were outside, I saw agents filing Dora into the Raider aircraft. She didn't look at me. I wondered if I'd ever see her again.

Probably not.

Well, good riddance. Traitors were not on my list of favorite people.

"I'm sure you like Texas barbecue," Michael said. "There's a new place in Lubbock at Avenue Q and 24th Street called Tom and Bingo's Hickory Pit Bar-B-Q. You'll love it. If you take off now you'll be in Lubbock in time for dinner."

That sounded damned good to me. "Okay, Michael, thanks. See you later."

I got in my car and waited. Brinkley climbed the steps to the plane, turned and waved at me, and I gave him a little salute. It took a few minutes for the Raider to taxi to the appropriate runway, and then it took off into the sky.

Four or five days of driving did not particularly appeal to me, despite my love of the open road. I should have felt good about it, but my heart was heavy. My senses were also telling me that nothing was what it seemed, especially considering the other item Masters had given me and what he'd whispered in my ear.

31

ROSWELL, NEW MEXICO AND ENVIRONS

The road out of the air base was a straight shot up Highway 285 and then east toward Texas on 380. I still had plenty of gas. I likely wouldn't have to fill up until I stopped for the night somewhere in southern Missouri. From Lubbock, I'd head into Oklahoma and go through Oklahoma City and Tulsa, then across Missouri to hit St. Louis. Onward to Indianapolis and over to Pittsburgh. Navigating back to New York from there was easy-peasy.

My jacket and sweater were off and in the passenger seat. It was still warm and sunny. My window was down and the fresh air was intoxicating. Maybe the trip wouldn't be so bad.

The landscape going out of Roswell's city limits was just like West Texas—barren, dry, flat, and boring. The wild west, for sure. The road was surprisingly lonely and unpopulated, provoking a bit of daydreaming and introspection. It was natural that I'd ponder everything that had occurred over the last twenty-four hours.

How did I feel about Dora Wysocki? Certainly it was

a combination of sadness and anger, whatever that might look like. What a fool I'd been to believe we had become close on that long trip from New York to Texas. The woman was a traitor. She had lied to me.

I missed her, though ...

And why the hell was she smiling inside that sedan after being taken into custody?

Then there were the red flags thrown on the play while I was talking to Brinkley. The man had always been good to me for the short time I had worked for him after moving to Manhattan from D.C. He was attempting to get me reinstated to the CIA. We were friends, as much as one could be buddies with a supervisor. And yet ... I didn't tell him everything. Why? What had come over me?

And then I knew. It was because I believed Dora over him. She was not one of the Prometheists.

I'd been driving about ten minutes when I saw a bridge in the distance. It spanned the Pecos River, not a particularly wide body of water, but one that runs vertically nine hundred miles from northern New Mexico down into Texas, ultimately connecting to the Rio Grande around Big Bend.

The bridge was not a long one. But on the far side of it, way in the distance, an unmoving dark car sat perpendicular to the road. I slowed as I approached the bridge. Something wasn't right. Now going about twenty miles per hour, the Packard made it onto the bridge and ...

POP! POP!

The front tires.

THE HOOK AND THE EYE

POP! POP!

The back tires.

Oh, no ...

I stopped. My car was in the middle of the bridge. I got out and did a walk-around. Sure enough, all four tires were flat. And I saw why ...

My lane on the bridge was littered with caltrops. Tetrahedron-shaped spikes. No matter how one falls, it forms a tripod with at least one spike pointing upward.

The car in the distance revved its engine. It was some two hundred yards away. It straightened and began coming toward me. The closer it got, the better the black vehicle became defined.

My blood pressure skyrocketed. It was the black Buick Roadmaster.

This was a trap.

What was I going to do? Run? Get into a firefight?

The sun reflected off the Buick's windshield, making it difficult to see inside it at that distance. Eventually it was a hundred yards away, gaining speed. It began to slow at fifty yards, then forty ... thirty ... Only then could I make out the driver's silhouette. The rounded shape of the head was recognizable.

Marko.

My training and instincts kicked in. I immediately cross-drew my Iver and stood straight and tall with my left arm extended.

Twenty yards away now, traveling maybe ten miles per hour. An arm reached out the driver's side window. A handgun, likely the Tokarev, pointed at me.

I was fully exposed, but my standing beside the Packard was the only way I had a chance of hitting the guy.

His gun fired. The round shattered the Packard's windshield right next to me. Had he missed on purpose? Was he playing with me?

Aim!

Closing my right eye, I stared down the Iver's barrel with my left.

Breathe!

Another gunshot from the Buick. This time, the round took a chunk of metal and paving out of the bridge's surface just a few inches in front of my feet. Luckily, the bulk of the splatter hit my BK leg, so I didn't feel it.

Hold! Don't move!

The Buick was ten yards away. I had only a second or two.

Fire!

I squeezed the trigger, my wrist jerking from the mild recoil. A spiderweb pattern instantly formed around a hole on the windshield directly in front of the driver. The Buick suddenly lurched forward, burning rubber, as if the driver's foot had slammed into the gas pedal.

Again, the survival impulse kicked in. My body involuntarily bolted to the left side of the bridge. From there I scrambled over the rail in the blink of an eye and leaped off without thinking. As I dropped the thirty feet down toward the murky water, the Buick simultaneously crashed into the Packard. I splashed into the shockingly cold river just as the Buick exploded in a fireball of noise and debris. Surfacing, gasping for breath, and then treading water, I was surprised that the Iver was still in my left hand. I managed to holster it as I kept bobbing.

Above me on the bridge, the two flaming cars, pushed by the Buick's momentum, scooted and spun to the right side of the bridge. They broke through the railings with startling force, and then the two hulks of twisted, burning metal plummeted into the river not far from me.

I quickly ducked under as the massive wave pushed my body away from the wreckage. When the intensity subsided somewhat, I concentrated on swimming as fast as I could toward the western shore. It was the first time I'd ever attempted to swim with my prosthesis. When I was a Marine, I was quite adept in the water, but not anymore. Nevertheless, I managed to reach the river bank quickly and safely. The doc in Florida would have been proud that I could actually do it. My feet felt solid rock and I pulled myself up to a standing position, holding on to the outcrop of stone and earth.

The two cars were half submerged and slowly began to sink. The Buick was in worse shape. The entire back end had been obliterated.

What could have caused such a detonation?

Then I remembered. The trunk of Marko's Buick had been stocked with sweaty dynamite. That wetness was pure nitroglycerin! Old dynamite had a tendency to sweat the stuff, which could crystallize or pool and be extremely touch-sensitive. Its volatile nature reacted to the collision.

It wasn't Operation Ivy's "Mike" test, but to me it was just as spectacular.

Climbing up to the road was more difficult than the swim, but I succeeded. Standing on the bridge and gazing down at the bubbling cauldron was a surreal, out of body sensation.

The river couldn't have been too deep, but I waited until both autos, and the corpse, were gone.

Presently I took stock of myself. My gun was in my holster, my wallet with my money was in my trouser pocket. I'd lost none of my loose change. My prostheses were still attached, although I had to take a few moments to empty water out of the BK leg. I could live without my jacket, suitcase and the other stuff in the trunk, and there would always be another car. Once I realized I was unharmed, just wet and terribly shaken, I felt an overwhelming joy.

I had finally hit the target with my left hand! The urge to holler, "*WA-HOO!*" overcame me, so I did, scaring all the rattlesnakes, lizards, and buzzards for a mile around.

The sun would set in an hour or two. The desert could get mighty cold in the dark. I needed to get back to Roswell in a hurry. It was, what, ten miles, perhaps?

But as I walked away from the bridge, one thought took up all the space in my brain.

Michael Brinkley had set me up.

32
October 31–November 1, 1952

Roswell, New Mexico – Lubbock, Texas

The most important business at the moment was to get back to New York as quickly as possible. Babanin's press conference was Sunday. The only way that was going to happen was by flying. Unfortunately, I was walking on a highway ten miles outside of Roswell, New Mexico on a late Friday afternoon with the sun threatening to drop below the horizon within an hour. I'd been in worse scrapes before, but this was right up there on the top ten list.

The one good thing was that Michael Brinkley would assume that I was dead. He likely wasn't planning to hear from his operative, Marko-Whatever-His-Name-Was, until tomorrow. Maybe Sunday. *Maybe* even Monday. That gave me an advantage of sorts.

Sheesh. Marko worked for Brinkley. He wasn't SMERSH at all. It was clear that Brinkley used the SMERSH moniker as bait to lure me into the plot. Marko was just a hired thug whose directive was to make sure Dora and I got to Texas in one piece, but he also had a penchant for eliminating the smuggling team when it was convenient.

Roswell wasn't a major airline hub by any means. Getting to the air force base didn't seem like a viable plan. I had no authority there. I had no government credentials.

Every now and then a car passed me on the way to Roswell as I walked. I quickly held up my left hand thumb, but that's awkward when you're on the right side of the highway. Would my prosthesis elicit sympathy or turn away prospective rides? There was only one way to find out.

When the sound of a car behind me grew louder, I turned and held out my hook. But I also raised my left arm, stuck out the thumb, and repeated a flex motion at the elbow. The vehicle zipped past me. After a while, a succession of automobiles heading my way came along. Same routine, same thumb, same hook. Zoom, zoom, zoom. None of them wanted to help a poor, helpless hitchhiker.

The sun was dipping close to the horizon. The sky had turned red-orange in the west but blue-black in the east. I'd probably trekked three miles. It would be pitch dark in twenty minutes, and it would be dangerous for me to be strolling on the side of the highway. My shirt was a light blue, but it might be too late by the time a pair of headlights picked it up.

My stump was in agony. The left leg above the prosthesis was sore. The left hip hurt. Perhaps I'd pulled a muscle when I jumped off that bridge, or it happened when I frantically attempted to swim. I needed a rest.

Dusk was just about to transition into night when a lone sedan drove toward me in the oncoming lane. The bright headlights almost blinded me. Even though the driver wasn't going my direction, I thought, why not, so I did my waving thumb and hook act.

Surprisingly, the car began to slow. I stopped walking and waited, and sure enough, the guy pulled over to the shoulder. The auto's silhouette told me it was a Chevy Fleetmaster, late 40s model. The driver lowered his window and called out in a deep baritone voice, "You need a ride?"

I crossed the road and stood at the side of the car. The driver was a man about my age, blond hair, blue eyes. I said, "I'm going to Roswell since that's the closest town, but what I'd really like to do is get a ride to Lubbock. That's probably got the nearest and biggest airport, right?"

He raised his eyebrows. "You're correct about the airport, and guess what ... I'm on my way to Lubbock. Hop in."

I went around to the passenger side and got in the seat beside the man. And then I was in for another surprise.

He also had a right prosthesis. The driver was using the hook on the column shift the same way I did.

"We must be twin brothers," he said.

I laughed. "My name is Felix Leiter."

"I'm Weston Hurt. Glad to meet you."

He took off, pulled onto the highway, and picked up speed. My kind of driver.

"So ... what's your story? If you don't mind me asking."

"You mean my prosthesis?"

"Yeah."

"I was attacked by a shark. The damn beast took off my arm and part of my leg, too." I reached down and knocked on the wood.

He whistled.

"What about you?"

"Normandy, Omaha Beach. First Infantry Division. June the sixth. 1944. A day I'll always remember because I still dream about it. Every. Single. Night."

"What happened?"

"Mortar. My whole right side was in the wrong place at the wrong time. Hit with shrapnel. The scars go up and down my rib cage, hip, and right leg. I was in the hospital a while."

"Sorry to hear that."

He shrugged. "Got me a Purple Heart out of it."

"I was in the Marines. Pacific theater."

"You see action?"

"I did. I was on Iwo Jima. Came out alive and unharmed." I tapped my BK again. "Knock on wood."

"Good for you. You sound ... I'm picking up a Texas accent, but it's more refined."

"I am indeed from Texas, but I spent a lot of time after the war in Europe and I've lived up north in D.C. and now currently in New York City. I hear a southern accent, too."

"I'm from the Houston area. Why were you hitchhiking in the middle of nowhere?" He nodded at my waist. "I noticed you're wearing a piece."

Yeah, it was in plain sight. What should I tell him? "Look, I'm law enforcement. Really. I ran into some trouble. If you don't mind, I'd rather not go into it."

"That's okay. I believe you."

"What are *you* doing out here?"

"I'm on the GI Bill at Texas Tech University, took a few days off from music school, and I'm heading back now to resume classes on Monday." He grinned. "I got the crazy idea that I might want to sing opera."

The drive to Lubbock would be roughly two and a half hours. After chit-chatting for another half hour, I finally told Hurt that I was dead tired and thought it might be wise if I tried to count some sheep. He told me to go ahead and that he'd wake me when we were at Lubbock Municipal Airport. I removed my BK leg to ease the pain on my stump.

Then I was out.

*

New York, New York

It was a long haul but I made it back to New York on Saturday night. My new buddy Weston Hurt had dropped me at Lubbock's airport around eight o'clock Friday night. Before getting out of his car, I realized I probably shouldn't try to walk onto a plane wearing a handgun. I'd noticed that Hurt had a small duffel bag with handles in the back seat. I asked him what was in it, and he told me it was just dirty clothes. He took me up on my offer to buy it from him. It was perfect for storing my weapon and holster. I could carry it right onto the aircraft and no one would give it a second thought.

I'd caught the last and only flight on Pioneer to Love Field in Dallas. I'd had a few minutes before boarding the plane, so I made a long distance phone call to the Roswell police to report the "accident" on the bridge over the Pecos River. I'd said the drivers didn't make it, and then I hung up before they asked for identification.

Unfortunately, I had to wait until Saturday morning for a one-way ticket to LaGuardia on American. Cost me a whopping eighty-nine dollars, but it had to be done. At first I was afraid I would run out of cash, but I had just barely enough to pay for the ticket, buy some food, and purchase a damn jacket to wear because of airline dress codes. The flight took almost all day with a few stops in between. Alas, I didn't have enough money left over for a taxi into Manhattan, but I promised the cab driver that if he waited outside my apartment while I ran in and grabbed some bills out of a safe I kept in my bedroom closet, he'd get a nice tip. That worked.

The IRT subway took me downtown to City Hall and the Pinkerton's building. Expecting no one to be around on a Saturday night, I was surprised to see a light on in Robert Pinkerton's office. He heard me, looked up from whatever he was working on at his desk, and did a double-take with his jaw open.

"Hello, Robert. I'm back." I stood in the doorway. "What are you doing here so late on a Saturday?"

"The real question is what are *you* doing here? I thought you were *dead*!"

I shook my head. "Whatever you've heard, it ain't true."

He ushered me inside, and I sat in the comfortable chair in front of his desk. Pinkerton held up a telegram. "This came today from the police in Roswell, New Mexico. It says your car and identifying registration were found in a river some miles out of town along with another vehicle. The body of the other car's driver was there with a bullet hole in his forehead. *You* were missing but presumed dead. They suspect foul play!"

The fact that my round had perforated Marko's head gave me an immense amount of perverse pleasure.

"Robert," I said, "the job I was on is not resolved yet. Once it is, I'll fill you in on everything. But how did the Roswell police know to contact you?"

"Oh, it says your Pinkerton's ID was in a piece of bloody clothing recovered from the sunken car."

A-ha. I recalled placing it in my jacket pocket at the Roswell air base.

"Well, Robert, I'm sorry this gave you a shock, but it's important that 'Mr. Parker,' the employer who put me on this job, believes I'm dead for another day. We'll talk later, but right now it's vitally important that I contact a friend of mine at the FBI."

33
November 2, 1952

NEW YORK, NEW YORK

The United Nations Headquarters had bounced around a bit since the organization was established after the war. They started off at Hunter College in the Bronx and then moved to a place in Flushing Meadows, Queens. But thanks to the multi-million dollar gift of a tract of land on the East River in Manhattan from John D. Rockefeller, the current home was built on eighteen acres and six city blocks between E. 42nd and 48th Streets on First Avenue. The thirty-nine-story Secretariat Building opened in 1950, and the brand new General Assembly Building just opened in October. It's an impressive structure of aluminum and blue-green glass with a sweeping wave of a façade.

The current state of diplomatic relations between the USA and the U.S.S.R. was complicated. While the Soviet Consulate-General in New York was closed, there was still a Soviet ambassador and Soviet Embassy in D.C., and the Soviet Diplomatic Mission to the United Nations still operated from the Percy R. Pyne House on Park Avenue and E. 68th Street.

There had been a small piece buried on page six of *The New York Times* yesterday saying that visiting diplomat Rurik Babanin was meeting over the weekend with the Soviets' representative to the U.N., Valerian Zorin, and was scheduled to fly back to Moscow on the afternoon of Sunday, November 2.

The presence of communists in the USA was a touchy subject. There was an angry mob atmosphere among the public toward the Soviets. But there was also a segment of the population that was sympathetic to those who may have had interaction with the Communist Party in the 1930s and 40s, or to those who believed they were simply exercising freedom of speech.

New York was a melting pot of ethnic populations, including a Russian enclave. There were Russian neighborhoods and restaurants. That didn't mean every Russian was a communist or that they supported the Soviet regime. The Russian Tea Room was still a popular "continental restaurant" in midtown Manhattan. Whenever bigwigs from the Soviet Union visited New York, though, often protesters on one side of the street had signs reading, "Commie Go Home!" There were also usually a small group of supporters on the opposite side. After all, it wasn't illegal to be a member of the Communist Party in America, at least not yet. There had been talk in political circles speculating that Eisenhower, if elected president, planned to sign a law that criminalized being a communist.

It was a cool, but sunny day. Babanin and Zorin were traveling with personal interpreters and bodyguards from the mission HQ on Park Avenue to the United Nations, where Babanin was scheduled to hold a brief outdoor press conference on the space between the North Garden and the General Assembly building. About fifty folding chairs and a podium surrounded by temporary roped barriers had been set up for the press, VIPs, and a tiny audience that was vetted to attend. As Babanin's address wasn't particularly newsworthy, the representation by the press was minimal. *The New York Times*, *Washington Post*, and *New York Daily News* were there. I wasn't sure who else.

Traffic up the one-way First Avenue had been blocked and detoured for two hours at 42nd Street, so the avenue was empty up to 47th Street. Complicating that, though, was the construction mess of the underground traffic tunnel that was in progress—the "First Avenue Tunnel"—which was scheduled to finally open in the spring of '53. Luckily, November 2 was a Sunday!

Naturally, a group of anti-communist protesters had shown up with the usual placards and signs. Police relegated them to stand in the middle of First Avenue behind sawhorse barricades positioned roughly between 45th and 46th Streets. This placed them maybe fifty feet from the podium and audience present to hear Babanin's remarks.

Several NYPD officers were scattered about the area. The FBI was also surreptitiously on hand. Steve Sandlin and several agents in plainclothes were among the attendees. At least two posed as press photographers.

I was among the anti-communist protesters on the

sidelines, dressed in my trench coat and fedora and equipped with a tiny pair of binoculars so that I could watch the proceedings up close. Sandlin hadn't wanted me to participate in the operation. It was not my job. Nevertheless, I had talked him into allowing me to be present at the site. He then agreed it would be useful for me to be an eyewitness.

The guests had begun to gather in front of the General Assembly building at one-thirty and police directed them to the folding chairs. I noted that a woman dressed in black and wearing a hat with a black veil sat in the front row. Those around her treated her with deference. The reporter from *The New York Times* attempted to ask her questions, but she held up her hand to indicate a refusal to talk.

Eventually a limousine was allowed through the police barricades on First Avenue. It pulled into the circle drive in front of the Secretariat Building and stopped. Three U.N. security met them there.

Four men in total emerged from the limo. I verified through the binoculars that Babanin was one of them, for I had seen his photo in Ava Spence's house. Babanin and a grey haired man, presumably Zorin, plus the other two from the car, obviously assistants or interpreters, trailed behind the U.N. guards as they walked across the space along the General Assembly Building to the event area.

At that moment, I noticed that another black sedan limo—obviously a federal vehicle—was allowed through the barricades at 42nd. It slowly drove along the west side of First Avenue, behind the protesters, and parked on the west side curb at about 46th Street, just uptown of the protesters. I figured it contained more of Sandlin's FBI men. Zorin and Babanin's limo remained parked in the circle.

Babanin's entourage reached the podium. With the binoculars, I studied the faces of the presenters and audience. The face of the woman in black was hidden because of the veil. Why was the widow special?

Zorin addressed the audience in Russian. There were quite a few present who understood the language, but the interpreter from the Soviet Mission also translated his words into English for those gathered who didn't, as well as for the press. He also spoke loudly enough for the protesters to hear. The gist was that he and Mr. Babanin had conducted productive meetings about the future of the Communist Party in America. The U.S. government was threatening to crack down on American communists and he wanted to assure those present that the Soviet government would do everything in their power to protect them. After the press conference, Mr. Babanin would be on his way back to Moscow to deliver the results of their talks to Stalin. Zorin then introduced Babanin, who stood at the podium.

He, too, spoke Russian. The interpreter said, "Greetings, comrades. I understand there are a few Poles among you." The man smoothly switched to speaking Polish, and the interpreter went along with it. "I, too, am of Polish origin. As my guest today, I have invited the widow of Charles Kaminski, who was tragically murdered in a U.S. prison last month."

I vaguely recalled the name and then put it together. One of the defendants in the Smith Act trial of 1949 had recently died in prison. The Alien Registration Act enacted in 1940, also called the Smith Act, set penalties for anyone advocating for the overthrow of the United States government. Several leaders in the Communist Party based in New York had been arrested on what may or may not have been trumped-up charges alleging they were guilty of this crime. A handful of men went to prison. One of them, Charles Kaminski, had been beaten by anti-communist inmates and suffered a brain injury.

The sound of a car door slamming shut behind me and the protesters averted my attention. A man wearing a dark suit and sunglasses had just emerged from the black limo parked on First Avenue, the one I thought contained more FBI agents. He stood by the passenger side of the car, his arms folded, watching the proceedings at a safe distance from the opposite side of the avenue.

Michael Brinkley.

So far, so good. We had expected him, but we didn't know where he would position himself. Brinkley didn't see me among the protesters. I was sure Sandlin had spotted him.

Last night when I had met with Steve, I told him of my suspicions. Brinkley's excessive drinking. His seeming lack of cash and complaints about the IRS. The fact that he had readily taken the quarter. Sandlin replied that the FBI was already on to him. Brinkley, being an Associate Director of the CIA, had Soviet contacts in the U.S. He obviously had been offered a great deal of money to betray his country.

Turning back to the ceremony, I watched as the woman in black stood and approached the podium. I studied her more closely with the binoculars.

She spoke in Polish. "Thank you, Mr. Babanin," the interpreter said.

Wait a second.

Her voice sounded awfully familiar.

So that was how they were going to do it! It suddenly all made sense. I wanted to shout out to Sandlin, but I figured he was smart enough to catch on.

"I want to thank you and Mr. Zorin for the support you have given me and my family in this difficult time," the woman said into the microphone with an Eastern European accent that I knew very well. "As a token of our appreciation, I want to present to you this family heirloom. It contains a ring that was a prized possession of my husband's. His father, Piotr Kaminski, received the Order of the White Eagle, the highest order of merit of the Republic of Poland, during the First World War. The Maltese Cross is enameled in red and white on a silver ring. Kaminski Senior gave it to his son when Charles emigrated to America shortly before the Nazis invaded Poland in 1939. Charles and I became acquainted here in New York in 1946 at a party meeting and we were married soon after. Mr. Babanin, I would like to give this precious heirloom to you in honor of my late husband."

The woman reached into her handbag and brought out a *small purple felt jewel box.*

Babanin took it and spoke softly to her. He placed the box in his jacket pocket and then asked her a question. The woman nodded. He gently raised the veil so that he could kiss both cheeks.

The woman was, of course, Dora Wysocki.

Babanin gave her a little bow and she returned to her seat. He continued his rather propaganda-oriented address, which was more about the "hysterical" reactions of Congress to communism in this country. He promised that as long as diplomatic relations could be continual and sensible, then progress might be made between our two countries. He ended by saying that Mr. Zorin would accompany him to the airport and that he was saying goodbye for now.

There was scattered applause among the attendees. Babanin waved to the group, shook hands with Zorin, and then they both allowed the U.N. security men to usher them and their assistants back to the circle where their limo waited. Once the entire party was inside, the limo took off up First Avenue to make its way to the Queens Midtown Tunnel and eventually out to Idlewild Airport.

As soon as it was gone, the FBI went into action. Eight plainclothes men, including Sandlin, shouted, "FBI! Nobody move!" They held up badges. Alarmed, the seated audience attempted to jump up and run, but the agents quickly moved around the perimeter of the roped-off section.

"Please stay seated!" Sandlin shouted.

Swinging my head back to Brinkley, I saw him bolt

away from the sedan and begin running across the avenue. He drew a Browning Hi-Power pistol from beneath his jacket and called out, "Hey! What is this?" He stormed toward Sandlin, sprinting past the protesters and me, probably hoping to use his CIA credentials to deflate whatever situation he thought might be happening.

Two FBI agents approached Dora, who was still seated in the front row.

Sandlin, his eye on Brinkley, made a gesture to two of his men. They immediately blocked Brinkley's path with guns raised. The realization that he was a target dawned on Brinkley. He halted, considered firing at them, but wisely grasped that that would be a huge mistake. Instead, he turned, looked at the gang of anti-communist protesters in the avenue where I was standing, and made a calculated decision to enact his exit sooner than he had planned.

Brinkley ran toward us, probably figuring that the crowd of protesters would provide civilian cover for him for the few moments he needed to run back to his waiting ride. What had been meant to be an official CIA lift away from the event had become his means to flee capture.

Unfortunately for him, though, he hadn't realized that *I* was standing amidst that crowd, and he was coming right at me.

Our eyes met. His widened with surprise.

I couldn't draw my Iver. Too many people around us. There would be shots fired, collateral damage, and an ugly horror.

"Leiter!" he yelled. He pointed the Browning at me. The surrounding civilians dispersed, screaming and running off the avenue to the streets.

Too late to draw. I held up my hand and hook in surrender.

Brinkley roughly grabbed me with his free hand, twirled me around, and held my body in front of his, hostage-style. He then marched me backwards toward his sedan, his gun aimed at my temple. "Stay back!" he yelled at Sandlin and his agents.

The NYPD had assumed firing positions but their captain ordered them to hold their fire.

"What are you doing?" I asked through clenched teeth.

"Shut up!" Brinkley growled. "You did this, didn't you!"

"I didn't do anything, pal, I was just here watching."

We got to the waiting car and stood with our backs to it, Brinkley behind me, his weapon still at my head.

"Let him go, Brinkley!" Sandlin shouted. He and a few agents, their weapons trained on us, were cautiously crossing the avenue. For a moment I didn't think this would end well.

"You're going to get in the car with me, Leiter," Brinkley said.

"No, I'm not."

He jabbed my temple—*hard*—with the gun barrel. He leaned in to my ear and growled, "*Yes you will!*"

That's when I was able to swiftly raise the forearm of my prosthesis and hook the terminal device onto the barrel. I then just as rapidly brought down the arm, pulling down the gun and throwing Brinkley off balance for the split second it took for me to lead with my left fist and twist my body. The pile-driver hit him directly in the solar plexus. The shock and pain caused him to gasp and bend forward. He dropped his weapon on the street. I then fixed my good leg behind his left one and *pushed*. Brinkley tripped and toppled backwards onto his backside. When he attempted to reach for the fallen Browning, I stomped on his arm with my wooden leg. He cried out in agony.

"Hold still, traitor," I snarled.

By then Sandlin and his men were there. Two of them stopped the driver of the getaway car from moving. The others had their weapons on Brinkley.

"You can step away now, Felix," Sandlin said.

I raised my shoe, retreated, turned, and crossed the avenue just in time to see an agent handcuffing Dora. It wasn't long before three unmarked vehicles pulled up in front of the site. The FBI wrapped up the scene, sent the civilians home, and took Dora, Brinkley, and the limo driver away in separate unmarked cars.

Sandlin approached me. "What a coincidence that you were standing where you were," he said. "Thank you, Felix. You saved us a lot of trouble."

"Steve, I don't believe in coincidence. It was fate. There's a difference."

He led me away and we strolled south along the General Assembly building toward the circle drive. He offered me a cigarette and we both lit up.

"I take it you're going to let Babanin get on the plane back to Moscow?"

"Of course," Sandlin answered. "That was the idea all along, right? It's what the Prometheists wanted."

I nodded. Last night I had told Steve the whole story of the twenty-five cent coin and the astonishing thing Stanley Masters had revealed in Carlsbad Caverns. The 1937 quarter did *not* have the hydrogen bomb specs on it after all. In a moment of conscience, he and Ava Spence had decided that the microdot affixed to the coin should contain what *appeared* to be the specs but were actually fake. Once any physicists attempted to work with the information, they would have found that nothing on it really worked.

"You know," Sandlin added, "Babanin delivering those phony plans to Moscow likely won't prevent the Soviets from eventually building their own hydrogen bomb, but it will certainly delay them."

"What happens now to Dora Wysocki?" I asked.

"Ah." He put a hand on my left upper arm and squeezed it. "I'm sorry about her. We thought she might show up. Had to keep some things close to the vest. We figured the coin would get delivered to Babanin disguised as some sort of gift. It was clever, to be sure. There she was, pretending to be the widow of that dead communist. And guess what ... Kaminski wasn't even married! She and Brinkley were surely planning to leave the country after Moscow paid them off."

"They both used me. It was an elaborate and finely tuned plot."

"Yep," Sandlin said. "But you ended up saving the day. Try not to let it get you down."

"Well, you know who's really good at 'elaborate and finely tuned' plots? SMERSH."

"Yeah, this whole thing stinks of them," Sandlin said. "I'll see you later, Felix. Thanks again."

"Say, Steve, I'd like a favor."

When I told him, Sandlin frowned and rubbed his chin. "Maybe. I tell you what." He gave me an address in lower Manhattan, not far from City Hall. "That's an unmarked federal detention facility. Come by tomorrow morning around ten o'clock." He shook my hand. "Good work today. It was all done with near-perfect precision and timing, we just didn't expect Brinkley to charge at the protesters and grab you."

I gave him the boyish grin. "But that's where the hook and the eye came in."

34

NEW YORK, NEW YORK

I had one more thing I needed to do that day.

At six-forty-five p.m., I walked into McSorley's Ale House and ordered a pint of their signature drink.

I needed it. The betrayal had cut me to the bone. Brinkley and Dora. Their scheme had been in place from the beginning. Manipulating me to get the coin and deliver it right into Brinkley's hands. All scripted. Marko abducting her was staged. That whole sham in Roswell, where Brinkley 'arrested' Dora, was one big cabaret act.

It was also bugging me that last night I had refrained from revealing everything to Steve Sandlin.

I hadn't told him about the Prometheists' Plan B.

Before I could do so, I had to satisfy myself about something.

Back when I had been in Karl Adamski's apartment and looked through his things, his calendar had contained several clues. The words "Hurricane" and "Ivy," for example, were on very specific dates that turned out to be significant and connected to those code names.

But there was still one date in question—November 2—where Adamski had scribbled, "MCS 7pm."

After a lot of thought, I had finally come to the conclusion that "MCS" stood for McSorley's. It was his favorite haunt. And I had witnessed him meeting someone there before.

Sure enough, at seven p.m., none other than "Biology Teacher" entered the place. The guy from the Consulate General of Poland building on Madison Avenue who had reminded me of my high school instructor.

I watched out of the corner of my eye from the table against the wall where I sat with the glass of ale in hand. Biology Teacher looked around the bar, searching for someone. He didn't find him, so he went to the counter and ordered an ale. Once he had his drink, he sat alone at a table. While he drank, he kept looking at his watch.

Finally, after a half hour, Biology Teacher finished his drink, got up, and left.

I then knew that the person he was supposed to meet was the deceased Karl Adamski's replacement. Jerry Bork.

In hushed whispers inside Carlsbad Caverns, Masters had explained that the intended, original plan was that the Prometheists were indeed attempting to steal and traffic the specs from New Mexico, but *not* to deliver them to Babanin and the Soviets at all. Adamski—and then Ava and/or Bork—was supposed to have brought them to New York and, on this date and at this time and in this bar, given them to Biology Teacher—whose real name was Mikolaj Rzepa—a Prometheist working at the Polish consulate general building in some capacity. Apparently,

Rzepa had the ability and clearance to travel back and forth from Warsaw to New York. He had his own spy network, and it was he who had informed Ava that Dora was working for the enemy. Rzepa was supposed to deliver the hydrogen bomb plans to Prometheist physicists in the hopes that *they* could develop their own weapon and use it for ... whatever.

That was Plan A, and the one that their opposition, that is, the Soviets, and, in turn, Brinkley and Dora, discovered and would believe was still in play. They knew the microdot with the specs would be on a quarter. And that's what the Soviet spies wanted to intercept and deliver to Babanin.

But after Adamski's murder, Ava learned that the Soviets were on to her. She and Masters then concocted *Plan B*. It would kill two birds with one stone, so to speak.

In case the Soviets got hold of the quarter, it would contain *fake* bomb specs that would go to Moscow and fool the Russians.

But in addition to the bogus plans on one coin, Masters was to hand over a *second coin* in the caverns.

A simple U.S. penny with a microdot containing the *real* hydrogen bomb specs that would be delivered to Biology Teacher.

The penny I had in my pocket.

35
November 3, 1952

NEW YORK, NEW YORK

The next morning, Monday, Sandlin honored my request for a favor.

The guard brought Dora into the prisoner visiting room at the appointed time. She was dressed in a red jumpsuit but she wasn't handcuffed. I was already sitting at the table. She sat across from me, her face expressionless. No makeup. Her hair a bit unkempt. The resemblance to Patricia Neal was long gone.

I tapped out two cigarettes from my pack of Chesterfields and offered her one. She nodded. A flick of the "Leiter" and both were lit.

"How are they treating you?" I asked.

She shrugged. "Okay."

Suddenly, my tongue was tied. I really didn't know what I had come to say, if anything. Maybe I had just wanted to *see* her one more time.

"What do you want, Felix?"

"Nothing. Well, maybe ... maybe I just want to know why."

"I don't have anything to say, Felix. Things didn't work out how I wanted. That's all."

"Jesus, Dora, it was all a lie. Everything. You hiring me. Your 'mission.' You and me. Could you explain to me how your role in all this came about? Pretend I'm your attorney. I'll keep whatever you say between us."

"It doesn't matter," she said with a sigh. "I've already spilled my guts. It will all come out at my trial anyway. I'm thinking of just pleading guilty and not having to go through it." She looked away, considering, and took a deep drag on the cigarette.

"How did you get involved with Michael Brinkley?"

She allowed a slight laugh. "I met him at a jazz club. In July. Birdland. He knew all about Ava and her network and their operation. He was CIA. Ava's communication network was poor and old-fashioned. There were leaks. Ham radios." Dora rolled her eyes. "So Michael *targeted* me. Once he knew my history with Ava, well, he knew I was vulnerable to his influence. When he told the Soviets about the Prometheists, Moscow dangled a *huge* amount of money as a carrot. Enough for him to retire and leave the country. He also told them about me."

"And then they came to you, too."

"The money was tempting."

I slapped my hand on the table, causing her to jump. "Bullshit! It was more about betraying Ava. Admit it. You were so consumed by your hatred of her for what happened to your boyfriend in Poland that you betrayed your goddamned country!"

After a beat, Dora whispered, "I'm such a fool."

"How did the Russians know they could trust you?"

"They tested me. I was to get Karl Adamski to date me. He knew of my history with Ava, but we had no chemistry together. Ava likely wanted him to find out what I knew. I was told to lead him on and find out what I could from him, and then ... finally steer him to his appointment with Marko on Bleecker Street. I'm telling the truth when I say that Marko was supposed to get Karl in the car and take him away for interrogation. I didn't know Karl would be shot. Marko acted on impulse. He sometimes overstepped his boundaries."

"You think? Throwing dynamite at us wasn't going to keep me alive for your scheme!"

"He was a psychopath. What he did that night at Bork's house was not part of the plan." After another pause, she added, "Felix, SMERSH planned the whole thing. They recruited Michael and set everything in motion. Whitehall was supposed to be acting as SMERSH's insurance policy to make sure we succeeded or, if not, take over the job."

I grunted and said, "But he went rogue, obviously. He turned against the Soviets and wanted to get the coin for himself. Likely to sell on the open market."

She shrugged in defeat, nodded, and met my eyes. "If it makes you feel any better, Felix, know that you did foil SMERSH."

Well, that was something. Perhaps not much, but something.

I rubbed my chin. "Dora, you're really not afraid of flying."

"No. That was part of the act. The long trip together was intentional so that—"

"—so that I'd become infatuated with you and trust you."

Dora looked away. "Yes."

That should have been enough. I'd heard almost all that I wanted to hear. My chest felt full. It would do me no good to remain in the room. But there was one last thing...

"Dora." I leaned in to her. "All that happened between us. On the road. In the hotel rooms. Was that just part of your act, too?"

She looked at me with those slow, dreamy eyes. "No, Felix. I wanted you. You are an attractive man. Somehow, giving us pleasure, giving *you* pleasure, made up for the fact that I was being deceitful. It was real. You are very much a *whole man*."

We sat there for a full minute in silence. Then I stubbed out my cigarette in the ashtray that sat on the table. I stood, gazed at her one more time, and said, "Goodbye, Dora. Take care of yourself."

She just nodded and extinguished her own cigarette.

Both butts emitted curling, intertwining wisps of smoke into the air.

*

And now I'm on the edge of the seaport near Fulton Market watching all the boats and ferries on the East

River. My reflection of the past several months has come to its end. Briefly I flash on how the authorities in West Texas and New Mexico won't know what to make of the crime scenes I left behind. Cold cases forever. Sometimes that's part of the game. Best to put all that out of my mind.

In the meantime, I'm left with the goddamned penny in my left hand, just as it was when I began my exercise of remembrance. How long have I been standing here? I don't know. Memories flit by at their own pace. They're just snapshots and little snippets of movies in the mind. Voices fading in and out. Like dreams.

Was the stroll across City Hall Park, the cigarette, and the replay of the recent events therapeutic at all?

Not much.

I stare at the coin.

The fate of the world.

Immense power. Indescribable destruction.

There is no need for me to tell Steve Sandlin about it. What the FBI doesn't know won't hurt them. Or anyone else.

But I ain't kidding myself. I'm sure I could find someone who knows someone who would pay me an obscene amount of money for it.

God, it's tempting. It really is.

Using my hook, I pick up the coin from my palm and examine it more closely. Can I make out the microdot? I think so. It's a tiny speck on top of Abraham Lincoln's Adam's apple.

Whatcha gonna do? my father asks.

With two flexes of my shoulder muscle, the prosthesis flings the coin out over the East River. It spins and sails thirty feet and drops into the dirty water.

Gone forever.

After a deep breath of cool autumn air, I turn away and limp-walk home.

Acknowledgments

I wish to thank Terry Busby (Carlsbad Public Library), Janice Diaz, Terri Francell, Robert Harvey, Lon Howard, Len Johnson, Mark W. Joop, Thomas Karolewski, Chandra Lagunas Lewis-Qualls (Dallas Historical Society), Jim Lindenas, James McMahon, Doug Redenius, my wife Randi Frank, and the entire team at Ian Fleming Publications Ltd.

For Ian Fleming fans everywhere.

–R.B.

About the Author

As of 2025, Raymond Benson is the author of over forty published books. He is most well-known as the first American to be commissioned to write adult continuation James Bond novels (six original adventures, three film novelisations, and three short stories published between 1997 and 2002). His critically acclaimed and best-selling five-book serial, *The Black Stiletto*, is in development to be a possible feature film or television series. Recent notable suspense titles include *The Mad, Mad Murders of Marigold Way*, which won the 2022 IPPY Gold Medal in Mystery from the Independent Publisher Book Awards; *Hotel Destiny: A Ghost Noir*; *Blues in the Dark*; *In the Hush of the Night*; and *The Secrets on Chicory Lane*. Raymond is also a sought-after media tie-in scribe and ghostwriter, having penned books for such series as *Tom Clancy's Splinter Cell*, *Metal Gear Solid*, *Hitman*, and more. He is a concert-level pianist with a lengthy background in theatrical composing, and he has his own YouTube channel. As a film historian, Raymond writes for *Cinema Retro* magazine, has taught college-level courses, and continues to lecture on film in the Chicago USA area. You can find him at www.raymondbenson.com.

James Bond Works By Raymond Benson

Original Novels
Zero Minus Ten (1997)
The Facts of Death (1998)
High Time to Kill (1999)
DoubleShot (2000)
Never Dream of Dying (2001)
The Man with the Red Tattoo (2002)

Film Novelisations
(based on the respective screenplays)
Tomorrow Never Dies (1997)
The World is Not Enough (1999)
Die Another Day (2002)

Short Stories
Blast from the Past (1997)
Midsummer Night's Doom (1999)
Live at Five (1999)

Non Fiction
The James Bond Bedside Companion
(1984: US; 1988: UK)

IAN FLEMING PUBLICATIONS

Ian Lancaster Fleming was born in London on 28 May 1908 and was educated at Eton College before spending a formative period studying languages in Europe. His first job was with Reuters news agency, followed by a brief spell as a stockbroker. On the outbreak of the Second World War he was appointed assistant to the Director of Naval Intelligence, Admiral Godfrey, where he played a key part in British and Allied espionage operations.

After the war he joined Kemsley Newspapers as Foreign Manager of *The Sunday Times,* running a network of correspondents who were intimately involved in the Cold War. His first novel, *Casino Royale,* was published in 1953 and introduced James Bond, Special Agent 007, to the world. The first print run sold out within a month. Following this initial success, he published a Bond title every year until his death. His own travels, interests and wartime experience gave authority to everything he wrote. Raymond Chandler hailed him as 'the most forceful and driving writer of thrillers in England.' The fifth title, *From Russia With*

Love, was particularly well received and sales soared when President Kennedy named it as one of his favourite books. The Bond novels have sold more than 100 million copies and inspired a hugely successful film franchise which began in 1962 with the release of *Dr No,* starring Sean Connery as 007.

The Bond books were written in Jamaica, a country Fleming fell in love with during the war and where he built a house, 'Goldeneye'. He married Ann Rothermere in 1952. His story about a magical car, written in 1961 for their only child, Caspar, went on to become the well-loved novel and film, *Chitty Chitty Bang Bang.*

Fleming died of heart failure on 12 August 1964.

www.ianfleming.com

X TheIanFleming

◉ Ianflemings007

f IanFlemingBooks

The James Bond Books

Casino Royale
Live and Let Die
Moonraker
Diamonds are Forever
From Russia with Love
Dr No
Goldfinger
For Your Eyes Only
Thunderball
The Spy Who Loved Me
On Her Majesty's Secret Service
You Only Live Twice
The Man with the Golden Gun
Octopussy and The Living Daylights

Non-fiction

The Diamond Smugglers
Thrilling Cities

Children's
Chitty Chitty Bang Bang